THE RETREAT

BOOKS BY KAREN KING

THE
RETREAT

KAREN KING

Bookouture

Published by Bookouture in 2023

An imprint of Storyfire Ltd.
Carmelite House
50 Victoria Embankment
London EC4Y 0DZ

www.bookouture.com

ISBN: 978-1-83790-673-4
eBook ISBN: 978-1-83790-672-7

PROLOGUE

I'm here. At last.

The warm air hits me as I step out of the minibus and I'm immediately struck by the beauty of the sprawling white villa nestled in the Spanish mountains. It looks so peaceful with blue skies, luscious green-leaved palm trees and the song of cicadas filling the air. I can't see it from here, but I know that there is a sparkling blue pool at the back of the house surrounded by beautiful fruit trees. I've pored over every inch of the photos you proudly display on your Facebook page.

I gaze around at the other guests. There are six of us, all come for five days of total relaxation. And there you are, your arms wrapped around each other, looking so happy. This is your dream come true and you didn't care who you trampled on to achieve it.

Your eyes fall on me and there is no guilt in them as you smile briefly then move on to greet the next guest. The bubbly pot of anger simmering inside me burns brighter and stronger. I've thought about what you did for so long – years – imagining my revenge. You took everything from me. You cruelly destroyed my life then built yourself a perfect one. Look at you, you don't have a care in the world.

Well, you soon will. I'm going to make you pay for what you did.

1

NOW

Her eyes scanned the room, looking for something to use to protect herself, pausing as she spotted the poker by the log fire. That would have to do. A few minutes later, holding the rod of cold metal in her hands, she opened the back door and stepped outside. The night air was cool and the velvety blackness surrounded her like a cloak. It was still. Quiet. Too quiet. She paused for a moment, peering into the darkness, ears strained for any sound, the poker clenched tightly by her side. She would use it if she had to, she wasn't going down without a fight. She gazed up at the handful of stars and the sliver of moon hanging like a hammock over the pool. She could do with a full moon to light up the sky tonight, she could barely see in front of her. Taking her phone out of her pocket, she switched on the torch then slowly walked down the steps guided by the small beam of light.

She was halfway down the steps when she heard a loud splash. The hairs on the back of her neck stood up as a chill ran through her. What was that? She couldn't see the pool clearly enough from here, not in the dark, her phone torch wasn't strong enough to light more than a few metres in front of her.

She paused, heart thudding, as she listened for the splashes indicating that someone was swimming across the pool. There were none. It was deadly quiet.

Too quiet.

She quickened her pace, stepping carefully so she didn't slip.

'Hello! Is someone there?' she shouted, her voice trembling.

Reaching the bottom, she hurried over and shone the light on the water. A scream rose up her throat when she saw a pool of blood on the surface then her horrified gaze rested on the body floating by it and the scream burst out, shattering through the silence.

2

THEN

José

'Well, that's it, the last place taken. We're officially in business, Eva.' José got up from his laptop and wrapped his arms around Eva, hugging her tight. 'This is it! This is our dream come true!'

It was such a relief, after all their hard work. The holiday retreat had been José's dream long before Eva had come onto the scene but luckily Eva had been happy to make it her dream too, and they had worked together to convert his grandparents' run-down house in southern Spain into the comfortable villa it was now. José's grandparents had built the rambling villa in the Andalucian mountains themselves, with help from family and friends. They'd lived in a caravan on the land, raising their two sons – José's father, Pablo, and his older brother, Diego – as they worked on the house every spare moment they got. They'd named it El Sueño, the dream. José wanted to keep the name, and Eva had happily agreed because it was their dream too, although they had replaced the chipped and faded house sign with a new one. They had both ploughed so much time and energy into restoring the villa over the last two years, painting, building, renovating, making new furnishings, taming the land, in between working part-time – Eva as a wellness coach in a luxury spa and health centre in Marbella and José as a chef in a restaurant in Malaga port. They'd taken a week's holiday to run this retreat, and hoped it would be eventually successful enough for them both to give up their jobs. Finally they were ready to welcome their first guests. He had gambled everything on this, more than Eva knew. It had to succeed.

It had been his idea to have a trial run before they officially opened the retreat for the summer. They'd planned on opening for the beginning of June, taking bookings for the three main summer months of June, July and August but had both been a little nervous about whether they had got everything right so José had suggested putting a notice on the Facebook page offering a fifty percent discount for the first six guests on this Easter trial run.

Eva had been a bit wary. 'It's a great idea but that's a big discount,' she'd pointed out. They'd really thought about prices and kept them down as much as possible to make the retreat competitive, especially as they were a new business. Reducing the price so much would be barely covering costs but José thought it was a chance worth taking and managed to persuade Eva too.

'I know but if we give them such a good discount they might be more forgiving if anything goes wrong. We'll make it a condition of the offer that the applicant shares the holiday retreat page to their own profile which will increase our visibility and give us valuable feedback before we get booked up for the summer, so we will have time to make any adaptions we need to. It's a win-win.' He'd been so sure of it but, as usual, Eva had still fretted.

'It's a bit short notice, Easter is only three weeks away. It doesn't give us much time to get everything ready.'

'We are ready. As ready as we will ever be.' This was what

their relationship was like, José full of ideas and enthusiasm, Eva always more cautious, worried that things would go wrong. 'Stop worrying, *guapa*.' *Guapa* – 'beautiful' – was his pet name for Eva. And she was beautiful, with her cascade of fair hair, eyes as blue as the sea and long, long legs. He had fallen for her as soon as he had seen her and had been delighted to discover that her nature was as lovely as her looks, she was gentle and kind, but suffered from bouts of anxiety, and he could see that she was stressed about the retreat being a success. She would be even more stressed if she knew about the big loan he'd taken out, using the house as surety. He felt sick every time he thought about it. He hated keeping it a secret from Eva, betraying her trust, but she wouldn't have wanted him to take the gamble and he knew he had to take a big risk if he wanted El Sueño to be prosperous.

'We are only offering six places as we don't want to be inundated with offers and have to disappoint people,' he continued. 'Most people will have made plans for Easter so probably only a few people will be able to make it.'

'Inundated with offers?' Eva playfully tapped his nose and he knew that he had won her around as he usually did. 'I admire your optimism. It's such short notice that we might not get any takers at all!'

They spent some time phrasing the post before finally agreeing on the wording and put it up on their page right away.

To their delight the six places were taken by the end of the day, which was amazing as they didn't have a massive page following yet, just a couple of hundred people.

Eva smiled as José tilted her head up, raising one hand to caress her cheek and winding the other hand around the back of her neck to gently pull her towards him, then he kissed her and she kissed him back which resulted in them being locked in a steamy embrace for a few minutes. The chemistry had always been electric between them and showed no sign of waning even after two years.

'That's brilliant,' Eva said, easing out of his embrace. 'Do we know any of them?' She knelt so that she could read the names on the messages showing on the screen. 'Wow! There's a couple from America! It's a long way to come for five days. They'll have just about recovered from jet lag and it will be time to go home!'

'Apparently they're in Marbella on business so are extending their stay to come to our retreat,' José told her.

'Carlos Lopez. Isn't that your cousin? Doesn't he live in Rome?' Eva looked up at him questioningly. 'I didn't know you were in touch with him.'

'I'm not. I haven't seen him since Abuelita's funeral. I hadn't realised he followed our page. I bet he's just coming to be nosey.'

He was as surprised as Eva was that Carlos was coming. He had never met his two-years-older cousin or Carlos's father, Tío Diego, until they had turned up at José's – and Carlos's – grandfather's funeral five years ago. Not that they had stayed long. He felt that they had only come to see what they had been left in the will, which had been nothing as his grandfather had left everything to his wife, naturally. They had stayed longer when they came to his grandmother's funeral two years later. José had wondered if they had come to pay their respects, or in the hope that Abuelita – he always referred to his grandmother by the Spanish term for granny – had left them something in the will, maybe even hoping to inherit the house as Tío Diego was the eldest son. Abuelita hadn't much money but had left Carlos, his father, Diego, and José's father, Pablo, a few thousand euros each. She had bequeathed the house to José because it had been his second home ever since he was a child.

'You are welcome to it,' Tío Diego had said. 'It is falling down and derelict. You will need a mortgage to fix it.' Which is exactly what José's father had said, almost begging his mother not to leave it to him, saying he didn't have the time or the money to renovate it. They were both right, the house was in a state but Abuelita had known that José would do it, he loved El Sueño as much as his grandparents had.

Over the last couple of years, in between working, José – and then Eva too – had lovingly restored the villa. Carlos must have been following the page, curious to see what progress José had made and couldn't resist the chance to come and see for himself. He would probably report back to Tío Diego. José just hoped that he wasn't coming to cause trouble. His uncle and cousin had barely spoken to him at Abuelita' s funeral and completely ignored José's father. He had no idea what the feud was about all those years ago but it was obvious that Tío Diego had made no attempt to make up with either his parents or his brother, and Carlos had shown no interest in them either. Which made it even stranger that he was coming to the retreat. *Don't pre-judge*, he warned himself. *This might be Carlos's attempt to reconnect.* After all, the quarrel was nothing to do with the two cousins. But he couldn't help feeling uneasy, the last thing they needed was any sort of tension at their first retreat.

Eva

'That's great. Where are the others coming from?' Eva scanned the messages then paused, her hand shaking when she saw a familiar name. Saskia Bader. She hadn't heard from her for years. Saskia had latched onto Eva at college and they'd been good friends for a while. Eva had trusted her completely – until Saskia had let her down in the worst way possible. She'd apologised, Eva reminded herself, and had been gutted about what had happened but Eva had always felt a bit wary of her after that and over the years they had lost touch. She'd forgotten that they were still Facebook friends and she had no idea that Saskia was following the retreat page, or she would have blocked her from seeing the message about the trial stay. Saskia was the last person she wanted here, she belonged to Eva's old life. The life she wanted to forget. She wished now that she'd checked the bookings instead of leaving it to José, she could have messaged Saskia back and pretended that the six places had gone.

'Someone you know?'

José's question broke her chain of thought. She nodded,

pointing to Saskia's name. 'We were at college together. I haven't seen her for years.'

She clicked onto Saskia's profile and saw that her former friend worked in promotions now and lived in London. They had both studied Social Studies and Media at college, but it looked like neither of them had followed it through to a career – although the course had certainly come in useful for setting up the social media accounts for both her wellness page and the retreat page. She guessed it had come in useful for Saskia's promotions work too. She decided to check out her old friend's Facebook page later and bring herself up to speed on what Saskia had been up to, ready for when they met again.

'Someone we each know then, a couple from the US and a couple from England.' José pushed the chair back and stood up. 'I think this calls for a celebration. White wine or sangria?' he asked.

'Wine, please,' she told him. They both followed a healthy lifestyle but they enjoyed the occasional glass of wine or sangria – although the latter was for hot summer evenings as far as she was concerned. 'We've got a bottle chilling in the fridge.'

They had a lot to celebrate, she reminded herself. Their dream was coming to life. Excited as she was about their big venture, the knowledge that Saskia was one of their first guests made her feel uneasy. She didn't want her here. Saskia knew too much about her. Things Eva didn't want José knowing.

She had a bad feeling about this, Eva thought as she lay awake in bed that night, listening to José snoring softly. She could sense that he felt uneasy about Carlos coming to the retreat, and she was definitely worried about Saskia. She had betrayed Eva so badly, even if she had apologised contritely. Eve didn't want anything or anyone to come between her and José. He meant everything to her.

Eva had fallen for José's sultry Spanish looks the instant her eyes had rested on him, his thick dark hair tied up in a man bun, the neat moustache framing his top lip and just right amount of dark stubble smattering his square jaw, when she was having a meal out with her friend Katrina and had peeped through the open door of the restaurant kitchen on the way to the loo. He'd looked up from the carrots he was dicing, his fingers hovering over the blade of the large, sharp knife as his chocolate-brown eyes had met hers. He'd smiled and she'd smiled back. Then he went back to dicing the carrots and she went to the loo. When she returned the kitchen door was closed but the sexy chef was in her mind all evening. He'd obviously been thinking about her too because when they finished the meal he'd come over to their table and asked them if they enjoyed it.

'It was delicious,' she had told him while Katrina put her finger and thumb together and kissed them exaggeratedly in appreciation.

He grinned. 'I hope you will come back and eat here again,' he said. They promised that they would and he'd handed Eva a card – 'so that you can phone and book a table when you want to come again' – bowed then gone back to the kitchen. Eva had been about to put the card away when she saw some writing on the back.

Friday is my night off. Dinner? José x

A telephone number was written underneath.

'You must go!' Katrina had squealed, clapping her hands in delight. She'd been happily engaged to Brett for months and was always trying to set Eva up with someone. Eva didn't need much persuading and had phoned José the next day, agreeing to meet him for dinner. He was charming, funny, attentive, they talked as if they'd known each other for years and she laughed so much her belly ached. José told her that he'd done his chef training in England which was why he could speak the language so well, but missed the sunny climate of Spain and his grandparents. After that evening they were inseparable. When José took her to see the house his grandmother – who had died a few months previously – had left him in his will, Eva had immediately fallen in love with it, wild and uncared for though it was back then with its cracked walls, overgrown land and leaky roof. She remembered the first time she'd seen it. The sprawling villa stood in three acres of land, a sheltered terrace ran along the entire front and back of the house as did an upstairs balcony, and there was an additional room on the roof terrace. On the left of the house was a pool – empty then – sheltered by various fruit trees, and to the right a driveway for several cars. Lined with huge palm trees, it led down to the double gates. At the back was the olive grove, a couple of falling down casitas and a huge overgrown garden. It was such a perfect location, set halfway up the Andalucian mountains, and must have been a beautiful family home once, she thought. José had told her his dream of turning the villa into a holiday retreat, where people could relax and enjoy the healthy Mediterranean food that he intended to grow himself. 'I could organise a few day trips, but mainly I thought the guests could relax by the pool and enjoy the beautiful scenery, take time out to unwind.' She had seen the potential and suggested he might organise a few wellness activities too, a bit of yoga and mindfulness, telling him about how popular the health centre she worked at was. He thought it was a great idea and asked her to come on board, run yoga sessions, give massages and teach some basic wellness therapies, she'd agreed. She'd moved in two months later and they had finished renovating the house together. It had been hard work and they had both worked long hours but finally their dream was coming true. They were both excited and a bit nervous about opening the retreat, they had prepared for it so long and staked so much on it. Eva didn't want anything to ruin it.

Nothing would. She was overthinking. Saskia had sent her a Facebook message earlier saying that she was looking forward to seeing her again and having a catch-up. They had been good friends once. Eva had to let the past go. What was the saying? Don't let your past ruin your future. She had no intention of doing that.

5

The next three weeks were hectic. As this was their first ever relaxation retreat, Eva and José were anxious that it would be a success, and the fact that they each knew one of the guests personally pushed them even more to check every tiny detail. José was tending to the large vegetable patch now, his pride and joy and an additional source of income as he had been selling the surplus produce at the local market until the retreat was up and running, while Eva tidied up the flower beds. They both wanted everything to be perfect and knew that the first impressions were the most important.

Eva could tell that José was anxious about his cousin Carlos coming, and small wonder as they had only ever met twice before and that had been at his grandfather's funeral, and then a few years later, his grandmother's. José had told her that a family feud had divided the Lopez family before either he or Carlos was born, and no one had ever made any attempt to reconcile. Eva thought that was so sad, she was very close to her younger brother in the UK and her parents and older sister, who now all lived in Australia, her parents moving over when they retired a few years ago, wanting to be near their grandchildren. They might live in different countries but they all kept in regular contact with each other and she couldn't imagine any situation where they would fall out so drastically. José had told her that he had tried to find out the cause of the fall out several times but the family refused to talk about it. Eva was pleased that Carlos was coming to the retreat. It was time someone made the first move. Even if José was right and he was only coming to be 'nosey' it was still a big step. She really hoped both cousins got on and it was the start of repairing the feud. José was determined to impress his cousin with how he'd transformed their grandparents' former home, especially when his uncle Diego, Carlos's father, had responded to the news that José had inherited El Sueño by remarking that it was a 'falling-down dump' and José was welcome to it.

She guessed that José had mixed emotions about his cousin arriving. Just like she did about Saskia. They had been such close friends once, so close that they told each other everything, which was why Saskia's betrayal had rocked her to the core. Was Saskia coming to be nosey too? Or did she want to rekindle their friendship? Whatever the reason, Eva wanted to impress her former best friend as much as José wanted to impress his cousin. They both worked every hour they could up until the arrival date, cleaning, repairing, planning workshops and activities, meals and healthy drinks. They were out of bed at the crack of dawn and didn't crawl back into bed until midnight. But it was exciting. Their dream of turning the much-loved family villa in the Andalucian mountains into a peaceful retreat where people could come to unwind, enjoy healthy food and fresh air, exercise and learn some relaxation techniques, was on the first steps of its journey. And they were both determined to make it a success.

She couldn't believe the transformation they had made, she thought as she looked over at the freshly painted, large, three-storey, white house, gleaming against the bright blue sky –

ducking to avoid a huge black carpenter bee heading her way, knowing that while these bees were mainly harmless they had a tendency to fly smack into your forehead. It was such a pretty house with the white balustraded terrace and balcony running along both the front and back, the cerise bougainvillea creeping up the side and winding around some of the balustrades and the huge jacaranda tree with its mass of blue-violet flowers resplendent in the middle of the garden. Sunbeds were laid out by the side of the sparkling aquamarine pool, waiting for the guests to lounge in them, scarlet hibiscus bushes added a splash of colour and palm trees reached up to the sky like multi-fingered green hands trying to catch the sun. There was a big wooden table and chairs on the terrace where the guests could sit around to eat their meals outside, a swinging seat and a smaller mosaic table with matching chairs. Brightly coloured pots of pretty plants were dotted about here and there, including on the steps leading up to the roof terrace, while the inviting aroma of orange blossom, honeysuckle, lavender and rosemary filled the air. They had spent so much time, money and energy renovating it, but it was all worth it now. The retreat was going to be a success. She was sure it was.

It had to be. They had sunk all their savings into this. Their future depended on it.

6

MONDAY – DAY ONE

José

'What do you think?' José dipped a clean dessert spoon into the country vegetable soup that was simmering on the stove and held it out for Eva to taste. He'd picked the vegetables – courgettes, carrots, potatoes, peppers and tomatoes – from the plot at the back of the house that morning, and was making the soup as a welcoming lunch for their guests who were due to arrive any moment. Eva had baked a loaf of rustic bread to go with it. José was the main chef but Eva loved making different breads, quiches, healthy juices and salads.

'Delicious,' she said approvingly.

'Not too much ginger?' he asked. He always followed an old recipe of his grandmother's which included fresh ginger and garlic as well as a mix of dried herbs.

'It's perfect. As always.' Eva turned to the window as a loud toot of the horn announced the arrival of the minibus bringing their guests. José had opened the gates earlier, ready for Mario, their friendly neighbour who also acted as a paid handyman, airport pick-up and taxi driver, to drive in with the guests. 'They're here.'

José's eyes locked with hers for a moment, the air tingling with a mix of excitement and nerves. She looked gorgeous, as always, today opting for a pair of white cropped trousers and a yellow vest top – summery and casual, as he had with his beige shorts and white rolled-up-sleeved shirt. He whipped off his apron, hung it on the hook by the fridge and gave her a reassuring hug, sensing her nervousness. 'It's all going to be fine.' He kissed her on the cheek. 'Come on, let's go and greet our first guests.' He draped his arm loosely around her shoulders and they both walked outside together just as Mario opened the driver's door and stepped out of the silver minibus.

'*Bueno,*' Mario said cheerily in his thick Andalucian accent, chopping off the end of *buenos* as he always did, and not bothering to add *días*, as was the Andalucian custom. 'Your guests arrive.'

Our guests. José repeated the words in his mind. He had done it. He'd completed the renovations and now their holiday retreat was open for their very first guests. They were actually in business! He was determined the retreat was going to be a success so if his cousin had decided to be awkward he must handle it carefully and not get into an argument with him. *Give Carlos a chance*, he reminded himself. *He might want to end the feud as much as you do.*

He gave Eva's shoulders a squeeze then stepped forward smiling as Mario slid open the side door, ready to greet the first couple to get out. A man, tall and broad-shouldered with closely cropped brown hair dressed in dark chinos and a short-sleeved crisp white cotton shirt stepped out then turned back to help a petite woman in an expensive-looking red dress that skimmed her knees, her expertly cut blonde bob dancing on her shoulders. They looked like they were going out to a meal in a posh restaurant rather than a holiday retreat in the Andalucian mountains, José thought. He was sure that the clothes were designer, the handbag the woman was holding looked like an original Gucci. The man held out his hand. 'Sean Wallis, and this is my wife, Adrienne.' He nodded towards the woman beside him, whose eyes rested on José, a small smile playing on her lips.

'*Hola*,' she said softly.

'*Hola*. Welcome to El Sueño.'

Feeling a little uncomfortable with the way she was staring intensely at him, José first shook the hand Sean offered to him then briefly kissed Adrienne on both cheeks. 'We're delighted that you've decided to spend a few days at our retreat.'

'We hope you've had a good journey and that the conference went well.' Eva was right behind him and kissed both Sean and Adrienne on each cheek.

'Thank you, it was very informative and we made some useful contacts. It was intense though, as we knew it would be, which is why we chose to extend our stay and spend a few days here.' Sean turned to his wife and gave her a fond look. 'We've been talking for ages about having a few days away to reconnect with each other, we live such busy lives we barely see each other for days sometimes, so this was the ideal opportunity.' He looked around appreciatively. 'And I have to say that it's even more beautiful than I expected.'

'It's gorgeous,' Adrienne murmured in agreement, her blue eyes still fixed on José's face. 'I think that we're both going to have a wonderful time here.'

'I'm glad you think so.' He turned his gaze to Sean. 'My grandparents built this house themselves but I'm afraid it got too much for them as they got older and was in rather a neglected state when I inherited it a couple of years ago, after my grandmother died. We've worked hard to get this up and running, haven't we?' José turned to Eva.

'Blood, sweat and a lot of swearing!' she replied with a grin. Adrienne and Sean laughed.

'I'm sorry to hear about your grandmother passing away,' Adrienne said sympathetically.

José bowed his head slightly. 'She was old and ill, but...' His voice trailed away. The death of his beloved Abuelita had saddened him, she had been like a mother to him and he wished she had lived long enough to meet Eva. He knew that she would have approved of her. Eva was so kind and gentle. She would never knowingly hurt anyone.

He glanced over his shoulder and saw that the other guests had now stepped out of the minibus and Eva was greeting them.

'Excuse me,' José said as he went to join them. Out of the corner of his eye he saw Adrienne scowl and wondered what her husband had done to upset her. She seemed a bit intense. Sean had said the conference had been busy so maybe she was still in work mode, perhaps that's why she stared at José so intently – wasn't it the business mantra to hold someone's gaze as you spoke to them? It was good to have such high-flying guests. Hopefully they would enjoy their stay and recommend them to their friends.

7

Eva

'Eva! I can't believe that it's been so long since we saw each other!' Saskia exclaimed. She was dressed in red shorts that emphasised her long tanned legs, and a white tee shirt, her dark hair plaited into two coils and pinned each side of her head, which made her look not a day older than when Eva last saw her ten years ago. She flung her arms around Eva and hugged her tight. 'Oh it's so good to see you,' she said then stepped back, looking her up and down. 'You look amazing. Living in Spain certainly suits you.'

She sounded like she really meant it and Eva felt guilty for feeling anxious about her attending their retreat. 'Thank you. So do you. And it's lovely to see you again.' She meant it too. It was so nice to see a familiar face and Saskia had been such a good friend. Until... Eva pushed the memory from her mind, the past was gone, she had to focus on the here and now. 'Excuse me while I greet everyone, we'll catch up later,' Eva said, conscious that the other guests, a casually dressed couple and a man who looked a little like José so must be Carlos, were talking to José while Mario was taking their suitcases out of the back of the minibus.

'I hope you've all had a pleasant journey here,' Eva said, joining them.

'It's beautiful countryside,' the man from the couple said. 'I'm Nathan and this is my partner, Bianca.' They looked very relaxed and natural, Nathan in cut-off denims and a burgundy striped tee shirt, Bianca in a pretty floral midi dress – a direct contrast to Sean and Adrienne, who seemed so polished. Eva hoped everyone would get on. She knew from the forms she had asked everyone to fill in with information about their age, any health issues or dietary requirements to help her and José plan the activities and meals, that Nathan and Bianca were early twenties, a little younger than the rest of the group – Saskia was thirty, the same as Eva whilst Adrienne and Sean were mid-thirties, like José. They had been pleased there wasn't too much difference in the age of the guests, thinking it should make it easier for them to gel.

'Pleased to meet you,' Bianca said pleasantly, tucking her wavy fair hair behind her ears.

'So this is where our *abuelos* lived then, *primo*,' Carlos said, using the Spanish terms for grandparents and cousin. He thrust his hands in the pockets of his beige shorts, the olive-green tee shirt a little too tight over his belly, his gaze taking in the terrace and the villa. 'It is impressive.'

'Haven't you been here before?' Saskia sounded surprised. 'I thought you said on the way here that José was your cousin.'

'It is a long story...' José started to say but Carlos shook his head sadly.

'No. Unfortunately my father fell out with his parents many years ago, before I was born. I have no idea why. I was never taken to see my grandparents. Nor did they ask to meet me. José and I, we met briefly at first my grandfather's then my grandmother's funeral. I knew that José had inherited the family home so when I saw that he had turned it into a retreat and was offering half-price holidays I thought I'd come and have a look what my cousin has been up to.' He held out his hand and smiled. 'You've done well, *primo*.'

Wow! Eva hadn't expected Carlos to spill out all that personal stuff as soon as he arrived. She glanced quickly at José, who looked a bit taken aback too but quickly pulled himself together, took Carlos's hand and shook it. 'Thank you. You are very welcome here.'

Well, it looked like he was being friendly and wanted to bury the hatchet, Eva thought, which was a good thing. She hoped he wasn't going to come out with more personal stuff though, that would make things awkward.

Mario lifted the luggage out of the back of the minibus then called '*Luego*', waved and drove back out.

'Welcome, everyone,' José said. 'Let's start with introducing ourselves. I'm José. I am a chef in a restaurant in Malaga port, for the time being, until our retreat gets off the ground. I will be cooking all the meals here from food we've grown in our own garden, so everything you eat will be freshly picked and healthy. I use no pesticides or fertilisers.' He smiled his easy, charming grin, encompassing the whole group. Then turned to Eva. 'This is Eva, my partner – both business and otherwise,' he added with a twinkle in his eye. 'She is in charge of the wellness side of the retreat.' He paused, waiting for Eva to speak.

She smiled. 'I'm a certified wellness coach, mindfulness and healing are my passion. I presently work in an exclusive clinic in Marbella and am trained in massage, acupressure, yoga and natural healing.' All this information was on their Facebook page but by starting off the introductions they hoped it would make the guests feel more relaxed. 'I am happy to provide a personal wellbeing guide for each of you, if you wish. And we are both available to answer any questions you may have.'

'How on earth do you both manage to work and run this retreat?' Saskia asked.

'We're working part-time at the moment – and have taken a week's holiday leave for this week's retreat – but José is giving up his job in the summer when the retreat will be open full-time, and I'll continue working part-time for a while,' Eva explained.

'Well, I'm sure it will be a big success.' Saskia beamed. 'Should we introduce ourselves too?' she asked, pre-empting Eva's next move. She turned to the rest of the group. 'I'm Saskia, pleased to meet you all.' She held out her hand and shook hands with the other guests in turn. They all followed suit, introducing themselves and shaking hands.

'It's a pleasure to have you all here and we very much hope you enjoy your stay with us,' José said when the introductions were over. 'We want our relaxation retreat to be as pleasurable as possible which is why we have given you all a big discount to try it out and give us helpful feedback.'

'There's a book on the table in the hall for you to write in any comments you want, or you can come and talk to us if you prefer,' Eva added. 'We'll give you all a tour around later but for now, I'll show you your rooms so you can freshen up. You will find a list of the week's planned activities in your rooms and can decide which you would like to attend.'

'Of course none of them are compulsory, if you wish to spend your time here relaxing by the pool or exploring the area by yourself that is absolutely fine,' José continued. 'Oh and the wi-fi password is also on the list, but I have to warn you that we don't have a strong signal here, and that you might also have trouble with phone reception at times.'

'That's okay, we've come here to get away from everything. I'm sure we can manage without the internet for a few days,' Nathan said.

'The kitchen and dining rooms are on the right and the

lounge on the left, feel free to make yourself at home and relax in the lounge whenever you wish,' Eva said as she led the way inside, the guests following with their suitcases. She pointed to a large notebook on a coffee table in the hall. 'That's the comment book. We hope you'll sign it and are grateful for any feedback you give. Obviously, you can write anonymously if you prefer.'

'Lunch will be served in half an hour, we can all get better acquainted then,' José added before he went back into the kitchen to continue with the lunch preparations while Eva led the way down the hall to the stairs, the guests following with their cases.

'All your rooms are on the next floor,' Eva said as they climbed the stairs. 'They all have an ensuite, and there's also a communal bathroom and separate toilet at the other end of the hall. Each room opens onto a balcony, where you'll find a table and chairs in case you want to sit outside and admire the views.'

'I noticed the balconies, the balustrades look so white and pristine. Very summery,' Saskia remarked.

'Thank you,' Eva replied. The balustrades had been a mess up until a couple of months ago, the yellowing paint cracked and chipped but they had repainted them and were pleased with the results. Although there were still a couple of cracks on the balcony rail on the roof terrace you couldn't really see it unless you were close up and none of the guests were sleeping in that room. Besides, as José had said, fine cracks in the walls and balustrades were common in Spain due to the intense heat.

'Are you two sleeping in the big room on the roof terrace?' Adrienne asked. 'It's so private up there and the views of the mountains are stunning, aren't they?'

Her question took Eva by surprise, it was almost as if Adrienne had actually seen the large upper terrace room.

'Actually no, it's much more convenient for us to be in the room on the ground level so we're on hand if the guests need us.'

'Can we have the roof terrace room then?' Adrienne asked

eagerly.

'I'm afraid that it isn't ready for guests yet,' Eva told her as she reached the top of the stairs. It was the one room they hadn't got around to redecorating. It was where José had slept ever since his childhood when he had visited his grandparents, and where he was still sleeping when Eva moved in. Eva had suggested doing up the large bedroom on the ground floor with the French doors leading out into the garden and moving down there and José had agreed. She loved to open the wide French doors in the summer and let the fresh air into the room, then step out onto the terrace to sip her fruit juice and drink in the fragrant smells of the plants and trees.

'You have the first room on the front, Adrienne and Sean, all the rooms have stunning views,' she said, walking along the hallway. Eva opened the door so that they could see inside. 'I hope you'll be very comfortable here.'

Adrienne went straight over to the window and peered out, her hand shielding her eyes from the sun. 'Come and look, Sean. It's such a gorgeous view over the valley.'

Leaving them to settle in, Eva moved on to the next room, which was Carlos's – he and Saskia had the slightly smaller rooms. Carlos nodded when she opened the door, disappeared into his room and closed the door behind him. It must be strange for him to be here, Eva thought. There were still family photos on the wall in the hall, a family he had never known. She felt sad for him, all those years without knowing his grandparents or the rest of his family.

Nathan and Bianca were delighted with their room. 'I could stand here and look out of the window all day,' Bianca said as she gazed out at the pool and fruit trees below. 'I'm feeling more relaxed already.'

Saskia was just as enthusiastic. 'It's gorgeous, so light and peaceful.' She opened her arms wide. 'I'm going to love it here. I won't want to go home.'

8

'Everyone happy with their rooms?' José asked, looking up from laying the kitchen table as Eva walked into the kitchen. They'd decided earlier that it would be cosier to eat around the large wooden kitchen table, which was plenty big enough to seat eight, rather than in the more formal dining room.

'Yes, although Adrienne and Sean wanted the roof terrace room, she must have noticed it as they came up the drive.' Eva went over to the cupboard to get the loaf of rustic Spanish bread and placed it on a board with a breadknife between the two bowls of olives which José had placed in the middle of the table. 'I think that when we do have it ready for guests we should charge more for it than the other rooms.' The large upstairs room was so private, with the only access being the outside steps at the side of the house, and had a spacious ensuite. They'd painted the balustrades lining the steps and put two big Buddha heads on the top of each pillar, which made the tiled stairway look very impressive.

'Yes, I agree. It is still my favourite room, but I know it is better for us to be downstairs when we have guests in the house.' José set a brightly coloured soup bowl, a glass and cutlery wrapped in a white serviette at every place setting as he spoke.

Eva flashed him a smile. 'Maybe we can move back up there for the winter. We probably won't have so many guests then.' She knew how much he loved that room and felt a little guilty that she'd persuaded him to move downstairs, even if it was more practical. She opened the fridge and took out two jugs, one of spring water infused with cucumber, mint and peach and one containing a freshly squeezed mix of orange and ruby grapefruit that she'd made that morning – although the orange trees were full of blossom there were still some of last year's fruit which were fine for juicing – and placed them on the table too.

'You are very thoughtful.' He came behind her and wrapped his arms around her waist, kissing her on the cheek. 'There is no need though, I am happy where we are and I think it will be cosier there in the winter,' he told her.

He was right, the winters were short but cold. Spanish houses were built to keep the sun out, and they had no central heating at the villa. In the winter the house was chilly so they usually kept to the downstairs rooms, using either the log fire in the lounge to keep warm or a bottled gas heater – or both if it was very cold – and an electric heater for the bedroom.

'I could smell that delicious aroma upstairs,' Saskia announced as she came into the kitchen a little later. 'It's gorgeous here, Eva. You are lucky. I'm so pleased how you've turned your life around. I've often wondered how you were faring.'

Eva glanced quickly at José, wondering if he'd heard her but he was busy stirring the soup. She had to get Saskia on her own and talk to her. She was sure that her old college friend meant well and was genuinely pleased for her but José knew nothing about Eva's past life and she wanted to keep it that way. Now wasn't the time to say anything though, she could hear the others coming down the stairs. She'd find a quiet moment to talk to Saskia later.

Soon they were all sitting down at the table, tucking into José's soup.

'This soup is delicious, did you make it yourself, José?' Adrienne asked as she broke a piece off her bread roll and dipped it into the soup.

'I did. I make all the meals you will be eating here, while Eva makes the fresh bread and invigorating juices. Also all the fruit, vegetables and salads that you eat here are homegrown,' José replied. 'Healthy eating, healthy living is what the retreat is all about. Our aim is to help you all relax and unwind by providing nutritional food, exercise and time to think.'

'That sounds just what we need,' Nathan said. 'I'm interested in the "growing your own food" workshops you're running. I've often said to Bianca that I'd like a vegetable patch in the garden. I'm hoping to pick up some tips.'

'I'd like a herb garden,' Saskia said. 'I live in an apartment but I could grow some herbs in a window-box, couldn't I?'

'You can, they are very easy to grow. I will show you how to dry them too. I use a lot of herbs in cooking, they are vital for enhancing and bringing out the flavour of the foods.' José put a bit of bread roll in his mouth and chewed it before continuing. 'You will notice on the timetable that the "growing your own food" workshop is before lunch. That is so we can pick the vegetables fresh then I can use them to make lunch.'

'That sounds perfect,' Bianca said. 'I'm looking forward to Eva's mindfulness activities and yoga sessions too. I want to take part in everything.'

'Have you been a wellness coach for long, Eva?' Adrienne asked, pouring herself a glass of the infused water.

'Almost eight years. Mental and physical wellbeing is my

passion,' Eva replied. 'We live in such a fast-paced, cut-throat world that sometimes people forget how important it is to take time out to unwind and look after both their physical and mental wellbeing.'

'That's very true.' Saskia had finished her soup now and sat back in her chair, looking at Eva with interest. 'What made you make such a big change of direction?' She glanced around the table. 'We were both at college together studying social media,' she explained.

Why was Saskia asking Eva that when surely she could guess the answer? She knew how low Eva had got, how desperate she'd been. Eva pushed the memories from her mind and tried to scramble together an answer.

'We all change direction in our lives, don't you think?' José came to her rescue, Eva wondered if he could see how she was floundering. 'I've spent most of my life working as a chef in various restaurants but I've had the dream of running a retreat like this for a long time, I can hardly believe that it's coming true.' He smiled at Eva. 'Eva's social media skills and wellbeing training come in very useful. She created the website, Facebook and Instagram pages, although we both like to post and reply to comments.'

'I'm keen to take part in the mindfulness sessions too,' Nathan said. 'I think the mind is very powerful but unfortunately mine is always buzzing with things I need to do, so much so that I sometimes find it difficult to switch off and sleep. I could do with learning a few tips on focusing and shutting things out.'

'I'm up for all of that. I really need to destress. These last few months have been so difficult and I get really anxious,' Bianca said.

Nathan reached over and clasped his hand over hers. 'I know, darling.'

Was she referring to work pressures, or personal stuff? Eva

didn't like to ask. She hated anyone prying about her past and always thought that if people wanted to tell you something they would of their own accord. Maybe Bianca would open up during the personal wellness consultation.

'Adrienne and I just want to relax and chill out by the pool, don't we, dear?' Sean asked, smiling adoringly at his wife sitting next to him. 'Our work life is so insane we hardly have time to ourselves. The conference in Marbella was very intense so we thought that this would be a great opportunity to unwind and take some time out. We want to reconnect with each other and spend some quality time together but we will join in some of the events. I think Adrienne is particularly looking forward to the yoga and massage sessions, aren't you, dear? And I am definitely up for the nature walks and "relaxing through creativity" session.'

Adrienne nodded. 'I am. It will be heaven to have a few days to unwind and relax. Yoga is something I've been wanting to do for some time. I hope I can learn enough basic poses to continue at home.'

'As you've all put on your forms that you are new to yoga, I will be introducing you to the basics and I can give you information about YouTube tutorials, books and courses that you might find helpful when you return home if any of you wish to continue with it,' Eva said.

'That sounds good to me,' Bianca said.

Nathan glanced at her and smiled. He seemed very protective, Eva thought, whereas there seemed a bit of underlying tension between Adrienne and Sean. She knew that a lot of couples chose to go on wellness retreats to give them a chance to spend time together, reconnecting through both learning new skills and relaxing away from the daily grind of life. She also knew that sometimes this closeness could cause problems between a couple who weren't used to spending a lot of time together and found that they irritated each other. She hoped this wasn't the case with Adrienne and Sean, or Nathan and Bianca. That would affect the energy of the whole retreat. She would look out for any signs of tension in the group and try to diffuse it, she decided.

9

'I know you've all only just arrived but does anyone have any questions?' Eva asked. 'Please don't hesitate to raise any concerns or queries you have with us.'

'I was surprised to see from the list in our room that you expect us to do our own cleaning.' Adrienne didn't look too pleased about this.

'We have no staff so yes we expect you to be responsible for keeping your own rooms clean but we provide fresh towels whenever you need them. Simply bring the dirty towels down with you and we will replace them,' Eva told her. 'And do let us know if there is anything else you need to make your stay here comfortable. Toiletries are provided but I expect you've probably brought your own, and you're welcome to use the vacuum cleaner or any cleaning materials if you want to spruce up your rooms. They're in that large cupboard next to the fridge.'

'All your drinks and meals are included in the price so please ask if you would like additional refreshments,' José said. 'We keep a variety of fruit juices, smoothies and healthy drinks in the fridge.'

'We also have wine and sangria if any of you fancy a glass in the evening,' Eva added. 'Healthy living doesn't mean that you can't enjoy the occasional drop of wine.'

'Glad to hear it. I'm really looking forward to a relaxing week,' Sean said.

'Me too.' Carlos had been quiet up to now. 'And the opportunity to spend some time with my cousin. I barely know my father's side of the family.' Carlos picked up his glass and swigged back his juice.

'That's such a shame, especially as your grandparents are gone now,' Saskia said sympathetically. 'Still, at least you and José can get to know each other now.'

Carlos raised his half-full glass. 'We can.'

Eva glanced at José, wondering how he felt about his cousin making the family split so public yet again. He seemed unperturbed, she noticed with relief. Actually it could be a good thing that they were being so open, it might help everyone else speak more freely. They seemed to both want to bury the hatchet. Perhaps they could even persuade their fathers to meet and make up once the retreat was over. José had told her his uncle Diego lived in Barcelona, she wouldn't mind a trip up there.

'You're very welcome,' José said. He glanced around the table to include them all. 'We're delighted to have you all here and sincerely hope that after a few days with us you will all go home feeling refreshed and having learnt some relaxation techniques to help you cope with life's stresses.' He pushed his chair back and stood up. 'Now, let me get the second course. It's a kale salad with balsamic vinegar, parmesan cheese and home-made breadsticks with chard. I hope that suits everyone.'

'That sounds delicious,' Bianca said.

'Once we've finished eating, we'll give you a tour of the grounds, then we thought you might enjoy a nature walk to explore the area a little, followed by a creativity session. Although if any of you prefers to go to your rooms and relax there, please go ahead. I know that you had an early start this morning and must be tired.' Eva stood up too and started clearing up the dishes then followed José into the kitchen.

'They seem a nice bunch,' José said as he took the salad he'd prepared earlier out of the fridge.

'How do you feel about your cousin being here? He seems pleasant and it sounds as if he genuinely wants to get to know you and repair the family feud.'

'It's not our argument, it's nothing to do with us. It was between our grandparents, my father and Tío Diego. It will be good to get to know each other, as Carlos says.' José added parmesan onto the dish of salad. He raised his deep brown eyes to hers. 'I told you there was nothing to worry about.'

He had, but she was a worrier and all the mindfulness techniques in the world couldn't change that, but they did help her control her negative thoughts. José put a bowl of small, boiled herb potatoes onto a tray alongside the salad then carried them through into the dining area. Eva followed with more rolls and another jug of the infused water, which had gone down very well, she noticed.

It seemed as if the guests had already gelled with each other as a lively discussion was going on about holidays. Adrienne and Sean were entertaining everyone with stories about the exploits of some of the guests at the hotel chain they managed. Bianca was listening, wide-eyed. 'I can't believe it,' she gasped.

'A lot of people act completely differently when they're on holiday,' Carlos said. 'I'm a tour guide in Rome and you wouldn't believe the things the tourists get up to. One woman in my group stuffed a Tiffany lamp from her hotel room into her suitcase but was caught as she tried to leave. She pretended it was a mistake.' He shook his head. 'Guests are always trying to sneak out towels, bathrobes, even cutlery.'

'What exciting jobs you both have,' Bianca remarked. 'I'm a librarian. I love my job but nothing really thrilling happens – although that's the way I prefer it. I don't like drama or conflict.'

She glanced at Nathan. 'Whereas Nathan is a policeman, so his days are full of both! He could tell you some stories that would keep you awake at night.'

'I could, but I'm here to forget about work,' Nathan said.

'As we are,' Sean agreed.

'What about you, Saskia, what do you do for a living?' Adrienne asked.

'I work for a promotion agency, so my day can consist of anything from giving out free sweets at a shopping centre to dressing up as a chicken to promote a new meat range,' Saskia replied.

'That sounds fun,' Bianca said. 'What's the strangest thing you've had to dress up as?'

Saskia tilted her head to one side as if thinking. 'A doughnut,' she replied after a couple of minutes. 'A new Delightful Donuts store was opening in a big shopping centre and a few of us models had to dress up as the various doughnuts. I was a chocolate one with sprinkles. Actually I might have a photo of it.' She opened her handbag which was hanging on the back of the chair, took out her phone, selecting the photo gallery and scrolling through. 'There we are!' She held up the phone so they could see the photo.

'That's hilarious,' Carlos chuckled.

'Another time I had to dress up as a bee and walk up and down the High Street, that was to promote a brand of honey!' Saskia said with a grin. 'It was August and very hot. I thought I was going to faint.'

'I bet you've got an interesting portfolio of photos though,' Carlos said.

'I sure have, although luckily I'm not identifiable in some of them.'

Everyone laughed.

Eva listened in surprise. She hadn't realised that Saskia worked as a promotions model, she'd imagined she was working more with the admin, securing the contracts, or advertising. They were both different people now, life took you to places you hadn't planned. Look at her. Ten years ago, when she last saw Saskia, she had been planning on working in publishing.

'It's great that you and Eva have been friends so long,' Bianca said. 'I guess you lived in the UK then, Eva. What area did you live in?'

'The West Midlands,' Eva replied. 'I've been living in Spain for five years now.'

'Eva and I were at college together in Sutton,' Saskia was saying.

'You grew up in Sutton too, didn't you, Bianca?' Nathan asked.

Bianca nodded. 'For a while.' She bit her lip as she rubbed her finger around the rim of her glass. 'My father was killed in a road accident. My mother couldn't face living in the area anymore so we moved away to Devon.'

Eva stared at her, shocked to the core. It couldn't be. Could it?

10

There were gasps from the rest of the group, who all looked shocked. Eva could feel Saskia's eyes on her. *Please don't say anything*, she prayed, her heart thudding.

'Oh goodness, that's dreadful!' Adrienne said. 'I'm so sorry to hear that. Were you just a child?'

Bianca nodded. Eva could see that she was making a big effort to control her emotions. Nathan reached out and squeezed her hand reassuringly.

'Such a tragedy. I am so sorry,' José murmured sympathetically.

'It was, but I didn't mean to come out with it like that and put a damper on things on our first day.' She gave him a wan smile.

'Please don't apologise, this is a safe space for any of you to talk about things that are bothering you,' José said gently.

'I'm okay, really,' Bianca assured him. 'Anyway, that's enough about me. What about you, José? Your English is very good. Have you always lived in Spain?'

Eva desperately tried to pull herself together. She wanted to close her eyes and take a few deep breaths but that would only draw attention to herself so she muttered some affirmations in her head instead. *I forgive and release the past and look forward to the future. I forgive and release the past and look forward to the future.* She could feel herself relaxing and tried to focus on José's reply.

'Sí, apart from a couple of years I spent training to be a chef in a London restaurant. I grew up in Marbella, my parents have a business there. Always they were busy, so I spent most of my holidays with my *abuelos*. I have many happy memories of my time here, so when my *abuelita* left me El Sueño in her will I decided that I wanted to make it into a happy place for other people too.'

'That's a sweet story, and how lucky you were to be left a place like this. It's beautiful!' Saskia remarked.

'It is but I'm afraid it was in quite a bad state. It's taken me...' He looked at Eva. '*Us*,' he corrected, 'a long time to get it like this. Although it was easier when I met Eva and she moved in and helped me.'

'And how long have you lived here?' Bianca asked Eva.

'I moved in two years ago, but José had already done a lot of work.' José always acknowledged the work she had put into the renovations too, and she loved him for that, but he'd done a lot of the structural work before they met.

'So why didn't your grandmother leave the property to your father?' Sean asked.

'My father didn't want it. He likes living in Marbella and this villa was too much work for him. He was pleased for it be passed to me and to see it renovated.'

'Then why not split it between you and Carlos, if you are cousins?' Adrienne asked.

'Because we are the – how do you say – black sheep,' Carlos said. He had been so silent through the conversation, Eva had almost forgotten he was there. 'As I said, my dad fell out with his parents and brother, José's father, before I was born.'

This was so awkward, Eva thought. Eva wondered if it had bothered Carlos that José had inherited the house rather than him, especially as he was the eldest grandson. It only seemed fair though as José had been very close to his grandparents and had looked after his grandmother when his grandfather died. Not that it was José's fault, but it wasn't Carlos's either. Both of the men had missed out on a relationship with their only uncle and cousin. It seemed dreadfully harsh to abandon one son and his child like that, yet José had often told her how kind his grandparents were, how they had the time to give him the affection his busy parents didn't.

'So you've never even been here before?' Saskia asked curiously.

'No, that's why I signed up. Thought I could pay my cousin a visit and take a look around the place too. Papá said it was practically a ruin so I'm very surprised to see it looking so well-cared for.'

'It was still in quite a state when I moved in and José had been living here and working on it almost a year by then. We've kept a scrapbook of how the house used to be and have recorded the renovations we've made if you want to see it,' Eva told Carlos. She was proud of the work they'd done here, and José was too. Perhaps if Carlos could see how bad the villa was when José inherited it and realised the amount of money and work they had put into it, he wouldn't resent José's inheritance.

'I do,' Adrienne said. 'It sounds fascinating.'

Eva fetched the scrapbook from the table in the hall and passed it around. There were lots of gasps of surprise and admiration over the photos recording the transformation from a run-down house in desperate need of care to the beautiful gleaming white villa it was today.

'Wow, you've worked wonders, mate,' Nathan said.

Carlos had flipped back the pages and was studying the first photograph, which showed a young José and his grandparents sitting in the terrace. What was he thinking? Eva wondered. Did he wish that he had known his grandparents too?

'You've certainly spent a lot of money, and time, on the place. I don't envy you. Although it would have been nice to have known my *abuelos*.' There was a hint of wistfulness in his voice. He shut the album. 'You did well, *primo*.' He patted José on the back in what Eva thought was a condescending manner but José simply nodded.

'Thanks.'

Eva wasn't surprised that Carlos was glad he hadn't had the bother of doing up the villa. There were many falling-down houses in Spain that had been passed to grandchildren who couldn't be bothered or didn't have the funds to do them up so left them to ruin. She knew that José had spent a small fortune on the place, and they had both put in a lot of hours. It had been very stressful at times.

The meal now finished, José suggested giving the guests a tour of the grounds, first taking them out of the back to see the pool, which was a beautiful clear blue, pristine sunbeds lining each side against the backdrop of orange, lemon and olive trees.

'This is gorgeous, I don't need to see anything else,' Saskia exclaimed. 'I'm happy to spend every day here just enjoying the view and smelling the orange blossom and jasmine.'

'Me too, it looks idyllic,' Bianca agreed. 'I wouldn't mind living here myself.'

After giving them a chance to admire the pool for a few minutes, José led the way over to the vegetable patch to the right, proudly pointing out the variety of vegetables and salads that he grew.

'Hey, that's a fantastic selection!' Nathan said admiringly. 'You're even growing artichokes and asparagus, I see.'

'Yes, I grow a large variety. All the food you eat here will be homegrown,' José said proudly. 'And all the juices we make ourselves too.'

'Do you make your own wine?' Sean asked, nodding over at the grapevine growing along the top of the terrace.

'That's something we plan to do in the future,' Eva told them. 'For now you'll have to make do with wine from the local supermarket. But it is very nice, I promise.'

They carried on along the path to the two casitas. 'Hey, are these for the guests too?' Saskia asked.

'They will be, but they aren't quite ready yet,' Eva told her. 'We hope to have these and the terrace room ready for use next year.'

Behind the casitas was the olive grove. 'This is amazing, do you make your own olive oil?' Sean asked.

'No, we cure them ourselves, so all the olives you eat here are our own, but we take the surplus olives to the local olive mill to be pressed to make the oil.'

'How fascinating.' Carlos looked around.

'Where does that little gate lead to?' Saskia pointed to a small wooden gate at the bottom of the garden.

'Up the mountain. We're going for a nature walk there shortly. Please make sure you keep that gate locked otherwise the goats will get in and chew up everything on site,' José told her.

'You get goats here, how quaint!' Adrienne exclaimed.

'The goatherd takes them up the mountain every morning and brings them down every afternoon,' José said. 'You'll hear them if you don't see them!'

On the way back to the villa they stopped to look at the studio apartment where Eva would be giving massages and wellness consultations. Then, tour over, the guests went to their rooms to unpack and relax for half an hour before the nature walk. Eva was surprised when they all said they wanted to go on that, she was expecting Adrienne and Sean to say they would prefer to stay home and sit out on the terrace. They didn't seem the sort to enjoy walking up a mountain.

'It looks like we're off to a good start. They all seem to be getting on fine, and are eager to take part in the activities,' Eva told José. She was excited for the coming week.

11

José

'I didn't realise that the grounds were so big. How many acres are there here?' Carlos asked in Spanish, ambling into the kitchen, hands in his pocket.

José turned from the fridge, the jug of homemade lemonade in his hands. 'Almost three,' he replied back in Spanish.

Carlos raised his eyebrows. 'That's a lot to look after. And all those olive trees too. Surely that is too many olives and too much oil for you to consume?'

'It is. We sell the surplus oil, it brings in some much-needed income,' José replied.

Carlos pursed his lips. 'So our *abuelos'* house is turning out to be very lucrative for you,' he muttered.

José put the jug down and looked his cousin in the eye. 'We are recouping some of the money we spent on doing it up, yes, thankfully. You have seen the photos how the house was,' he reminded him. 'Our *abuelos* were old. It was too much work for them. I came over as much as I could and when Mario's parents died he came to live in their house nearby and helped too, but he has his own house and land to look after. Gradually this villa got into a real state of disrepair. Eva and I, we had a lot of work to do.'

'And what about Tío Pablo, didn't he come and help?'

José kept his voice calm. He didn't like his cousin's attitude but then maybe he had the right to ask questions, they were his grandparents too. Then again, Carlos could have contacted them. Tried to visit. Once he became an adult, he could have made his own decisions.

'My father is a busy man, he has a business to run.' He smiled ruefully. 'He never had time for me, never mind to run this place. He did offer to pay for someone to come in and do the garden and any repairs needed but our grandparents were proud and refused.' That was his father's answer to everything, throw money at it, José thought sadly. His father had even sent gardeners and decorators to the villa but Abuelo had turned them away and told him that if he didn't stop he would fall out with him too. Although, José was sure that if his *papá* had turned up to help then Abuelo would have been glad of that, he was always pleased when José came for the weekend and helped pick the fruit, rotavate the land, clean the pool, anything he could see needed doing. He would have liked to help more but he had to work too and his own apartment to take care of. 'It is a pity *your* father didn't try to make it up with Abuelo,' he said. 'It is sad for families to fall out.'

Carlos pulled out a chair and sat down. 'Do you know what the argument was about?'

José shook his head. 'My father refuses to talk about it.'

'As does mine.'

'We can do nothing about their fall out but we can end it. You are welcome here.' José held out his hand.

There was a slight hesitation then Carlos held out his hand too and the two cousins shook hands.

José looked over Carlos's shoulder and saw Eva standing in the doorway smiling at them. Although he and Eva mainly spoke English to each other he knew that she understood enough Spanish to have caught the gist of the conversation and was pleased he and Carlos were getting on.

12

Eva

Bianca's reveal about her father's death played on Eva's mind. Saskia had kept quiet, although she must have been wondering the same as Eva, and would surely know how much it would be playing on Eva's mind. She had to talk to Saskia, make sure that she didn't say anything in front of José.

The bedroom door was half-open. Eva knocked on it and poked her head around. Saskia's suitcase was open on the bed and she was unpacking. 'Hi, I'm just checking that you have everything you need,' Eva said cheerily. 'We'll be leaving for the walk in ten minutes.'

'It's lovely, you've thought of everything.' She looked up. 'Come on in. We can have a catch-up for a few mins if you have time.'

'Sure.' Eva walked in and shut the door behind her. 'It's been a while, hasn't it?'

'Ten years. And you look really well. I'm so relieved. It was part of the reason I wanted to come here. You were broken when I saw you last. I thought you would never recover.'

Eva swallowed. Broken was a good word to describe the despair that had taken over her and wrecked her life, plunging her to a place so dark she thought she would never get out. She'd worked hard to pull herself up from the guilt and despair that had consumed her. 'I wanted to talk to you about that.' She sat down on the edge of the bed. 'The thing is, José doesn't know anything about it. I've never told him. And I'd rather he didn't find out.'

Saskia gave her a hug. 'He won't find out from me. We've all got stuff in our past that we want to keep there. I'm so pleased that you're over it all now.' She stepped back and studied Eva. 'I saw the look on your face when Bianca told us about her father and wondered if it had brought it all back to you.' She placed a comforting hand on Eva's arm. 'I'm your friend. I'm here for you. I won't let you down.'

You did before, how do I know I can trust you? The words shot across Eva's mind but she didn't voice them. The past was the past. She had to move on. She couldn't let anything drag her down into that dark place again. 'Thank you, that means a lot,' she said as she got up. 'I'll see you outside in a few minutes.'

'Just putting my trainers on and I'll be with you,' Saskia replied.

Before they set off for the mountain walk, Eva checked that everyone had changed into comfortable shoes for the walk and handed out small bottles of water. 'It's important to keep hydrated even though it's not too hot at the moment,' she said. In the summer they would do the walk earlier or later in the day. 'Remember to take notes of anything that interests you for the "relax through creativity" session later.'

'How far up the mountain are we going for our nature walk? We're not walking all the way to the top, are we?' Adrienne asked as José led the way out the small gate at the back of the garden that led up the mountain.

José glanced back at her. 'No, don't worry. We will walk for twenty minutes or so then we'll stop for a rest and refreshments before we continue. It's more about using your senses to notice your surroundings than the exercise, although that's important too, of course.'

Eva closed the gate and pulled the bolt across, it was a bit stiff and took her a couple of minutes, by which time the others were a little ahead all apart from Saskia, who waited for her.

'Having trouble?' she asked.

'The bolt needs some oil on it. I'll do it when we get back,' Eva said, quickening her pace to catch up.

'Isn't it beautiful?' Saskia asked as Eva fell into step beside her. 'If I lived here I'd want to take a walk every day.'

'We do walk here as often as we can,' Eva told her. She loved living on the mountain – although it could be terribly windy, it was invigorating, wild and stunning with the pencil-trunked pine trees dominating the landscape and the occasional black-winged kite or eagle soaring across the cobalt-blue sky sometimes disappearing behind a whisper of cotton-wool cloud then reappearing again.

José was up the front talking to Sean and Adrienne, with Nathan, Bianca and Carlos a little behind. It wasn't a steep track and Eva and Saskia chatted as they walked side by side, it was almost as if the last decade had never happened and she and Saskia were best buddies at college again. They'd always chatted away easily, shared confidences, kept each other's secrets.

Until Saskia had betrayed her.

As if she could read her thoughts, Saskia reached out and gently touched Eva's arm. 'I'm glad that you're so happy now and really sorry about what I did. It's so good to catch up again. I hope we can keep in touch when I go back?'

'I'd like that too,' Eva said. She'd put the past behind her since moving to Spain, her life was a different one now. She had to focus on the future not the past.

13

After a while they sat down by a stream to have a drink and rest for a few minutes.

'This would be a good chance to take a few notes or make some rough sketches for our session this afternoon, but first let's focus on being present and mindful of our surroundings,' Eva said. She sat cross-legged, arms in front of her, palms open on her knees, turned up to the sky. 'Close your eyes, take a few breaths and feel the clear mountain air going into your body, reviving it. Breathe in through your nose, hold the breath for the count of three, then breathe back out through your mouth.' She demonstrated. 'Feel the mountain air cleanse and relax you.'

They all copied her and for a few moments it was quiet apart from the sound of breathing and the occasional bird tweeting. 'Now take one last deep breath, hold, release it and slowly open your eyes,' Eva said softy. She waited until everyone had done that and were sitting with their eyes open. 'How did that make you feel?'

'Peaceful. As if nothing matters,' Bianca said.

'Invigorated,' Nathan added.

'Relaxed.' This was from Sean.

'Refreshed,' Saskia said.

'Clear headed.' This was from Adrienne. 'It's a good focusing exercise.'

Eva was pleased with their responses. She glanced over at Carlos, who hadn't said anything. 'What about you, Carlos, how did it make you feel?'

A wistful look came over his face. 'That I wish I had come to see my grandparents and visited this beautiful place when they were alive. I hope they know that I am here at last. God rest their souls,' he said softly, making the sign of the cross.

Saskia reached out and touched his arm comfortingly. Was this retreat going to be upsetting for Carlos? Eva wondered. She looked over at José to see if Carlos's remarks had troubled him but his expression was impassive.

She didn't know what to say after Carlos's comments so left everyone to their thoughts for a couple of minutes before addressing the group again.

'Now let's practise a bit of mindfulness. Sit still and take a few minutes to be present and really notice your surroundings, the sights, sounds, and smells. Try to use all your senses. You might find it helpful to close your eyes,' she added.

Again everyone was quiet. Eva wondered if like her they were noticing the fresh mountain air, the smell of the lavender, the chirping of the cicadas, and the warmth of the afternoon sun on their skin. She opened her eyes, checking for any sign of restlessness. People often found it difficult to still their minds at first. Carlos was looking fidgety, she noticed. Adrienne seemed quite serene, as did Sean and Nathan. Saskia opened her eyes and stretched then Bianca snapped open her eyes and stared at Eva, a slight frown on her face. Eva's breath caught in her throat. She swallowed, took a deep breath and continued.

'Now, open your eyes and think about how you felt, the things you heard, the smells. Write a few notes in your notebook, ready for this afternoon's creativity session. You could describe the impression the mountain has made on you. Perhaps a particular plant has caught your eye, or the scenery has inspired you to write a short poem.'

They all got out their notebooks and pencils and started writing away. Eva always found her and José's walks relaxing and inspirational, often jotting little quotes or drawing sketches in her wellness journal. She was pleased to see that their guests seemed inspired too.

After fifteen minutes she suggested that everyone got up and stretched their legs. Bianca and Nathan both walked over to the side of the mountain and looked out at the valley. 'All those little white houses scattered about like sugar cubes on the grass,' Bianca said. 'I feel like I want to paint this valley, but I'm no good at painting.'

'That doesn't matter,' Eva told her. 'What matters is that you do something you enjoy. Paint for the pleasure of it, no judgement.'

'I'm not sure,' Bianca said hesitantly. 'I don't want to waste my time doing something I'm no good at.'

'A lot of people feel like that—' Eva started to say but Nathan interrupted them, pointing eagerly up at the sky.

'Look, an eagle!' The majestic bird, wings outstretched, was soaring above them. He put his hand in his pocket for his phone.

'It's a booted eagle, we get a lot of them here,' José said as Nathan zoomed in on the eagle with his phone camera. There were several clicks as others captured the sight too.

The eagle disappeared behind the mountains and they resumed their walk for a little while, finally stopping by a rippling stream. 'Oh I must have a paddle!' Saskia exclaimed, sitting down and pulling off her trainers and socks then heading for the stream. Carlos followed suit and they were soon both fooling around in the water. Eva watched in amusement as Saskia splashed Carlos and he retaliated by scooping up a handful of water and throwing it over her.

'I think those two have the hots for each other,' Bianca said.

Saskia was roaring with laughter now, her head thrown back, her eyes sparkling. She looked so vibrant and alive. She had always been fun, Eva remembered, she had turned everything into a party. It seemed that she hadn't lost that ability, she was already bringing fun to the retreat. Eva was glad Saskia had come, she was lightening the atmosphere.

'I think you might be right,' she agreed. Maybe that would be a good thing, if Saskia kept Carlos occupied he might not have time to reflect over the past too much. She looked around for José and saw that he and Sean were both standing side by side, looking down at the valley as they chatted. Adrienne was sitting on the grass, watching them. Eva got up and walked over to join José to suggest that they walk back now, she wanted time to run the 'relax through creation' session before dinner. As she passed by Adrienne she noticed that her gaze was fixed on José not Sean. She couldn't seem to take her eyes off him. She'd stared at him when she got off the coach too. Was she attracted to him? Eva hoped not. That could make things awkward.

14

José

José turned and smiled as Eva joined him and placed her hand on his arm.

'I think we should head back,' she said.

He glanced at his watch, she was right. The day had fled by. At least everyone seemed to be enjoying themselves. They were all getting on well and were an interesting group. Even his cousin had started to relax and gel with everyone. Carlos's remark about wishing he'd come to visit their grandparents sooner had seemed genuine and José felt for him because, through no fault of his own, he had missed out on a relationship with two warm and loving people.

'I'm hungry now,' Bianca said as they set back home. 'There's nothing like a walk to give you an appetite.'

'Me too,' Nathan agreed.

'Don't worry, it will only take me a few minutes to put together a few bits that will keep you going until dinner,' José told them.

He quickened his pace and carried on ahead so he could

start preparing the snacks, and as El Sueño came into sight he heard the tinkle of bells that announced the goats were approaching. Sergio, the goatherd, was obviously taking them on their daily stroll up the mountain. Their guests would probably like to see the goats going by, he thought with a smile, there were some young ones amongst them now and it was quite a sight to see them all coming up the mountain, herded by the three border collies. He used his hands to shade his eyes as he peered ahead. It looked like the goats were clustered around the gate to El Sueño as they often did, nibbling at the hedge. Then the smile froze on his face as he realised that the back gate was wide open and the goats were piling into their grounds.

Dios mío! His vegetable patch! José raced down to the gate, looking around wildly for Sergio. He was at the back of the goats and obviously hadn't seen what had happened yet. José waved his arms. 'Sergio! The goats are going in my garden!' he shouted.

He saw by the panic on Sergio's face that he'd heard him. The herdsman immediately whistled for his dogs and one of them managed to squeeze through the mass of goats piling into the garden while the other two dogs ran around, trying to stop more goats going through.

Much as he longed to push his way through, José knew that the gate opening was too small and he would be risking getting knocked over and trampled on so he held back, hoping that Sergio could deal with it quickly. Two of the dogs had now managed to round up and prevent the rest of the goats going into the garden but José knew that the errant ones would be trampling over everything and chewing anything edible. Including his precious vegetable patch.

'What's happened?' Eva had joined him now, with the guests.

'Someone left the gate open, the goats are everywhere!' José snapped, running his hand through his hair. He needed to get in there, to stop them, but goats were still milling around the gate, preventing him access.

At last, he could get through. He dashed through the gate and up the garden then swore under his breath when he saw that, as he had dreaded, there were goats all over his vegetable patch, nibbling away at the lettuces and other vegetables. One of the border collies was trying to round them up.

'*Mierda!* They will destroy them all!' He dashed over, clapping his hands loudly to try and scare the goats off. '*Vete! Vete!*' *Go away, go away.*

'*Lo siento,*' Sergio, the herdsman, apologised in Spanish as he ran to join him, another border collie at his heels. José glanced up and saw Eva and the guests were now in the garden, and Eva pulled the gate closed behind them. A bit late now, he thought bitterly.

'I'll open the front gate, it will be easier for Sergio to get the goats out that way.' Eva was running off around the side of the house, down the drive.

It was a good few minutes before Sergio and his dogs managed to round up all the goats and get them out. Sergio was still apologising profusely as José locked the front gate behind him, muttering, '*No pasa nada.*' It wasn't actually fine at all, but neither was it Sergio's fault. The gate shouldn't have been left open. José walked back down to the vegetable patch and stared in horror at the remnants of chewed cabbage, lettuce, cauliflowers, beans, aubergines and other vegetables strewn over the soil. It looked totally destroyed. What hadn't been nibbled by the goats had been trampled all over, he noticed in despair. He'd be lucky if there were enough vegetables and salad to see them through the rest of the week, thank goodness they only had six guests and he had picked some before everyone arrived this morning. He wiped the back of his hand across his forehead. All that planning and hard work growing the vegetables. He might be able to salvage enough for the retreat but there would be none to sell at the market, he would lose regular customers. And it also meant there would be no vegetables to pick for the gardening and cooking session tomorrow. If only that damn gate hadn't been left open.

'*Dios*, what a mess!' He looked up to see Carlos standing over him, his hands thrust in his pockets, a look of almost triumph in his eyes as he surveyed the damaged vegetables. 'Are there enough vegetables left for the retreat?' he asked in Spanish.

He was pleased, José realised. All that talk of wanting to end the family feud and bond with José was just an act. Carlos was glad that things were going wrong. He didn't want him to succeed. He was jealous.

Had Carlos left the gate open? They had mentioned about keeping the gate locked to stop the goats getting in when they were showing everyone around earlier. He wouldn't put it past his cousin to have left it open on purpose.

Before he could reply his cousin shrugged and continued in Spanish. 'Shame that Eva left the gate open. She and Saskia were the last ones out, weren't they? Still, these things happen.' He sauntered back to the house leaving José reeling. Carlos was right. Eva and Saskia had been the last ones to leave. They had been at the back of the group. Eva must have been so busy chatting she'd forgotten to check that the gate was securely locked. It wasn't like Eva, she was usually very careful but she had seemed a bit distracted today.

He would have a word with Eva about it later. Thanks to her carelessness most of the vegetables were ruined. And he was looking a failure in front of his cousin. He wasn't sure which of those things annoyed him the most.

15

Eva

Eva could see that José was distraught, but there was nothing she could do and the guests needed refreshments, plus the creativity session was due to start soon. She had to get on with everything. She and José had talked about the possibility of something going wrong when they were planning the retreat and had both decided that whatever happened they had to carry on and keep to the timetable as much as possible. She just hoped that there was enough fresh produce for the rest of the week – the whole ethos of the relaxation retreat was to provide the guests with healthy, homegrown food. It wouldn't make a good impression if they had to buy in most of it. She couldn't understand how the goats had got in, she had locked the gate, she knew she had. It was a disaster. Even if there were enough vegetables for the week it would still mean that José had to plant more to grow for their own food, and future retreats though. Would it even be possible? They had been planning to officially open the relaxation retreat at the beginning of June, just a few weeks away.

As she walked to the terrace she glanced back at the front entrance and saw Adrienne talking to Mario through the gate. He was probably on the way to Toria, their nearest town. and had dropped by to see if they needed anything. He was such a kind neighbour, always ready to offer help. She'd had a text to say the box of massage oils she'd ordered had arrived, she needed them for this week so if Mario could pick them up for her it would save her a journey tomorrow morning. There wasn't time for her to go now. She turned around to go back and as she got nearer she realised that they were talking in Spanish, and that Adrienne was fluent. '*Hola*. Mario, did you want us?' she called.

'*Hola*, Eva, I come to see if you need me to fetch anything while I am out collecting the post. I was about to ring the bell but Adrienne saw me. I have just seen Sergio and he told me about the goats ruining your vegetable patch,' he replied in Spanish. He could only speak a little English so used his native Spanish when talking to Eva and José.

'Yes, it's a right mess. I'm hoping we have enough vegetables to see us through the week. We definitely have enough for a couple of days, José picked some yesterday,' Eva replied in Spanish too. She'd become quite fluent herself during her time living in Spain. 'Are you going down to the town now? I've a parcel to collect if you have time to pick it up.'

'Of course,' he said. 'I will be back very soon, an hour most.'

'Thank you, that's so kind of you.' She waved to him. '*Luego*.' She turned to walk back with Adrienne but the other woman had already carried on ahead. When Eva reached the back terrace she saw that Carlos was there too but not José.

'Are all the vegetables ruined?' she asked him.

'I'm not sure. It looks bad. I offered to help but...' He shrugged his shoulders. 'I thought it was better if I left José to it.'

That shrug said a lot. José's vegetable patch was his pride and joy. He'd be going frantic, no wonder Carlos thought he was best to leave him to deal with it. It was nice of him to offer to help though. 'Probably wise but thank you.' She nodded. 'I'm sure he will sort it. Now I'll organise some snacks and then we'll get on with the next session.' She tried to keep calm and sound professional. They were running a business and it was her job to ensure the guests remained relaxed.

'I can see that you're both used to this! All part of Spanish living then?' Saskia quipped.

'It is in the *campo*,' Eva replied lightly. 'You never know what's going to happen next!'

'Well, I think the gorgeous scenery makes up for it,' Bianca said. 'Imagine waking up and seeing those mountains every morning.'

'It is a wonderful place to live,' Eva agreed.

She left the guests sitting outside while she went in to get some snacks. When she came back out a few minutes later she was carrying a tray loaded with bowls of dried nuts and fruit, a platter of cheese and grain crackers and two jugs of juice and some glasses. 'Please help yourselves. I'll just go and get the canvases, paints and paper and pens and we can get started. I won't be a moment.'

She went indoors to get the materials from the store cupboard, and Saskia followed her. 'Let me help,' she said as Eva opened the cupboard door.

'Thanks.' Eva passed her a stack of paper and placed some paints on top.

'Is everything really okay?'

Eva took out a couple of canvases, closed the door and met Saskia's worried gaze. 'I hope so. The goats have pretty much ruined the vegetables.' She bit her lip. 'I did bolt the gate, didn't I?'

'Definitely,' Saskia said. 'Look, it's a rubbish thing to happen but if they are all destroyed you can always buy vegetables from the market, can't you?'

'Yes, but our aim is to serve up food we've grown or made ourselves as much as possible. Still, the food in the market is grown by local farmers so it's all fresh and high quality.' It would mean an extra expense for them though and they were already on a tight budget. Plus José would lose the extra money from selling the surplus fruit and vegetables to the market. It wasn't a good start to the week.

They took the equipment out to the back terrace where everyone was waiting for them. Eva shot a quick glance down the garden and saw that José was still tending to the vegetable patch. She wanted to help him but knew he was best left to deal with it himself. She turned her attention back to their guests, who had now placed the canvases, paper and pens on the table.

'We're ready to start,' Saskia said.

'Great.' Eva slipped into warm but professional mode. 'In our busy lives we often don't take time to relax, to do things that we enjoy, or to do something simply for the pleasure of it. Creating something is a wonderful way to relax, so for this session I want you to express your creativity by either painting an abstract based on the landscape from our walk this morning, remembering the colours or shapes to inspire you, or write a few words or so about your experience, perhaps in the form of a poem or haiku.'

'Is that compulsory or can we paint or write anything we want?' Adrienne asked.

'Nothing is compulsory here, so they are just suggestions to get you thinking,' Eva assured her. 'The aim is to relax through creation, create whatever you wish, paint multi-coloured streaks across the paper, write about the things you saw on your walk or explain how it made you feel. It doesn't matter how you express yourself. We're not here to judge your work but to encourage your freedom of expression.'

She put on some classical music playing softly as the guests settled down to write and paint. Apart from the soothing background music it was quiet. No one talked, they all seemed intent on their task. Eva hesitated for a moment, wondering whether to go around and see what everyone was doing or whether to leave them to it and finally decided to leave them to it for a bit while she checked how José was doing. She was halfway down the garden when José started walking up.

'Is everything ruined?' she asked.

'Most of it but we have enough to get through the week, thank goodness. I will have to plant some more though to feed us and for our next guests.'

'So the gardening session can go ahead tomorrow?' she asked.

He nodded. 'Although we no longer have a wide selection.'

'That's a relief.' She turned to walk back side by side with him. 'I did bolt the gate, José, I promise I did.'

He stared ahead, hands in his pockets. 'I believe you think you did,' he said, his voice measured. 'But you were the last one out, so if you bolted the gate how did the goats get in?'

He was right. She must have not latched it properly. There was no other explanation. How could she have been so stupid? She bit her lip. 'I'm sorry, I was sure...'

'It's okay, we will manage.' José's voice had softened now. He turned towards her. 'Now I must make dinner. Have you started the creativity session?'

She nodded. 'I put some snacks out too. I've left them all busy writing and painting. I'm interested to see what they come up with.'

She turned around at the sound of the horn. Mario was at the gate. 'Mario is back with my oils,' she said, hurrying down the path to the gate.

'*Hola*,' Mario greeted her cheerily as she opened the gate and went to take the large cardboard box from him. 'It's heavy, do you want me to carry it in for you?' he offered.

'*Gracias* but it's fine.' She took the box from him. It was heavy, but not too heavy. 'Thanks for collecting it.' Mario was always so helpful, she didn't know what they would do without him.

She carried the box down towards the little studio apartment, placing it down outside the studio so she could open the door. Then she heard a shout from the terrace so left the box there while she hurried to see what had happened now. It seemed like it was going to be one of those days!

16

Sombra, the black cat who had adopted them as a stray, frail kitten shortly after Eva moved in, had jumped down on the table, spilling water all over Nathan's painting. It was drenched but Eva could make out green and brown triangular shapes which she guessed were mountains. He'd gone for the abstract idea, she noted. She should have given them easels to put the canvases on, Sombra wouldn't have been able to do any damage then.

'I'm so sorry, but let's put it in the sun to dry then hopefully it will be fine. It really is a good abstract,' she added.

She fetched a plastic tray from the kitchen – José looked up questioningly from the paella he was preparing and she quickly explained what had happened then dashed out with the tray.

'We'll put it on this tray and move it out to the table on the sun terrace. It will soon dry there,' she suggested. Eva carefully lifted the painting onto the tray and carried it over to the table beside the pool which was already basked in sunlight. She hoped that Sombra wouldn't walk on it there. It wasn't like him to come around when they had visitors, he was really wary with strangers and it had taken her months of feeding him before he would come to her or allow her to fuss over him. They had called him Sombra – Shadow – because he was always hiding in the shadows, watching them.

'How are the rest of you getting on?' she asked.

'I've written a haiku,' Saskia said rather proudly.

'I've made up a poem, it was really therapeutic,' Bianca said. 'I'm surprised how much I enjoyed it.'

'I've written a song,' Carlos said with a grin. 'I'll sing it to you all later, if you want.'

'That would be great, maybe José can play his guitar and accompany you?' Adrienne suggested. 'It would be fun to have a musical evening.'

Eva shot a surprised glance at her. How did she know José played the guitar?

'I saw the guitar in the living room – unless it's you who plays it,' Adrienne said, obviously noting Eva's surprise. 'Sorry, it was a bit sexist of me to automatically think it was José.'

'You were right, it is José's guitar. He plays it very well,' Eva replied. José had often serenaded her with a song, especially in the early days of their relationship, when they would sit outside with a cold drink in the evenings. Not for a while though, they had been so busy doing up the villa they had hardly had time to relax, never mind sit outside and chat. They needed to fix that, she decided, remembering how Adrienne and Sean had said that they were so busy they hardly had time for each other and were hoping to reconnect on the retreat. Well, she and José needed to find time to reconnect *after* the retreat. It had been ages, months, since they had sat down and chatted about anything other than their plans for the retreat. When they first got together they had talked about getting married, having a family, but that had been put on the backburner. She was thirty-one this year and would like to have a child within the next couple of years, while she was still in her prime. An image of their baby, a little boy with dark hair and brown eyes like

José, flashed into her mind. Or maybe a little girl with fair hair and blue eyes like hers. Or one of each.

'What do you think of this?' Adrienne's question interrupted her thoughts. She paused to look at the painting on the canvas. It was of a large yellow and blue Spanish jug, with green ferns growing out of it, placed against a wall. She hadn't gone for abstract then. And it was pretty impressive, definitely not her first attempt. Eva looked at it a little closer and frowned. It was a typical urn, one that you would see in a variety of pottery shops in Spain, but something about it niggled her, it seemed familiar. And it was almost too precise, with the chip out of the top and crack running up the front, as if the urn was standing on the table in front of Adrienne when she painted it. What had made her paint that rather than any of the plants or scenery they had seen today? 'That's lovely, Adrienne, what inspired you to paint that?'

'I saw it in someone's house once. It was so pretty I had to take a photo of it,' she replied. 'The walk today brought it back to mind again. I imagined picking some of the wildflowers and putting them in the urn.'

'Did you see it in Marbella when you were at the conference?' Eva asked, surprised.

'No, when I came to Spain many years ago.'

'Is that when you learnt to speak Spanish so fluently?' Eva asked.

Adrienne shot her a surprised look. 'I can't speak Spanish fluently. I know a few basics, that's all.'

Eva was about to protest that she'd heard her speaking to Mario when Sean came over to look at the painting. He whistled and put his arm around Adrienne's shoulder. 'That's fantastic, Adrienne, you are really talented. I had no idea you could paint like that.'

She smiled. 'Thank you.' And she kissed him on the cheek.

'How's your painting? Has the cat ruined it?' Sean asked

Nathan.

'Very wet, but at least he didn't walk all over it. Eva's put it out to dry,' Nathan replied.

Sean walked down to the table to take a look at the painting then nodded in approval. 'That's a pretty good abstract of the mountains and stream.'

'Thanks.' Nathan seemed pleased at the praise. 'I enjoyed it. I think I might take up painting, to help me unwind.'

'Good idea,' Bianca said. 'We could both use a hobby. I was thinking of taking up painting too but I really enjoyed writing that poem so I might attempt some more poetry. It's a good way of expressing your feelings, getting emotions out.'

'Can I read it?' Eva asked.

Bianca handed her the piece of paper and a lump formed in Eva's throat as she read it. The poem was describing Bianca's sadness at her father's death, stating he was still here, in the sun shining down on her, the mountain breeze, the water trickling in the stream. Eva swallowed. 'This is beautiful, Bianca.'

Bianca's eyes seemed like they were boring into her. 'He would have been sixty last week. It's been a hard time for me imagining planning his birthday but somehow, sitting up that mountain, I felt that he was near me.'

'I'm glad,' Eva whispered, guilt consuming her.

You don't know. Stop jumping to conclusions.

José came out. 'Dinner will be half an hour,' he said. He stopped in front of Adrienne's painting and a strange look came over his face, then it was gone. 'Who did this?'

'Adrienne. She saw it in someone's house when she was in Spain one time,' Eva told him. 'It looks familiar, doesn't it?'

He rubbed his bearded chin. 'There are urns like this all over Spain,' he said with a shrug. Then he turned and went back into the house.

How strange. He'd looked at the painting as if he'd recognised it, just as she had, Eva thought.

17

It was a pleasant evening. They all sat out on the terrace at the back to have some cool drinks and chat. Eva lit some citronella candles to keep the mosquitos at bay and put a spray bottle of homemade rosemary water repellent on the table. 'Help yourself to the repellent, there are only a few mozzies about at the moment, thank goodness. They come out in swarms in the summer. That's why we have rosemary and lavender growing around the house and pool, mozzies hate them,' she explained.

They all sprayed themselves, just in case, apart from Carlos, who said that mosquitos rarely bit him. 'If they do I put an ice pack on it, that soothes it,' he said.

'José does that too,' Eva told him. 'I prefer to use honey or aloe vera.'

José brought out snacks of homemade crisps, nuts and berries again, while Eva made a jug of sangria, a jug of pomegranate-flavoured sparkling water and one of homemade lemonade so that there were a few choices to drink.

'We've kept this evening free so that you can all get to know each other a little more,' José said. 'Is everyone happy to relax and chat? We can play some music if you wish?'

'How about a bit of a sing-song?' Saskia suggested. 'Carlos made up a song today and we thought you might play some music on your guitar while he sang it to us tonight. We saw it in the living room earlier,' she added, seeing that José looked surprised.

'I didn't know you were a songwriter,' he said to Carlos.

Carlos met his gaze steadily. 'And I didn't know you played the guitar, but then we hardly know each other, do we?'

'Well, here's the chance to rectify that,' Eva butted in, anxious to break the underlying tension between them. 'It will be great to finish off the evening with a sing-song.'

For a moment she thought that José was going to refuse but he got to his feet. 'Sure. I'll go and fetch my guitar, I moved it into the bedroom earlier. I'll only be a few seconds.'

'I'll go and get more sangria.' Eva picked up the jug and took it into the kitchen. She'd just refilled it when José came back with the guitar. He didn't look too happy. She was surprised – José was usually pretty easy-going and loved the opportunity to play. 'You don't mind, do you?' she asked. 'You normally like to play your guitar for people.' She paused. 'Is something going on with Carlos? I thought you were both getting on well.'

He stroked his beard, as he always did when something was bothering him. 'I thought so too but when we were at the vegetable patch it was...' He paused.

'Go on.' She half-turned to him and placed her hand on his shoulder. 'What did he do?'

'Nothing. But the way he acted, it was almost as if he was pleased that the goats had trampled all over it.'

'Why do you think that? What did he say?'

'It was the expression on his face. He looked... triumphant.'

No wonder José was troubled. Eva cocked her head to one side. 'You don't think he's come to cause trouble, do you?'

'I don't know. I think that perhaps he isn't as okay about me inheriting El Sueño as he is pretending to be.'

Small wonder really, Eva thought. It was hardly Carlos's fault that his father had argued with his parents and brother. And as Carlos was the older grandson she could understand him being peeved that their grandmother had left José the villa rather than him, or at least split it between them. 'Maybe he hadn't realised all the work we have done on the villa, seeing it look so splendid could be a shock if he was expecting it to be half falling down,' she suggested.

'I think perhaps you are right. Come, let's forget about it. If Carlos gives me the words to his song I will make up a tune. It's only a bit of fun,' José said. 'It would be good if we could get on. After all, he's my only cousin.'

It turned out to be a really enjoyable evening. Carlos's song was a catchy tune about meeting a Spanish flamenco dancer and being entranced by her, José soon picked up the tune and strummed along with it. Soon everyone was joining in the chorus, clapping and singing at the top of their voice. When it was finished, Saskia stood up and asked everyone to applaud Carlos and José, which they all did. But Adrienne kept staring at José whenever she thought no one else was looking. What was that all about? Eva hoped that Sean hadn't noticed too, the last thing they needed was a couple falling out while they were here.

Finally, one by one the guests went up to bed, saying they would see Eva tomorrow morning for the sunrise yoga session by the pool.

Eva and José sat out for a little longer to unwind.

'It sounds like your yoga session is going to be popular,' José said. 'They all seem interested in that.'

'They might feel differently when it's time to get up in the morning,' Eva told him. The yoga session was before breakfast and although it was light and quite warm then she wondered if the guests would feel like getting out of bed at six-thirty. She loved that time of morning herself, and always did her daily yoga session then. 'I guess we ought to be going to bed ourselves otherwise I might not feel like getting up in the morning either.'

Eva got out of her seat and walked over to the table to pick up the tray of dirty glasses when she heard a loud crack.

Spinning around in alarm, she saw that the Buddha statue from the right pillar of the roof terrace was lying on the seat where she had been sitting, the nose had broken off and rolled onto the floor. If she hadn't moved it would have hit her on the head – and with some force from that height.

She could have been killed.

18

'*Mierda!*' José leapt out of his chair. 'How the hell did that happen?' he exclaimed, looking down at the statue.

Eva shook her head, she was too shocked to speak, she couldn't tear her eyes away from the Buddha head. It was huge, and very heavy. It had taken both of them to lift each of the two heads and put them on top of the posts. If she hadn't moved it would have landed on her. A shudder ran through her at the narrow escape she had had.

José took the two steps to reach her then wrapped her in his arms. 'Are you all right, *cariño?*' He held her tight, and she knew that he was thinking, as she was, what a close shave she'd had.

'Oh my God. I'm so sorry. Are you okay?' Bianca's panicky voice shouted down.

They both looked up to see Bianca, Nathan, Adrienne and Sean peering over the balustrade. 'We all came up to have a look at the sky then Adrienne bumped into me and I slipped and fell onto the Buddha head, knocking it off. I'm so sorry.'

'Fortunately Eva had just got out of the chair otherwise it would have smashed onto her head. She could have been killed,'

José replied curtly. 'We didn't realise that you were up on the roof terrace.'

'I think you should have made sure that it was securely cemented on, mate,' Nathan said. 'That could have fallen off anytime. It could have landed on one of us.'

She heard José take a deep breath and knew that he was fighting back his anger but Nathan was right, he should have cemented it on. Eva had suggested it when they bought the Buddha heads last week but they had run out of time, and José had pointed out none of the guests would be staying up there and there were no winds forecast so it would be safe to do it after the retreat had ended. The Buddha heads were so heavy and they fitted perfectly on top of the posts so there didn't seem any danger of them falling off. They hadn't even considered that the guests would wander up to the terrace and knock them off.

'You said that we could look around,' Adrienne reminded them as they all came down the steps. 'We wanted to see the constellations. The sky is so clear up there.' She looked at Eva. 'Are you okay, Eva? I tripped into Bianca, sorry.'

Eva had now moved out of José's embrace and turned to face her. 'I'm fine, just a little shook up.'

'I should think so! That head's heavy! If it had landed on you...' Bianca shuddered.

'Well, as Nathan pointed out it obviously wasn't placed securely on the pillar. It could have fallen on any one of us when we were sitting out here,' Adrienne said sharply.

She was right, Eva thought. One of the guests could have been badly injured. They should have made sure the statues were safe.

'We didn't expect anyone to go up there, otherwise we would have warned you not to lean on the Buddha heads. I'll cement them both in place first thing tomorrow, until then we'll have to ask you to stay off that terrace.'

Sean nodded briefly. 'You should have done that in the first place. Customer safety is a major priority at our hotels. I realise that hospitality is new to you, so there are obviously going to be some corners that need rounding off. I think it's a good idea for you to have a trial run like this, hopefully we can help identify anything that needs improvement. We're quite happy to share our expertise, aren't we, dear?' he asked Adrienne.

'Of course.' Adrienne nodded. 'Now I'm tired and would like to go to bed. Can we have a glass of juice to take into our rooms?'

'Of course. What flavour would you like?' José went to the kitchen to get the juice, and Sean and Adrienne followed too leaving Nathan and Bianca with Eva.

'I think we'll go to bed too, sorry about your statue,' Bianca said. 'I'm glad it's not broken too much. It's a good job there was a cushion on the chair to break its fall.'

It's a good job that I'd got up from the chair, Eva thought, but she merely replied, 'It's fine, José will be able to fix the nose back on.'

'At least let me lift it off the chair for you.' Nathan took hold of the statue, and Eva could see that it took all his strength to lift it off and put it on the floor. Then he and Bianca said goodnight and went inside.

That statue was really heavy, it would take a big push to knock it off the pillar, Eva thought. Had Bianca pretended that Adrienne tripping had caused her to knock it off or had she deliberately pushed it off, knowing that Eva was sitting below?

Had Bianca wanted to harm her?

Did she know who Eva was? Was that why she'd come here?

*

I don't know what I expected when I came here, a run-down villa, an amateur affair. But you've transformed it to something spectacular. I can see it will be a thriving concern. And that you're thriving too, in a happy relationship. You really have got it all, haven't you?

I don't think you've given me a moment's thought all these years. You've carried on with your life, chasing your own happiness, not caring that you took everything from me. Your selfishness takes my breath away. How can you do this? How can you build your life on the ashes of someone else's?

19

TUESDAY – DAY TWO

Eva

All the guests turned up for the early morning yoga session, apart from Carlos. Eva wasn't surprised, she hadn't got him down as the sort who did yoga. If fact, she wasn't expecting him to take part in any of the wellness activities, he'd made it clear that he'd come to see how José had transformed their grandparents' home, and to get to know his cousin. Not that she minded that, she hoped they would become closer. They always spoke Spanish to each other when they were together, she noticed, which was understandable as it was both their native language.

She asked everyone to take a yoga mat from the pile she had placed on the sunbed, put it down on the ground, slip off their shoes and get ready to start the exercise.

'You may find that you ache a little at first after the session, but that's because you'll probably be stretching muscles that you don't usually use. The important thing is not to push yourself too hard, and to breathe through the exercises.' She showed them how to breathe first, then started with some warm-up exercises, followed by a few standing postures, next sitting poses and

finally relaxation on the mat ending with the *Savasana*, the
popular corpse pose that was ideal for relaxing the body and
mind.

'That was great, I feel very relaxed. I could have fallen
asleep when we were lying down,' Saskia said as they all put
their shoes back on, ready to go inside and shower before
breakfast.

'I ache,' Nathan groaned, rubbing the back of his neck.

'As I said, that's only natural at first but it should soon wear
off,' Eva told him. She'd noticed that Sean and Nathan had
been very competitive, really pushing themselves in the exercises, so wasn't surprised that he ached. She bet Sean did too
although he didn't say anything.

'Breakfast will be on the back terrace in half an hour,' she
said as the guests went off to their rooms to shower and change.
She had a quick shower herself then helped José take the breakfast of fruit, nuts, yoghurt, homemade croissants and two jugs of
juice – celery and beetroot – outside, placing them onto the
table alongside a jug of iced sparkling water. The others came
out a few minutes later, and were tucking into the breakfast
when Carlos finally joined them, wearing another pair of shorts
and a vest top – rust-coloured shorts and black vest top this
time. 'Morning everyone, how did the yoga session go?' he
asked.

'Great. You should have joined us instead of being a lazy-
bones,' Saskia told him.

'*Qué va!* I like my sleep too much.' Carlos reached out to
take a croissant off the plate. 'This looks delicious.' He broke a
bit off the end and buttered it.

'Anyone want jam?' Eva indicated the dish of homemade
strawberry jam. She made a range of jams and was quite proud
of them.

'I will. Thanks.' Saskia reached out for the pot. 'If anyone
would have told me when we were at college together that you'd

be living in a villa in the Spanish countryside and making your own bread and jam I would never have believed it,' she said.

'And I wouldn't believe that I'd be doing yoga at six-thirty in the morning,' Sean said, rubbing the back of his neck again. 'I think I'll be aching all day.'

Adrienne shot a furious look at Sean. She didn't like him talking to Saskia, Eva realised. Didn't she trust him? Did he have a roaming eye? He and Adrienne seemed so close, sitting together holding hands, doing yoga together, yet Adrienne was always watching Sean as if she was insecure. She was always watching José too and scrutinising everything. She made Eva feel a bit uneasy, it was as if she was constantly assessing everything and everyone and finding them lacking. Why did Adrienne come here when it obviously wasn't the sort of place she was used to staying at? It couldn't have been because of the discount, she and Sean didn't seem short of money. Why didn't they stay at one of the luxury retreats in Marbella? Then a thought crossed her mind: did they run a blog assessing different holidays or retreats? Had they come along to see how well-organised El Sueño was? Was that why she'd suggested them all going up onto the roof terrace? Could she have tripped into Bianca to test if the statue was secure? The thought made Eva panic. She hoped that she was wrong but if she was right then she had to make sure that there were no more mishaps. The last thing they needed was to be slated online before the retreat even properly got going. They needed this to be a success. Their whole future depended on it.

20

After breakfast, Eva headed for her studio to prepare for the massage and acupressure sessions. As she walked down the path she noticed that the storage shed door was open. How strange. Perhaps José was in there looking for something. She walked over and opened the door wider. 'José?'

The shed was empty, but several things had been moved so she guessed he'd been in there earlier. It was unusual for him not to close the door after him though, there were all sorts inside the shed, tools, pool cleaning stuff, broken picture frames... perhaps he'd taken something out and was coming back for something else. She turned to go back out, intending to close the door behind her, when her gaze caught a large gold-framed painting of a yellow and blue urn, leaning against the wall. It was almost identical to the one in Adrienne's painting. Right down to the chip at the top and the crack. Suddenly she recalled where she'd seen it before – it had been on the wall in the upstairs terrace room when she moved in. José had taken it down and put it in the shed, hanging Eva's Buddha painting on the wall instead, wanting her to feel at home. Had José remembered where he had seen it too and been looking for it?

And how strange that Adrienne had seen a similar one.

Then she recalled Adrienne asking if they were sleeping in the upper terrace room, remarking about the wonderful views from there. Had she been to El Sueño before? Had she been in the large room and seen the painting on the wall?

Had she and José met before when she was in Spain? Was that why she kept staring at him? And how she knew that he played the guitar, she suddenly remembered. If so, why hadn't José told her?

'Morning, *guapa*, are you looking for something?'

Eva spun around at the sound of José's voice. 'I saw the shed door open as I was on my way to the studio. I thought you were in here.'

'No...' Suddenly José's eyes rested on the painting too. '*Dios mío!*'

Eva scrutinised his face as she saw the realisation dawn in his eyes.

'It's the urn Adrienne painted. The painting used to be on the wall in the upper terrace room,' she said slowly.

He nodded. 'What a coincidence. Is that why you came in here? Did you remember it and wanted to check if it was the same?'

'I told you I found the shed door open. I came in to see if you were in here and saw that painting standing against the wall. What's going on, José?' she demanded. 'Adrienne seems to know a lot about you, that you slept in the roof terrace room, this painting, that you can play the guitar. And she speaks fluent Spanish although she pretends she doesn't.' Her eyes met his. 'Do you know her?'

21

José

Adrienne. Only he had known her as Addie, her surname had been Miller then and she'd been less sophisticated, her dark brown hair in a short, choppy cut, not sleek and blonde as it was now, she had been curvier too and he remembered her laughing a lot. No wonder he hadn't recognised her at first, this sleek, polished woman was a far cry from the laughing, impetuous Addie he used to know. Then, this morning, he had seen her standing on the balcony outside her room, her hair wrapped up in a towel, and suddenly it had hit him who she was. The shock had rendered him speechless, and as if she sensed he was staring at her she had looked down and met his gaze. Her lips had curved into a slow smile, as if she had planned this, knew that if he saw her without her makeup and her blonde hair concealed he would recognise her. Why was she here? It couldn't be simply a coincidence, she had been here before so she knew that it was his home. Why didn't she introduce herself when she came, remind him who she was? Both of them had been single, it wasn't as if they had to keep their past relationship a secret. And why had she gone into the shed to hunt for that painting? It was almost as if she wanted to remind him, and for Eva to know too. Perhaps that's why he had caught her staring at him, waiting for him to recognise her. Was that why she'd painted the jug? To remind him?

He sat down on an upturned crate, resting his elbows on his knees, clasping his hands together. 'This is true. We had a holiday romance many years ago, long before I met you.'

Eva frowned. 'Then why didn't you tell me? So this is why she keeps looking at you. And she obviously wants me to know, otherwise why would she have painted this jug, and then searched for the painting in the shed and left it out for me to find?' Her forehead puckered even more. 'How did she even know it was in the shed? How long ago were you seeing each other?'

So many questions. José unclasped his hands and rubbed his forehead with the base of his palm. 'About ten years ago. I can't remember exactly. And I didn't tell you because I didn't recognise her. I've only just realised who she is.'

'Oh, there were so many women it was hard for you to keep track of them all!'

Eva looked hurt and angry. He stood up and reached out for her but she stepped back.

'Eva, I was single, I don't question you on your past relationships,' he said gently. 'And Addie...'

'Addie...' she repeated, her arms now crossed across her chest.

'That is how I knew her. She was not the woman she is now. She looked very different. We met at the restaurant, we dated for a while then she went back to America. I've not seen or heard from her since.'

Eva seemed to be struggling. He tentatively reached out for her hand and this time she didn't pull away from him.

'If I'd have remembered I would have told you, but Eva, it is not important. A brief, long ago romance.'

'How could it be that long ago? She obviously stopped over here at El Sueño, she knew that painting was on the wall in your room,' Eva pointed out. 'She told me that she'd taken a photo of the urn when she saw it, that's why she could remember it in such detail.'

'She stayed here a couple of nights when my grandfather was still alive. We came to visit my grandparents and discovered that they both had the flu. If we hadn't arrived when we did...' He closed his eyes briefly as he remembered how ill his grandparents had been. In hospital they discovered that his grandfather had pneumonia, they saved him but it weakened him and he died five winters later. He opened his eyes again. 'We called an ambulance and they were taken to hospital. Addie and I – we stayed here to look after Zorro until Mario's father returned from holiday and took him in.' Zorro was his grandparents' dog, he had died last year. 'Addie loved the place and took some photos, she must have taken one of the painting.' José gazed intently at her. 'This is not important enough for us to quarrel over, Eva.'

'Well, she seems put out that you don't remember her. Actually I would say that she's doing her damnedest to jog your memory, wouldn't you?' she demanded. 'How dare she mooch through our shed to find the painting? Who does she think she is?'

José nodded. 'You are right, she should not have done that. I will speak to her – on her own in case she doesn't want her husband to know,' he added, suddenly realising that was why Addie might have kept quiet. 'It's nothing for you to worry about,' he promised Eva, kissing her on the forehead. 'Please, let's not fall out over it.'

She nodded. 'It's not that I'm jealous, as you said we all

have past relationships, but I don't like the subterfuge and sneaking around. Anyway I'd better get to the studio, Saskia will be along for her massage in a minute. Then it's Adrienne's turn.' She screwed up her nose. 'Awkward or what?'

'Maybe don't mention anything to her until I get a chance to speak to her?' José suggested.

'Don't worry, I'll be totally professional,' she told him. Then her eyes widened and she put her hands to her mouth. 'I've just remembered that I forgot to unpack the bottles of oil Mario picked up for me yesterday. I'd better get a move on.' She turned to dash away but he reached for her hand and pulled her in for a brief kiss.

'*Te amo.*'

'I love you too. See you later.' And she was gone.

He turned to close the shed door.

'Maybe you should keep it locked.'

Addie. He spun around to find her standing behind him. 'Addie, we need to talk,' he said.

'So, finally, you recognise me!' A triumphant smile played on her lips. 'Well, I can't talk now, Sean will be along in a minute. I'll meet you later. At the fountain.' Her eyes challenged him.

He nodded solemnly. 'Eleven-thirty,' he replied, taking control so that she didn't think she could give him orders.

He cast his mind back to when he'd said goodbye to Addie. She had been on a six-month training session in Spain, so they had always known it was a short romance, but they'd had fun. Addie had been a bit upset when they parted at the airport, she had suggested keeping in touch but he had told her a clean break was best for both of them. 'We have our memories, now we both need to move on.'

She'd smiled a little too brightly, they'd hugged and she'd set off through departures. He'd never heard from her since. He had no idea what she was doing here, but he knew she had come for a reason. She had remembered him, had come here to see him. Whatever it was she wanted to say he would make it clear that what they had was over.

22

Eva

Eva hurried down to the studio, thank goodness Saskia was first to have a massage. She had to compose herself a bit before she could deal with Adrienne. It seems that she was wrong about Adrienne and Sean running an online blog and intending to assess the retreat, but why had she come here? What was the woman playing at? Okay, she could understand that she might be a little upset that José didn't remember her, but why not simply talk to him and remind him – in private if she didn't want Sean to know? It was seriously weird to replicate the painting that used to be on the terrace room wall, then mooch through the shed to find it and leave it out for them to discover. How did she even know it was in there? She felt like giving Adrienne a piece of her mind rather than a massage, she hated anything underhand, people doing things behind your back.

But you're keeping a secret too.

Eva took a few deep breaths. *Keep calm, composed and professional and don't mention anything unless Adrienne does,* she told herself.

Her ears pricked as she heard a load miaow coming from the studio. Sombra! How had he got shut in there? He must have been in there all night! Oh no, he must have been terrified – and she hoped he hadn't done much damage. She grabbed the door handle and flung it open. A black streak shot out, belting up the path and an overpowering smell of oils hit her. She groaned, Sombra must have knocked the oils over, she'd left them on the table. Her eyes darted to the now-empty table and then the box of oils on the floor. *Please don't let any of the oils be broken.* She covered the distance to the box in three strides and bent down to open it, holding her breath as the strong smell filled her lungs. To her dismay the bottles were all smashed. How was she going to give any massages now?

'Morning, am I too early?' Saskia appeared at the doorway. 'Oh goodness! What's happened?'

Eva looked up at her. 'Sombra must have sneaked in yesterday without me noticing. He's been locked in all night. And he's knocked the box of oils over, all the bottles are smashed.' She swept up the broken bottles and put them in the bin.

'Don't you have any left at all?' Saskia asked.

'A little. I'm not sure I even have enough for this morning.' She wiped her hand across her forehead. 'This is the last thing I needed. I ordered these oils especially.'

'How long will it take you to get some more?'

'A couple of days if I pay for premium postage.' She sighed. 'I might be able to get some from the health shop in Toria to tide me over, they're not the make I prefer and are a bit more expensive but they'll have to do. The trouble is, I have three massages booked in this morning, and others might turn up. It doesn't look good letting people down.' Especially as it was the first full day of the retreat.

'Look, forget my massage. I'll help you tidy this up, and get ready for Adrienne, she's next, isn't she? I don't mind not having a massage at all while I'm here. Save the oils for the others. Do you mind if I open the window first though, get rid of this smell? It's making me feel a bit nauseous.'

'Of course not. And thanks so much,' Eva said. She was so grateful for the support she could have hugged Saskia.

Saskia walked over to the window and opened it wide. As she turned around her eyes rested on something on the floor. 'I think I know why the cat came in here.'

'What is it?' Eva asked anxiously, hoping that Sombra hadn't left her the remains of a rat or a gecko like he often did.

'There's a fish head here. It looks like he got hold of a fish and dragged it in to eat.'

'Really?' Eva walked over to see for herself and stared at the fish head underneath the chair. 'How could he get hold of that?' Then she remembered that José had cooked paella for dinner yesterday. Sombra must have sneaked into the kitchen and stolen a piece of fish.

'That's cats for you, sneaking up everywhere. Now let's get this all cleaned up before Adrienne comes along for her massage. She's a bit of a snobby one, isn't she? You don't want to be giving her something to complain about.' Saskia grabbed the dustpan and brush by the door and started sweeping up the mess while Eva wrapped the fish head up in some paper and put it in the bin outside.

'There you are, good as new,' Saskia said.

'Apart from the overpowering smell of oils.' Eva chewed her lip anxiously. 'Thank you so much for helping.'

'Hey, it's no problem but are you okay?' Saskia reached out and touched her shoulder. 'You look upset. Accidents happen. I'm sure everyone will understand if there aren't enough oils to go around. We're all here to give the retreat a trial, after all, so you can get feedback on anything that you need to tweak.' She smiled. 'Maybe not leaving fish about, checking that the cat hasn't snuck in before you close the studio door and keeping an extra supply of massage oils should be top of your list.'

She was right, they were common sense precautions. Sombra had never snuck into the studio before though, he rarely came into the house only on the coldest of winter nights. He was an outside cat, always had been, turning up in their garden about eighteen months ago, all skin and bone. Eva bit her lip. 'It's not just the oils, is it? It's only the second day of the retreat and already so much has gone wrong. The goats running over the vegetable patch, the Buddha head falling off the terrace post and just missing me.' Seeing Saskia's puzzled face, she told her about it. 'And now this.' She chewed her lip anxiously. She and José had worked so hard to make this retreat a success but they were failing already.

'Hey, you need to get this in perspective. Accidents happen.'

'Are they accidents though? Or is someone deliberately trying to sabotage the retreat?' The words were out before she could stop them. She hadn't meant to confide her fears to Saskia but her friend had been so understanding. 'It's strange that fish being in here. Almost as if someone deliberately put it there to lure Sombra in then closed the door.' Eva knew how far-fetched this sounded. Would Saskia think she was becoming delusional again?

Was she delusional again?

'I know it sounds crazy but I closed that gate. You know I did.'

Saskia nodded. 'You did close the gate, but maybe the catch didn't quite connect and the wind blew it open again.' She squeezed Eva's hand. 'I think you're over-worrying. After all, why would anyone want to ruin the retreat?'

Eva swallowed. 'Because they've got a grudge against me.'

'And why would anyone have a grudge against you?'

'Because I killed their father.'

Saskia's eyes widened. 'What?' Then realisation dawned in her eyes. 'Bianca?' She shook her head. 'Have you been worrying over that? There must be lots of road accidents in Sutton. Don't jump to conclusions.'

Eva nodded. 'That's what I keep telling myself but I can't help wondering if the man I ran over was her father. What am I going to do? I've never told José about this.'

Saskia squeezed her hand. 'You're not going to do anything, not before we find out if it was Bianca's father that you...'

'Killed.'

'Accidently ran down,' Saskia corrected.

Eva nodded, she knew that her friend was right. It had been an accident. But the guilt had overwhelmed her. And now it was all coming back to haunt her. She could feel her hand shaking, her heart racing, the knots of panic forming in the pit of her stomach.

'Take a second and breathe, Adrienne will be here in a minute. Leave it to me to sort this out,' Saskia said. 'It will all be all right.'

She hoped it would be, Eva thought as Saskia left. She was grateful for her help. But she wasn't sure she could trust her. She'd made that mistake before.

23

José

While Eva was doing her massage sessions, José went to check
the other Buddha head on the terrace. It was secured firmly, it
would take a hefty shove to push it off. He paused at the empty
space at the top of the other post where the broken Buddha had
been standing. How had Bianca managed to knock that over?
She said that Adrienne had bumped into her. Could she have
done it on purpose, knowing that Bianca would fall onto the
Buddha head and dislodge it? Wanting to draw attention to the
fact that she was on the terrace? To remind José that she had
been to his family home before and spent a couple of nights
with him in the terrace room when his grandparents were ill?
She wouldn't have realised that it could have fallen on Eva
below, she probably just wanted to startle him. Addie had
always hated being ignored, he remembered.

Why had she come here with her husband?

He looked down at the ground below, there was such a good
view of the land from here. He could see Mario picking some
oranges and talking to Adrienne. The trees were full of orange

blossom and the oranges left on them, weighing down the branches, were last year's crop only suitable for juicing. Mario had less land than them and mainly lemon trees. He often brought them a bag of lemons over to swap for a bag of oranges. He and Adrienne seemed to be having quite a conversation, he wondered what she was asking him. He'd have to ask Mario to help him carry up the broken Buddha head and place it onto the post, it was too heavy to lift by himself and he didn't want to ask any of the guests, he couldn't risk them injuring themselves. He would securely cement both the statues in place to make sure they didn't fall off again, but for now, he'd border off the terrace just to be safe.

He was about to go back down the steps when something else caught his eye. Carlos and Sean, deep in conversation by one of the casitas. There was no sign of Saskia – he was sure that Eva had said she was the first one due for a massage this morning so she might already be in the studio. And no sign of Bianca or Nathan. They were probably in their room. They were a pleasant young couple, he thought, and it was such a tragedy about her father's accident.

Mario was walking down towards the gate with a bag full of oranges, Adrienne was walking up towards the house. Carlos was still talking to Sean.

José watched them thoughtfully. He wasn't sure what he thought about his cousin. He wanted to believe that he had come to the retreat because he was curious about José and longed to see their grandparents' home for himself. Carlos had seemed so genuine when he'd said yesterday while they were on the mountain walk that he regretted not coming here before. José hoped he had come in peace but he couldn't forget the look of triumph in his cousin's eyes when he'd seen the destroyed vegetable patch. He didn't trust him.

24

Eva

Saskia had just left when Adrienne came in.

'Goodness, what an overpowering smell of oils!' she exclaimed. 'I think you might have gone a bit overboard, Eva.' She pressed her thumbs to her temples. 'I have a terrible headache and the smells are making it worse. I think I ought to cancel the massage.'

'Sorry, Sombra got locked in and knocked a couple of the bottles over,' Eva said, feeling her cheeks flush. Adrienne's slightly condescending manner always made her feel a bit awkward and she was still annoyed with her about mooching in the shed. She longed to say something but she'd promised José she wouldn't mention anything to Adrienne until he'd had time to speak to her. 'I've opened the windows and the smell should disperse soon but I quite understand if you don't want to continue with the massage.' *Please say you don't,* she thought, she really didn't want to have to deal with Adrienne right now.

Adrienne pursed her lips. 'I guess I can give it a try,' she reluctantly agreed. 'I am finding it rather debilitating but I'll try to work through it.'

Eva focused on the neck, shoulders and head, first asking Adrienne to lie on her back while she gently massaged her head, then turn onto her front so she could massage her shoulders and neck. She could feel Adrienne relaxing as she softly kneaded with her fingers.

'I must say that this is a lovely home you have here and you both work well together. How did you meet?' Adrienne asked.

Eva bristled, not really wanting to discuss José with her but reminded herself that Adrienne was a guest so briefly explained about meeting in the restaurant, going out together and then moving in and helping with the renovations. 'José liked my idea of doing wellness activities and asked me to join him with the retreat,' she said. 'We're hoping to turn it into a full-time business eventually.'

'So you never met José's grandmother then?' Adrienne asked.

Obviously Adrienne had, José had told her that. It was all in the past, Eva reminded herself. 'No, she died the year before I met him, but I wish I had. He adored her.' She asked as she expertly massaged Adrienne's shoulders, 'How's this? Has the headache gone now?'

'That really does feel a lot better,' Adrienne said with a relieved sigh. 'You have magic fingers, Eva.'

'Thank you,' Eva replied, pleased with the compliment. She got the impression that Adrienne didn't praise often.

Well, that wasn't too bad, she thought in relief when Adrienne left. Then Nathan arrived for his massage. After saying hello and explaining that he suffered a lot with his lower back, he didn't make any attempt at conversation, lying silently on his stomach as Eva massaged his back. That wasn't unusual, some clients were chatty but others barely spoke.

As soon as Nathan left Eva pulled her phone out of her

pocket to see if there were any messages – she'd set it to silent while she worked – and saw one from José. Opening it up, she read it quickly. He had blocked access to the upper terrace to stop anyone going up until both Buddha heads had been cemented securely in place, and was meeting Adrienne this morning to find out what game she was playing. Good. The sooner Adrienne realised that Eva knew about their past relationship, and that it was firmly in the past, the better. She sent back a thumbs up with a couple of kisses then called the health shop in Toria to see if they had any aromatherapy oils she could buy. Luckily they had so she arranged to go down before lunch to get them when José was running the cookery session, she would be back in time to eat so she wouldn't be missed. She took a swig out of the water bottle she kept in the mini fridge in the studio then set off for the session on stress and relaxation techniques she was holding on the back terrace.

All the guests had turned up for that, Eva was pleased to see. 'I thought this might be one of the popular sessions,' she said.

'I guess it's one area we all need help in,' Nathan said. 'I know I do. I particularly find it difficult to unwind at night and sleep.'

'We all suffer from stress from time to time, it's difficult not to in the society we live in. And stress can make it hard to relax or to sleep. In this session I'm going to teach you ways to deal with this. Before I start, let me give you all a wellness journal.' Eva handed a light blue hardbacked notebook and a matching pen both decorated with the El Sueño logo (they'd had them printed especially) to each of them. 'This is for you to write and reflect in. You can write about your thoughts and emotions, what you hope to get from the retreat, any tips you pick up, healthy eating recipes, anything you like.'

They all discussed things they could do to help relax, such as taking a few deep breaths, making time to do things they enjoyed, sitting down with a soothing herbal drink, taking a walk or just sitting outside taking in the scenery and listening to the sounds of nature.

'Remember also to try not to allow yourself to get over-whelmed by doing too much,' Eva said. 'Some people find it really difficult to say no and end up over-committing themselves and then feeling stressed.'

Bianca raised a hand. 'That's me.'

'Others find it hard to leave the job at work and take work problems home with them.'

'Me!' Adrienne nodded, a rueful smile on her face. She turned to Sean. 'And you.'

They all discussed ways they could deal with this, and then moved on to sleep problems, going through the usual methods of keeping to a regular bedtime, no screen time or alcohol, a dark quiet room. 'I do all that but my mind goes into overdrive when I get to bed,' Nathan said, so Eva suggested he try the four, seven, eight method of breathing in for four seconds, holding his breath for seven seconds then breathing out for eight seconds, and the body relaxation method of starting with relaxing the muscles in your face then slowly working down through the body, exhaling and inhaling as you did so.

'There's some great tips there, thank you,' Nathan told her. 'With a job like mine it's difficult to relax.'

'My mind always seems to work overtime at night, thoughts just come into my head and I can't seem to stop them,' Bianca said.

Eva remembered Bianca's poem and wondered if it was the trauma of her father being killed that kept her awake. Losing a parent as a child could affect you all your life. The familiar panicky feelings started to flood through her and she fought them back. *I am not my anxiety. I am not my anxiety.* She repeated the words over in her mind, bringing herself back into focus.

'You might find it helpful to use guided imagery,' she said once she felt calmer herself. 'I sometimes use the palming method.' She explained about choosing a colour to identify with the different emotions. 'For example red could represent anxiety or fear, and green for calmness and healing. Place your palms over your eyes and imagine the colour you've chosen to represent what you're feeling, then replace it with another positive colour. So, in this case, replacing the red with green.'

'What an interesting idea,' Sean said.

'A popular guided imagery is imagining yourself on the beach, really visualise the scene, feel the sun basking on your skin, hear the waves licking against the shore, smell the sea air, taste the cool refreshing cocktail.'

'Now that I could go with,' Nathan said.

'Or if you have particular worries or pains, imagine a warm light over the area where your pain is, healing it, or putting your worries in a bin and closing the lid on them.'

Eva waited while they all made notes then she finished the workshop with some deep breathing exercises to help with relaxation and anxiety. She was really pleased with the questions and the response to her suggestions. Learning the various wellness techniques had helped Eva cope, prevented her from sinking into despair again, and teaching them to others not only gave her the satisfaction of knowing that she was helping people with their mental health but also made her realise that she wasn't the only one who struggled with anxiety and depression. Most people were carrying some mental baggage around with them.

'I do feel a little more relaxed,' Bianca told her. 'I'll keep trying these methods.'

'I'm going to imagine sleeping on the beach tonight,' Nathan quipped.

'Maybe I ought to give you our card in case it makes you want to book a holiday,' Sean jested and everyone laughed.

Eva was relieved to see the guests were getting on so well. 'Now, we'll take a short break for refreshments then José is running the healthy eating cookery session, which I know you've all signed up for. And we'll be eating your culinary efforts for lunch.' She smiled. 'I'm nipping down into the town for a couple of things but I won't be long. After lunch we've got a free session where you can all relax, go for a walk, rest in your rooms, journal, socialise. Anything you like. José and I will be sitting out on the terrace too so feel free to come up to us if you want to chat or ask any questions.'

Leaving José to serve up refreshments and chat to everyone, Eva headed down to the village to get the massage oils. Thank goodness the health shop had the oils she needed to get her through the next few days, she thought as she set off, otherwise she'd have had to cancel the massages and that wouldn't have looked good at all. Saskia was right, she should keep a back-up supply, she couldn't risk this happening again. She'd already decided to keep a reflection journal noting how the retreat had gone, what things had gone wrong and ways to improve things for the next retreat. The way things were going it would soon be full.

25

José

After refreshments, José went to the fountain to meet Adrienne, as they'd arranged. He was due to start the cookery workshop in fifteen minutes so their conversation would have to be short. He'd prefer not to have a conversation at all, the past was the past as far as he was concerned but Adrienne obviously had something she wanted to get off her chest. She was already waiting at the fountain and her face broke into a big smile as he approached.

'You came. You're late so I thought you had changed your mind.'

'Five minutes, I had to clear away.' What was her problem? 'Where's Sean?' he asked, wondering if he might not be suspicious why Adrienne had gone off by herself and feeling a little uncomfortable at how Adrienne was smiling at him.

'Making some business phone calls. He doesn't know I'm here. He doesn't know about us and I want it to stay that way.'

'Is that why you wanted to meet me, Adrienne?' He used her full name on purpose, to call her Addie now was too personal and this private meeting was making him feel uneasy. He didn't like being secretive. 'Well, don't worry, if you prefer him not to know then I won't mention it but really it was a long time ago. Too long for anyone to be jealous about.'

'You don't know Sean. He's insanely jealous. He can't bear me to even look at anyone else. That's why I didn't let on that I knew you when we first arrived. I thought that was why you didn't acknowledge me either, because of Eva, but you didn't recognise me, did you? I can't believe you've forgotten me so easily. I thought we had something special,' she said with a little pout. She looked hurt, he realised.

'We had fun but it was many years ago. A lot has happened in that time. I apologise for not remembering you but you have changed so much.'

'I'm not so naïve and trusting, you mean,' she retorted then took the sting out of her words with a sad little smile.

She had been more natural and unpolished back then and he preferred that Adrienne, now she looked like a confident woman who knew what suited her, what she wanted, but there was a harsh edge to her. And the anger in her that the smile didn't quite conceal had surprised him. 'Why are you so upset about it, Adrienne?' he asked. 'We were together, we had a good time, then you went home. We both knew it would be like that.' He wondered if she had wanted him to ask her to stay but he hadn't loved her enough to ask her to give up her whole life for him, and he thought she had felt the same. Had he got it wrong?

'I'm not upset. Why should I be?' she said quickly. 'As you said it was a long time ago. I wanted to meet you to ask you not to mention our past relationship to anyone else, I don't want it getting back to Sean.' Her eyes clouded over and she suddenly looked vulnerable, fearful even. 'He can be very... difficult if he gets angry.'

'Are you scared of him?' he asked quickly. This new Adrienne seemed too confident, too in control to be scared of her husband but that could be a front. She was obviously worried about Sean finding out she and José had been an item once.

She hesitated before answering then shook her head. 'No, of course not. I just prefer not to upset him.'

'Then why even mention it when you can see that I had clearly forgotten? It could have remained in the past. Yet you did the painting of the jug, then hunted out the original painting in the shed and left it out for Eva to discover,' he challenged her. 'And you knew this was my home but still booked in for the retreat.'

'I left the painting out for you, not Eva. To remind you who I was.' She blinked back the tears overflowing in her eyes. 'I still can't believe that you forgot me. After all that we were to each other. And Sean booked the retreat, not me. It was convenient for us to come so I wasn't going to cancel it just because we were once in love.'

Love. He looked at her, astonished. Is that what she'd thought? They had been lovers, yes, but he had never told Adrienne he loved her. It was a few months of fun, that was all.

'It was a long time ago,' he reminded her. 'Why would your husband be jealous? He must have had past relationships too.'

'Yes but he isn't holidaying at an ex-lover's place, is he?' Her eyes met his and he saw the pleading in them. 'Believe me, if I could have got out of coming here, I would, but Sean was set on it and I couldn't think of a reasonable excuse.' She reached out and touched his arm. 'Please say you won't tell him.' Her eyes widened as if the idea had just occurred to her. 'You haven't told Eva about us, have you?'

'Of course. We don't keep secrets from each other,' he said. 'Don't worry, I will ask her not to mention it to your husband.' He looked at her worriedly. 'Are you sure that you are okay? You seem a little scared of Sean?'

'Not at all. I just prefer to avoid arguments if I can.'

Her eyes didn't quite meet his and her tone didn't sound sincere.

'It's okay, neither myself nor Eva will say anything,' he promised. He gave her a reassuring smile. 'It's nice to see you again, Adrienne. I hope you and Sean enjoy the retreat. Now I need to get back, it's time to start the cookery workshop.'

As he walked back over to the house he kept replaying the conversation in his mind, wondering why Adrienne had acted so strangely. Why had she painted that jug, then hunted through the shed for the picture? Why hadn't she simply taken him to one side in the first place, jogged his memory and asked him not to say anything to Sean? And she seemed so hurt that he hadn't remembered her. He would do as she asked though, he didn't want her and Sean arguing about it while they were at the retreat. That would be very awkward. He knew that Eva would keep quiet too.

He glanced around and saw Sean standing by the shed. He looked steadily at José then turned and walked away. Had he spotted him and Adrienne talking? If so, surely he would question her. He remembered the look on Adrienne's face, the pleading in her voice. She was scared of Sean, he was sure she was.

26

Eva

As soon as Eva got back with the oils she went straight into the studio so she could put them away. She'd just unpacked them when there was a tap on the half-open door and Adrienne stepped in.

'Hello,' Eva said in surprise. 'Is everything okay? Were you looking for another massage?'

'No thank you. I heard you come back and popped in so we could have a quiet chat.' Adrienne closed the door behind her and smiled at Eva. 'José said that he's told you about us.'

And there was she wondering whether to broach it or not, Eva thought as she placed the last bottle of oil in the cabinet. 'You mean that you had a brief holiday romance years ago?' she replied nonchalantly. 'Yes, he did. He also told me that you'd arranged to meet him this morning to talk about it.' She turned around, leaning her back against the massage table. 'I presume that you've done that and everything is okay?' She kept her tone neutral although what she really wanted to say was, *Why did you act so weird about that painting, and keep going on about the roof terrace room?* Adrienne had obviously wanted Eva to know about her and José being an item once, what she couldn't figure out was why. She had no intention of saying anything to rock the boat though, they needed this retreat to be a success and there were still three days to go.

'A brief holiday romance? Is that how he described it?' Adrienne looked wounded. 'It was a lot more than that. Do you think I'd want to keep it from Sean if it was just a brief romance?'

Eva looked at her, puzzled. 'What do you mean?'

'We were living together. We slept in the room on the roof terrace and that painting of the urn was on the wall. I woke up every morning and there it was, facing me.'

Lived together? José said that Adrienne had only stopped over a couple of nights when his grandparents were in hospital. José's grandfather had died five years ago and he'd said that he and Adrienne had a holiday romance about ten years ago. It was impossible that they'd lived together here. José didn't move in until his grandmother died, until then he told Eva he had stayed in his flat in Malaga in the week and with his grandmother at weekends. She wasn't sure what to say, Adrienne was a guest, but it was apparent that she was telling massive lies.

'You lived here?' she repeated. 'With José's grandmother?'

'No, not here,' Adrienne admitted. 'In José's apartment in Malaga. But I stayed over when his grandparents were in hospital. We were that close.'

'Yes, José said. He came to see his grandparents and found them to be so ill they needed to go to hospital and you both stayed over to look after Zorro.' She nodded. 'It was a long time ago, surely Sean won't be jealous about that.'

'José was the love of my life, my first lover,' Adrienne said indignantly. 'I can't believe that I meant so little to him that he didn't even recognise me.' Her lips were pressed into a straight line. 'It's an insult to what we had.'

She looked so angry and upset that Eva wondered if she had booked this retreat so that she could see José again. Did she hope to pick up where they left off? And what reaction did she expect from Eva, telling her all this?

'I'm sure he wasn't being rude, people change a lot in ten years,' she said, her mind a whirl. Adrienne's account of their relationship was a lot different to José's. Surely he would recognise her if they had been that close? Or was he pretending he didn't in case it made things awkward with Eva or Sean? And had he really been her first lover? That was huge. *We all have a first time. You need to be adult about this.*

'We were together for months. I was over in Spain on a six-month contract with a hotel in Marbella,' Adrienne said. Tears pricked her eyes as she looked at Eva. 'I can't believe that he hasn't told you all this. That I meant so little to him.' She gulped. 'Perhaps I shouldn't be telling you, maybe José doesn't want you to know but you have a right to know about his past. About what kind of man he is.'

Did she? José didn't know everything about her past, did he? 'José is a good man, trustworthy and loyal,' she said. 'We all have past lovers, that's not important. For José and me it's the future that is important.' She wished that Adrienne would go, she wasn't really comfortable with this conversation. She trusted José.

She would have told him though if one of her past lovers had booked into the retreat. She wouldn't have kept it a secret.

He hadn't recognised Adrienne, she reminded herself.

Besides, she hadn't told him everything, had she? She hadn't told him what she had done.

27

José was laying the table for lunch when Eva went in. 'How did the cookery session go?' she asked.

'Very well. Everyone was interested and attentive – although Adrienne didn't join us until halfway through. By the way, I spoke to her and she doesn't want Sean to find out that we were together.'

Eva nodded. 'Yes, she came into the studio to ask me so I promised her I won't say anything.' It was on the tip of her tongue to tell him what else Adrienne had said, but she bit back the words. *Leave the past in the past and concentrate on the present.* That's what her therapist had told her when she was recovering, and it was advice that had helped her hold it together over the years.

'Did she? She seems very worried about him finding out. It sounds like he's a bit... controlling.' José looked worried.

Was that Adrienne's game, to worm her way back into José's affections by pretending to be vulnerable? Or was Sean really controlling?

'Well, he won't find out from me,' Eva said. 'I don't like being in this situation though, it's awkward.'

'I know,' José agreed. 'Thank goodness it's only for a couple of days. Did you get the massage oils you wanted?'

'Yes, I've plenty to see me through the rest of the week now.' She took a couple of jugs of flavoured water out of the fridge and laid them on the table as the guests piled in. Lunch was delicious, chicken and spinach pasta with lemon and parmesan served with sourdough flatbread and green smoothies and followed by chia pudding or fruit salad.

'This is excellent,' Eva said as she took a spoonful of the chia pudding. 'How did you all find the cookery lesson?'

'Really interesting. I'd have never thought of making chia pudding but it's very tasty,' Bianca said. 'José is going to email us some recipes that we can try out when we get home.'

'People often think that healthy eating is boring and you have to avoid desserts but there are so many nutritional ones – baked fruit, frozen yoghurt. Even dark chocolate as long as it's at least seventy percent,' Eva said.

'I'm definitely going to start eating healthier when I get home,' Bianca said. 'I can feel the benefit already.' She took another spoonful of dessert. 'I'm so enjoying it here. And it's lovely to wake up to the view of the mountains.'

'I agree. The fresh air and the walk yesterday helped me sleep better,' Nathan agreed. 'But there was a sort of humming noise outside the window. It carried on for ages but I was so tired I fell asleep.'

'That's the cicadas. They kept me awake at first but I soon got used to them and learnt to block the noise out,' Eva said. 'Hopefully some of the relaxation techniques I talked about earlier will help you fall asleep easier.'

'I have to say that I'm definitely starting to unwind and relax,' Sean agreed. 'We're enjoying it here, aren't we, dear?' He looked lovingly at Adrienne. He really didn't seem controlling, Eva thought. Although he could be putting on an act.

Adrienne nodded and smiled. 'It's good to have a few days away from it all.'

'I am pleased to hear that. Remember that there is no pressure, join in as little or as much as you want,' Eva told them. 'The important thing is that you all relax while you're here. We want everyone to go away feeling refreshed and recuperated.'

'And tell us if there is anything you need,' José added. 'We really want to hear your opinion of the retreat and the activities, the pluses and the minuses. If there is anything you particularly like do let us know, and similarly please tell us if there is anything we can improve upon.'

'There won't be any complaints from me. I think it's wonderful here,' Saskia said. She turned to Carlos, who was sitting next to her. 'Don't you?'

'It's a beautiful place, and the food is delicious,' Carlos agreed.

'We're both delighted to hear that. Now it's a free session for the next couple of hours,' José said, lunch finally finished. 'You can read, journal, socialise, go for a walk, go in the pool, whatever you wish. Eva and I will be relaxing outside so feel free to come and talk to us.'

'Later on there will be a chance to have another massage,' Eva said. It was such a relief that she had managed to get extra oils.

'Great, count me in,' Saskia said.

'I'd like a massage too, it might help me relax.' Bianca rubbed the back of her neck. 'I feel very achy today.'

Eva was glad that Bianca wanted a massage, this might be her chance to get her to talk about her father. Eva had to know, it was eating into her.

28

The guests had gone up to their room for a while so Eva took the opportunity to try and destress. She lay back in the sun lounger, closed her eyes and placed her thumb on the spot between her eyebrows, taking slow, deep breaths as she gently pressed down and made small circular movements. Adrienne's words about her former relationship with José were going over and over in her head. She couldn't understand why Adrienne had gone out of her way to force José to remember who she was if she didn't want Sean to know about their relationship. And why she was so upset that José hadn't remembered her when they'd only been seeing each other a few months. Did she still have feelings for him? Or was it a pride thing? She was also worried about the forthcoming massage session with Bianca. She had to encourage her to talk but would the information be what Eva wanted to hear?

'Is it helping?' José asked softly as he sat down in the sun lounger beside her.

She flickered open her eyes. 'A little.'

'I know there's been a couple of hiccups but everything will be okay, don't stress.'

Don't stress. That was José's mantra. And Eva tried hard not to. They were offering a retreat for people to destress yet here she was already getting worked up and it was only the second day.

'I'm trying not to but so much has already gone wrong. The statue almost landing on my head' – the memory of her narrow escape still made her shudder – 'that could have been one of the guests, and the goats getting in and trampling the vegetables, then Sombra being locked in the studio all night and breaking the oil bottles.' *And Adrienne, Saskia and Bianca,* she wanted to add but she didn't want José to think that she was jealous of Adrienne – although she felt that was exactly what Adrienne wanted – and she couldn't tell him her fears about Saskia and Bianca, could she?

'Some unfortunate things have happened, yes, but we have dealt with them. There are bound to be some teething problems, *guapa,* that is why we're doing this trial retreat.'

He was right, she was overthinking everything. It wasn't the first time the goats had got in, was it? Or that Sombra had sneaked into the studio – although he'd never taken a piece of fish in there before. As for Adrienne, yes it was an awkward situation but she'd be gone on Friday. All Eva had to do was to be pleasant and polite and not let it get to her.

'I know. We've worked so hard, I really want it to be a success.'

'It will be. And whatever goes wrong we will deal with it – together.' José leant over and kissed her on the forehead. 'As we always do.'

She felt the tension leave her. He was right, they would. They always did. They were a team and nothing or no one was going to come between them.

29

It was a warm, sunny afternoon and they were soon joined on the terrace by Nathan and Bianca both dressed in their swimwear and carrying towels and suncream. Bianca waved. 'We're going for a swim,' she shouted as they headed for the pool.

'The water is still a bit chilly,' Eva warned them. She and José swam every day from the beginning of April but a lot of people waited for the warmer months of May and June.

'We live in the UK, I bet this is warmer than our sea in the height of summer!' Bianca replied, running over to the side of the pool and jumping into it. Nathan followed her.

They looked so young and full of life, Eva thought as she watched them. They were about ten years younger than her. Ten years ago she had been a mess. Rock bottom. Suicidal.

She was over that now and as she had told Saskia she would never let anything plunge her down there again. She had worked hard to fight the demons and keep them at bay.

The others soon joined them, first Saskia dressed in tiny denim shorts and a vest top, with the orange straps of the halter-neck bikini she wore underneath visible around the back of her neck. Carlos followed, bare-chested with swimming trunks draped on his hips. Then Adrienne and Sean, hand in hand, Adrienne in a loose kimono and Sean in swimming shorts and tee shirt. Saskia padded over to the side of the pool. 'Is the water cold?' she called.

'Not once you're in!' Nathan told her. 'Come and join us.'

'Sure, why not?' Saskia walked back over to a sunbed and slowly unbuttoned her shirt to reveal a barely-there bikini top, then wriggled out of her shorts to reveal a thong, her eyes fixed on Carlos all the time. Feeling uncomfortable at this flirtatious display, Eva glanced to see if José was looking but he had gone, probably back inside to get refreshments. Saskia had been a flirt in college and it looked like she hadn't changed. She'd always had a bit of a loose tongue too. It had been thanks to her that Eva's breakdown, and what had caused it, had come to the attention of her manager at the coffee shop where she worked. She had been so sorry though, Eva recalled. She'd been distraught as she begged Eva to forgive her, promising that she had only told Rachel, her neighbour who worked at the same place as Eva, because she had been so worried and had no idea she would tell anyone, least of all the manager. It was a long time ago, and Saskia had promised that she would never mention it again. And if she did, what did it matter? Mental health issues were sympathetically treated nowadays. It surely wasn't a big deal if José did find out that Eva had had a break-down when she was at college.

Providing he didn't find out the reason she had cracked. And how bad it had got.

She noticed that Sean was watching Saskia too and Adrienne seemed to be struggling to control her fury. Not so much the happy couple then. Which one of them was the controlling one? She wondered. Adrienne said that she was worried about

Sean finding out she and José used to be an item yet she was angry that Sean had glanced at Saskia, who actually was being deliberately provocative – although her actions were aimed at Carlos not Sean.

'Are you two going for a swim?' Eva asked, wanting to defuse the situation.

'No, we're going to sit and relax around the pool, aren't we dear?' Sean dragged his gaze from Saskia and smiled at his wife.

'I'm wondering if that's such a good idea, maybe we should have stayed in our room,' Adrienne said pointedly and a look of irritation crossed Sean's face then it was gone.

'You really do have a beautiful home,' he said in what Eva sensed was an attempt to change the subject. 'It must be wonderful to sit out here every afternoon, enjoying the sunshine and having a dip in the pool when it's too hot.'

'It would be, but we are often too busy to do that,' Eva told him. She was sure that most people had no idea just how much work was involved in living in a place like this, the land and house both needed a great deal of daily attention. The retreat added even more work, but it would be worth it if they could make a success of it and give up their jobs completely.

Squeals of laughter came from the pool and she glanced over to see that Carlos, Saskia, Nathan and Bianca were throwing a beach ball to each other. They seemed to be having the time of their life. Saskia scooped up handfuls of water and sprayed it over Carlos, her head thrown back as she laughed. 'I'll get you for that,' he said, swimming after her. *It looks like we have a budding holiday romance here*, Eva thought. Would that be a bad thing though? If Saskia and Carlos hit it off, Carlos might be less inclined to cause any trouble. She could sense an undercurrent of resentment with him towards José and was hoping it wouldn't build into a big conflict.

Eva's big worry was that Saskia knew so much about her past. Would she confide in Carlos? If she did, it might get back to José. They were only here until Friday, she reminded herself. She would tell José herself when everyone had gone. Secrets never lay buried forever and it was best he learnt the truth from her rather than anyone else.

She was getting herself worked up over things that might not happen. She had to calm down before the anxiety overtook her. She raised her hand to her ear, located the acupressure point in the upper shell and pressed it firmly in a circular motion for a couple of minutes, feeling herself relax as she did it. She knew several acupressure points for anxiety but found this one, The Heavenly Gate, fairly inobtrusive so always chose to do it if she was in company. Ever since she had known that Saskia was coming to the retreat she had felt the anxiety rise. She had to keep it under control.

'I must get a cold drink.' Adrienne got up and went inside.

'I'll bring a jug of juice out for everyone,' Eva said, getting to her feet and going inside too. It was quite warm now and the others would probably appreciate a cool drink when they came out of the pool. As she stepped inside, she saw José lift out of the fridge the jug of sparkling water with a splash of pomegranate juice that she had prepared earlier and pour some into a glass. Adrienne took it from him, her eyes holding his gaze. He turned away to continue dicing the carrots and Adrienne stormed out, her face furious, not even acknowledging Eva.

Why was she still angry with José? They had both moved on and Adrienne had married. What did it all matter now? Unless she wasn't happy with Sean – maybe being here was bringing back happier memories for her.

'I feel relaxed already and this is only our first full day here,' Saskia said, coming into the kitchen. She held her arms out wide. 'It's all the fresh air and beautiful countryside.' She flashed a smile at José. 'And the delicious freshly grown food and homemade meals, of course.'

She linked her arm through Eva's as she used to do when

they were best friends at college. 'I think your retreat is going to be a big success. You'll be booked up all summer.'

Eva was grateful for her support even if it did feel a bit over-gushy. But then Saskia had always been over-the-top friendly and had a habit of over-sharing. Could she trust her to keep her secret?

30

Before dinner Eva got ready for the massage session, which Bianca and Saskia had signed up for. She knew from the form Bianca filled in that she suffered from stiffness in her neck and shoulder – a typical sign of tension – and had seen her massaging her neck this afternoon. She'd see if she could do anything to help her with that, Eva thought as she freshened up and changed into her white uniform, then lit some aromatherapy candles. She had soft music playing in the background and had just finished blending the oils when Bianca arrived, dressed in a kimono over a bikini.

'Hello.' She smiled warmly at the younger woman. 'Just in time.'

Bianca's smile was a little strained. 'You're not going to believe this but I've never had a massage before. My neck and back feel very stiff though so I'm really looking forward to it.'

'I'm sure you'll find it beneficial. Could you lie down on the bed then we'll get started.'

Bianca did as she asked and lay down, Eva rubbed a small amount of the warm oil in her hands then rubbed them together, ready to start. Moving her hands slowly, she started massaging Bianca's lower back then worked her way up either side of the spine until she reached the back of her neck. She could feel the young woman relaxing as she slowly massaged the oils into her body. She didn't speak for a while, knowing that some of her clients preferred silence during a massage while others preferred to chat, but somehow she had to get Bianca chatting. She needed answers.

'How's that? Can you feel the tension easing?' she asked after ten minutes or so.

'I can, this is so relaxing,' Bianca said. 'I'm glad Nathan persuaded me to come along. He said that the massage yesterday really helped him. As you can imagine, his job is so stressful and he never seems to unwind.'

Eva continued massaging gently as she replied, 'I'm sure a policeman's job is really full on – and dangerous. And although being a librarian sounds very calming I imagine you have tough days too.' Eva poured more oil onto her hands before massaging across her shoulders.

'Now and again but I love it. It's the only job I've ever had. I love it.'

'You must enjoy reading – or does everyone say that?' Eva worked her way gently down Bianca's upper arms.

'I do. It's been my escape ever since I was a child,' Bianca said.

'I love reading too,' Eva told her. 'It's good therapy to lose yourself in a book.' She paused, carefully rephrasing the question. 'You said your father was killed in a road accident, that must have been devastating for you. Did reading help you deal with your trauma?'

Bianca stiffened and Eva wondered if she was going to clam up but then the younger woman let out a long breath, as if letting go of her tension. 'I guess it did. When my dad was killed my mum was so devasted, she had a total breakdown. And to make it worse she blamed me for it all. I felt like she couldn't bear to look at me and decided that it was best to keep out of her way so would go to the library, I spent hours there. I loved the peace and quiet, and losing myself in the books. Going to the library saved my sanity, brought peace into my life. It was a natural career choice for me.'

How awful. 'I'm so sorry, that must have been so upsetting for you,' Eva said sympathetically, not quite sure what to say. She often found that having a massage would relax some clients so much they talked about things they had kept buried for years and hoped that this would be the case with Bianca. She wanted to find out more about the accident, to know that it was a different one to the one she'd been involved in. 'I'm sure it was your mother's grief talking. Grief can affect people in so many different ways.'

Bianca's voice hardened. 'No, she was right, it was my fault because I was the one who had begged Dad to get us some fish and chips. He didn't want to go, it was a dark winter's night and raining a bit but I wouldn't shut up and he finally agreed. The fish and chip shop was only a few minutes away but as he crossed the road a car came out of nowhere and knocked him over. Killed him outright. And the driver got away with it because a witness said they had tried to brake and that Dad hadn't looked as he crossed the road.' There was a bitter edge to Bianca's voice as she suddenly sat up, her eyes filled with pain at the memory, met Eva's and her words spilled out hot, angry, accusing. 'It was an inexperienced driver, who had only passed their test that week. They didn't go slow enough to stop if someone came out in front of them. If they hadn't been going so fast my dad would still be alive.' She swung her legs off the massage bed, visibly upset. 'I need to get out of here.'

Eva's head was swirling and nausea rose up in her as Bianca ran out of the studio. She collapsed down onto the chair, trembling. It couldn't be. Surely it couldn't.

31

'Do you mind if I forget my massage? Me and Carlos are going for a walk... hey, what's up, you look like you've seen a ghost,' Saskia said, coming into the studio a few minutes later. 'You're literally shaking.'

She was right, Eva was trembling. She sank down into the chair and tried to compose herself, concentrating on her breathing. In, out, in, out. Finally she felt calm enough to talk to Saskia, who was now sitting opposite her looking very concerned. 'Tell me what's happened,' she urged.

'Bianca.' Eva swallowed. 'She was talking about her father's accident. And it just brought it all back.'

'That's understandable.' Saskia squeezed her hand comfortingly. 'Are you okay? Do you want me to stay with you? I can cancel the walk with Carlos. I don't mind.'

'No, you go. I'm fine. It was such a shock, that's all.' She needed time to think, to sort her head out. She hadn't told Saskia everything Bianca had said and she wasn't sure whether to. She didn't know if she could trust her.

They both looked around as there was a knock on the door then Sean stepped in. 'Is it too late to have a massage?'

'You're in luck, I've just cancelled so you can have my place,' Saskia said. She squeezed Eva's arm. 'I'm here if you need me.'

'Problems?' Sean said as Saskia went out.

'Not at all,' Eva said calmly, wishing that Saskia hadn't said anything. She was so careless with her tongue sometimes, it made Eva scared to confide in her.

'Adrienne said her massage this morning really helped her destress so I thought I'd come for one too,' Sean said. 'I can't tell you how much we need these few days' rest. Our life is crazy right now.'

He chatted all the while Eva gave him a back massage, telling her how he and Adrienne had been trying for a family for years but had been told she would never have children so they'd been having IVF treatment. 'We've stopped for a while now because Adrienne has been getting so stressed out,' he said.

'I'm so sorry, it must be awful to want a child so much,' Eva replied softly. It was strange how having a massage made some clients confide all sorts of secrets to you, while others – like Nathan – barely spoke at all. 'I hope it works out for you both.'

'The thing is the medication she is on makes her so... emotional and irrational at times,' Sean said in a confiding tone. 'I'm only telling you this in case she behaves a little strangely while she's here. I wouldn't want her to upset anyone, she can't help it. She gets confused, things get mixed up in her head and she thinks that people are talking about her or ignoring her.'

Was that why Adrienne was so fixated on her relationship with José? Eva wondered. Did she think that he had deliberately ignored her?

'She's always accusing me of chatting up other women and having affairs,' Sean went on. 'She's very insecure at the moment.'

'I'm sorry to hear that.' Eva thought about the look Adrienne had given Sean when he had glanced at Saskia. And the furious look she'd given José in the kitchen. Adrienne had given the impression that Sean was controlling but was she the controlling one, because of her insecurities? Was that why she was determined to make José remember her, why she wanted Eva to know that she and José had been an item? That she'd been with him first.

José had told her Adrienne had been so different back then, unsophisticated, fun. Eva envied her in a way, she and José had been so young, carefree, she'd met José's beloved grandparents, lived in the Malaga flat that Eva had never even seen. Adrienne had known a different José, they'd probably both lived for the moment, no cares and responsibilities.

Eva had been like that once. Before that terrible winter's night that had blown her life apart.

32

Somehow Eva had managed to hold it together all evening, but as soon as she climbed into bed and closed her eyes the memory of everything leading up to that fateful day came flooding back.

She turned off the engine and sat still, her heart pounding. She'd made a couple of mistakes, she knew that, but were they bad enough to fail? This was her third attempt and she didn't think she could afford any more lessons. She picked at her nails as the examiner scribbled something down on the piece of paper he'd been making notes on all through the lesson. Then he coughed, pushed back his glasses and turned to her. She held her breath.

'I'm pleased to say that you've passed,' he said. 'Congratulations.'

She squealed with delight, resisting the urge to kiss him on the cheek. 'Really! Thank you!' She could hardly believe that she'd finally succeeded, having a driving licence offered so many work possibilities to her. It was as if a whole new exciting world was waiting for her.

'You drove well, a couple of minors that's all,' the examiner said, handing her the paperwork to send off for her new licence. A full licence. At last. She was floating on air when her driving instructor drove her home, she practically ran into the house where her parents and little brother were waiting for her. She had toyed with the idea of pretending that she had failed again but knew that her face would give her away so instead she let the big, happy grin spread over her face.

'I passed!' she shouted, waving the much-longed-for certificate in the air. 'I actually passed!'

'That's marvellous! Congratulations!' Her mother beamed and hugged her, as did her little brother. Her father gave her a hug too then looked seriously at her. 'You've passed your test but now the real learning to drive begins. Never rush, never panic and always, always watch your speed.'

'I will,' she promised. There was no way she was going to risk losing her coveted licence now she finally had it.

They had a celebratory meal that night and the next day Eva drove her mum to work and her younger brother to school. She was a little nervous but she took her time. A couple of evenings later when her mum ran out of milk Eva drove to the corner shop to get some. It was getting dark so she remembered to turn on her lights and kept her eyes peeled on the road ahead. It was the first time she'd driven in the dark and she was nervous so took her time, keeping her speed well below 30mph. She was almost home, with the milk and a chocolate cake that she'd spotted in the reduced corner of the shop sitting in a carrier bag at the foot of the passenger seat, just one street away, when she turned the corner and a shadowy figure suddenly stepped out in front of her. Horrified, she hit the brake, the car screeched to a halt. She gripped the steering wheel, shaking. Had she stopped in time? She couldn't see the figure. Leaving the engine running, she flung the car door open, got out, ran to the front of the car. *Please God, let him be alive. Please God, don't let me have killed him.* Her heart thudding, she felt sick. Her hand flew to her mouth, her stomach heaved when she saw a man lying sprawled out in the road.

'Is he dead? Is he dead?' she screamed, backing away in horror. Someone was beside her, a woman, calming her down, calling the police, telling her it wasn't her fault, the man was wearing a black coat, barely visible, and had stepped out without looking. The woman bent down to check the man's pulse and to Eva's relief said that he was breathing. 'An ambulance is on its way, love. He'll be okay,' the woman reassured her. But he wasn't okay. He had a heart attack and died that night.

And part of Eva died with him. She had killed someone. No matter how many times she was told it wasn't her fault, despite the fact that the police didn't charge her because the witness had said she had no chance to stop, she couldn't stop blaming herself. She should have come around the corner more slowly, she should have stopped more quickly. She had destroyed a life, a family. The doctor gave her antidepressants and she tried to carry on but the guilt and despair were too much and she had a complete breakdown. She squeezed her eyes tight to block out the memory of what that breakdown had caused her to do, what Saskia had witnessed. She had ended up in hospital. She sunk into a dark, bottomless pit that she thought she would never get out of. Antidepressants, counselling, none of it had helped her cope with the guilt until Yvonne, a wellness coach at the hospital had helped her, taught her techniques to cope. Eva had thrown herself into healthy eating and mindfulness, driven by the desire to heal herself first, then wanting to help other people to look after their mental as well as physical wellbeing. It gave her a reason for living, helping others somehow helping to absolve the guilt of accidentally ending a life. It had taken her years before she could drive again but now she managed it although she always tried to avoid driving in the dark.

She remembered that the newspaper report said the man was married and had a young daughter. Was Bianca that little girl?

*

I've tried to be kind, to forgive you for destroying my life and to give you another chance but it's too difficult. To see you thriving, living in this beautiful place, happy and loved, a home where you will probably bring your children up, surrounded by the love of two parents, eats away at me. I've thought of you so much over the years and couldn't resist this opportunity to see how you were faring but I shouldn't have come because I can't stand your happiness. I want to destroy it like you destroyed mine. And I can, believe me I can. I can take it all away from you in a heartbeat. I've given you a couple of warnings to let you know how easy it would be to destroy all that you have but you ignore them. You think that you are charmed and will rise above everything. You dragged me down to a place I barely had the strength to climb out of and now your time is coming too. But for you, there will be no way back.

WEDNESDAY – DAY THREE

Eva

When Eva woke up the next morning there was no sign of José. She guessed he'd probably gone for an early morning swim before the guests got up, as he often did now the weather was warmer. Deciding to join him she pulled on her swimsuit and wrapping a kimono over it she went into the kitchen, poured herself an orange juice and took it outside. As she stepped out onto the terrace she heard hushed voices. It was someone making a telephone call, she realised, stepping back so as not to intrude.

'I'll be home at the weekend. We'll talk about it then. It's only a few days. I miss you too.' There was no mistaking the American drawl. It was Sean. Was he cheating on Adrienne? It certainly didn't sound like a business call. Yesterday he'd said that Adrienne was insecure, it sounded like she might have reason to be.

Eva went back inside and made a lot of noise opening the door as she came out again to alert Sean to her presence. He had his phone in one hand, and his other hand in his shorts pocket, staring at the pool, which was empty. José wasn't having a swim then. Perhaps he'd gone for a walk.

'Morning,' she said cheerily to Sean. 'I hope you slept well. It can be a bit noisy here with the cicadas and parakeets.'

'Very well, thank you.' He held up his phone. 'I had to make an urgent call. Work. Thankfully we have a signal at the moment. I know that Adrienne and I both agreed to take these few days off but unfortunately there's been a bit of a crisis at one of the hotels. It's all sorted now though.'

'I'm glad to hear that.' She looked over at the pool. 'I'm about to take a dip before everyone gets up. This is my favourite time of the day.'

'I'm the other end of the scale, I like the night-time. I love to sit out at midnight and look at the stars. It's so peaceful then.' He glanced around. 'I thought Adrienne might be out here, she wasn't in bed when I woke. Maybe she's in the kitchen.' He nodded then went back inside.

Had she misunderstood the call? His explanation sounded very reasonable. Although 'I miss you too' was a strange thing to say on a business call.

It was nothing to do with her anyway. She shrugged off her kaftan and dived into the pool, bracing herself for the coldness of the water. Once submerged she soon warmed up.

She swam two lengths, dried herself, pulled on her kaftan again and went into the kitchen to get a drink. There was still no sign of José and she could hear the others coming down.

'Morning,' Saskia said cheerily as she walked into the kitchen first.

'Morning.' Eva smiled at her. 'Help yourself to some juice. I'll be starting the yoga session in a minute.' Where the hell was José? She hoped he'd be back for breakfast.

Carlos came down next, then Bianca and Nathan followed by Sean.

'Still no sign of Adrienne so I presume she's gone for a stroll but I would have thought she'd be back now,' Sean said. 'I've tried calling her but it goes straight to answerphone.'

Eva didn't want to draw attention to the fact that José had gone out early too but her mind was going over and over. Was it a coincidence? They were lovers once. She recalled Adrienne's words. 'He was my first lover, the love of my life.' Adrienne was feeling insecure and maybe unloved now. Would she try and ignite that old flame?

She pushed the thought from her mind. She trusted José. He would never cheat on her.

'I'll get the yoga session started,' she said. 'I'm sure she'll be along soon.'

Adrienne and José both came back together just as the yoga session finished. Adrienne was limping and José had his arm around her waist.

'Look who I found lying injured on the mountain track,' he announced.

'Adrienne, what have you done?' Sean dashed over to her, and he and José helped her to an empty chair. 'Sit down and let me take a look at it.'

'It's okay, I think I've just twisted my ankle,' she said, tears brimming in her eyes. 'I couldn't sleep so I went for a walk but I tripped. Thank goodness José came along or I might have been stuck out there for hours. I took my phone but I couldn't get a signal.'

'I was surprised when I woke up and you weren't there,' Sean said, kneeling beside her. 'I thought you had gone for a stroll around the grounds. I didn't expect you to go up the mountain. That's a bit dangerous.'

'I know but it's such a lovely morning. I went out through the side gate – but I did close it after me – I didn't get far, before I tripped and fell on my side. My ankle hurt so much I couldn't get up.' She wiped away the tears. 'I shouted as loudly as I could, hoping someone was about and would hear me, then José came along. I've never been so pleased to see anyone in all my life.'

'Lucky that you were out and about so early too,' Sean said pointedly to José.

'I often go for an early morning jog, especially if I've had a restless night. I was on my way back when I head Adrienne shout.'

Eva couldn't recall José having trouble sleeping before. He was usually out like a light as soon as his head touched the pillow. But then, he had looked very tense yesterday, she reminded herself. They were both feeling the strain this week.

It was a good job that he had been out jogging though, otherwise Adrienne could have been there for hours. The last thing they needed was an injured guest.

'I wish you'd woken me. You shouldn't go out for a walk alone here. You don't know the area well enough,' Sean told her.

'Don't worry, I won't be doing it again,' Adrienne replied.

'Do you need a doctor to take a look at your ankle?' Eva asked.

Adrienne shook her head. 'No, honestly, I've just twisted it a little. It's feeling better already.'

Well, that was a quick recovery, Eva thought as she went into the kitchen to take a crepe bandage out of the first aid tin. Was Adrienne pretending she'd hurt herself so that José would have to put his arm around her to help her home? 'At least let me strap it up for a while, to give it some support,' she said, coming back outside with the bandage.

'Thank you,' Adrienne said as Eva wrapped it around her ankle.

'Why don't you go and rest? I'll bring breakfast up to you,' Sean suggested but Adrienne shook her head.

'I'm fine, honestly. José looked after me.'

'You were lucky I came by and found you,' José told her.

'Now, breakfast will be a little late, but I promise you it will be worth it.' He smiled.

Everyone went up to their rooms to freshen up before breakfast, giving Eva the chance to speak to José alone and warn him to be careful around Adrienne.

'Oh Eva, you're not jealous of her, are you?' he asked. 'It was years ago.'

'No I'm not but you were her first lover, José, and I think she still carries a torch for you.'

José's jaw dropped. 'I was not! Why do you think that?'

'Adrienne told me when I was giving her a massage. She said that she had stayed at this house with you, and that you both lived together in your flat in Malaga, and you were the love of her life,' she couldn't stop herself from adding.

José looked puzzled. 'She's making our relationship sound far more than it was, Eva. It was a holiday romance when she was working in Marbella for a few months. Yes, she stayed over at my flat a couple of times, and overnight here when my grand-parents were in hospital. I told you that. I wouldn't call that living together. And I'd be amazed if I was her first lover. She wasn't in the least inhibited or shy.' He looked a bit embar-rassed. 'Sorry if that's too much information but you were the one who brought this up.'

'Only to warn you. Sean told me yesterday that they've been trying for a child. Adrienne can't have children apparently and they've been having IVF treatment. It's left Adrienne feeling emotional and insecure.' She raised worried eyes to his face. 'And I overheard Sean on the phone today, it seemed a bit... personal. I'm worried that their marriage is breaking down and that you – we – might get caught up in the crossfire.'

34

José

As he started preparing breakfast, José replayed his conversation with Adrienne that morning when they had walked down from the mountain – he no longer thought of her as Addie, that woman had gone. He was sure that she had seen him go out jogging and had deliberately followed him, staging the fall so that he would stop and help her, give her time to talk to him. To tell him exactly why she didn't want Sean to know about them. And it had shocked him.

He thought back to when he had first met Adrienne, ten years ago. She and another woman had been having a drink outside the restaurant when he finished work, he recognised them as they'd visited the restaurant a couple of times. They'd invited him to join them and they looked a lively pair so he had. He'd been in his early twenties then, young, single, with an eye for a pretty girl. What was wrong with that? He wasn't hurting anyone.

Adrienne had told him that she was over from America on a six-month training course at a hotel in Marbella. Her friend was over on two weeks' holiday and due to go back that weekend. He and Adrienne had taken up with each other, become lovers. She was fun, they had a good time together. Eventually Adrienne had to go back to America, he'd gone to the airport with her, said goodbye. And that was it. Over. It hadn't been serious for either of them. They both knew that it wasn't forever. They had parted as friends, with no hard feelings. So he had thought.

'We loved each other, it hurt that you didn't want to keep in touch,' she'd told him. 'And that you've forgotten all about me.'

'It was a long time ago. We're both happy with someone else,' he'd reminded her.

'Except that I'm not happy with Sean,' she'd gulped. 'He's not the friendly, calm man you all see. He has another side to him.'

'You mean he's... abusive?' José asked, horrified. Adrienne seemed too strong and independent to put up with an abusive partner but he knew that relationships were complicated and abusive people could be very manipulative.

'Controlling is more the word but he can be very... difficult,' she said, her voice barely a whisper. 'He wants a child more than anything, we both do, but I can't conceive. We've been having IVF for years, it's almost bankrupted us, but nothing's worked. It's tearing us apart, and Sean is convinced that I'll leave him.' She swallowed. 'He's so jealous, he can't stand me even talking to anyone else. If he finds out about us he will be furious and I can't take any of his mood swings again. Please make sure you and Eva don't tell him.'

He was angry at Sean for being so cruel. Adrienne seemed really frightened. 'Of course, we won't say anything but, Adrienne, you should not put up with this. You should leave him.'

She had looked at him then with huge, sad eyes. 'I can't. I'm scared of what he will do.'

35

Eva

Carlos didn't come down for breakfast but the other guests tucked eagerly into the delicious wraps José had cooked and the healthy drinks Eva had prepared.

'I love this kombucha,' Bianca said as she took another sip from the glass cup. 'José said that it's rich in probiotics and antioxidants.'

Eva nodded eagerly. The fermented tea was one of Eva's favourite drinks, and she always had a cup before breakfast.

'It really is a heathy drink, experts believe that it can protect against lots of diseases such as cancer and diabetes.' She forced herself to look at Bianca and guilt flooded through her when she saw the bags under the young woman's eyes. She looked so pale and drawn. And she'd been so upset when she ran out of the studio last night. Was it all Eva's fault?

'It helps burn calories too.' Saskia's voice interrupted her thoughts.

Eva pulled herself together. She had to put this out of her

mind and focus on their guests. It might have been a completely different accident than the one Eva was involved in.

A lively discussion followed on the benefits of kombucha against other healthy drinks then, breakfast over, everyone went to their rooms to relax for half an hour.

'Are you okay, Eva? You look tired and you seemed really distracted over breakfast,' José said as they cleared the breakfast things away. 'Are you still fretting about Adrienne?'

She shook her head. 'Sorry, I was thinking about the water aerobics session, I was about to ask who was attending it when we got talking about the kombucha then I forgot. I'll just see who turns up.'

When she went out to the pool a little later she was pleased to see all the guests were on the terrace, waiting for her.

'I'll sit this one out, my ankle is still painful.' Adrienne looked nervously at the pool as the others eagerly stepped into the water. Adrienne never went in the pool, Eva realised. Perhaps she couldn't swim and was worried she would be out of her depth, which she would be if she went to the far end of the pool as the water was six feet deep there.

Adrienne turned to Sean. 'You go in. I'm happy to sit and watch.' She sat down in the chair and pulled her sunglasses down over her eyes.

Sean kissed her on the forehead and then took a run to the pool, leaping in at the deep end then swimming over to the shallower end.

'Okay, everyone, it's good to see you're so enthusiastic,' Eva said, getting down the steps into the pool herself. 'Now first let me say how beneficial doing exercises in water is. It's great for cardio and strength training and also improves flexibility which helps relieve pain so is really good for people with back problems.' She moved across the pool until she was facing them. 'First we're going to start with a warm-up. I want you all to lift up one knee as high as you can, then lower it and raise the other knee.' She demonstrated and they all copied her. After the warm-up exercises she followed with some cardio ones such as leg kicks, arm stretches and jogging in the water then cooling-down exercises. They exercised for twenty minutes then Eva suggested a short break before the next activity.

José brought out a tray of fresh drinks and snacks as soon as they came out of the pool. Adrienne joined them and they all sat around chatting for a while then José got to his feet. 'I'll be starting the "grow your own food" workshop at eleven. Who's joining me?'

They all raised their hands and Eva could see that José was pleased that everyone was interested. Gardening and cooking were his passions. Bianca rubbed her forehead. 'Actually I have one of my headaches again, I think I'll give it a miss and lie down for a while,' she said.

'Why don't you have another massage,' Nathan suggested. 'You said that it really helped yesterday.'

Bianca glanced at Eva. 'Can you fit me in?'

'Yes, give me ten minutes or so to get set up then come on along to the studio.'

Eva swallowed down her panic at the thought of being alone with Bianca again. What would the woman say? Would she confront Eva about what she did?

36

Bianca came into the studio looking pale and drained. 'I'm sorry I ran out on you yesterday, I get a bit emotional sometimes,' she said. She thrust a lock of her hair behind her ears. 'I'm always anxious, that's why Nathan suggested this break. We're both hoping that I learn some relaxation techniques.'

Was Bianca's anxiety Eva's fault? Losing her father at such a young age had clearly had a terrible effect on her. And having to cope with her mother's breakdown too. Eva knew how much her family had struggled to cope with her own breakdown, caused by her guilt. The guilt that was building up inside her again, threatening to suffocate her. All she wanted was for this retreat to be over with, for everyone to go home so that she didn't have a constant reminder of her past. She took a deep breath to compose herself before replying.

'We all have times like that. I find that concentrating on my breathing helps. I breathe in deeply then out, in, out, relaxing my body as I exhale and imagining that I am breathing out all my worries. I often find a few minutes of that helps me relax.'

'Thank you, I'll try it. The massage yesterday really helped, that's why I've come back today.' She lay face down on the massage table bed ready for Eva to start.

This time, to Eva's relief, Bianca was silent during the massage, Eva could feel Bianca's muscles relaxing as Eva's fingers gently moved over her back, rubbing in the soothing oils. Finally Bianca let out a long sigh. 'That feels so much better. I must book myself in for a regular massage somewhere when I go back home,' she said as she sat up. 'The difference it makes is amazing.'

'You might want to try a bit of acupressure too,' Eva told her. 'The Spirit Gate might be a good one to start with.' She held out her hand and pressed her right thumb on the little crease on her wrist on the little finger side of her left hand. 'Press down firmly on it for a couple of minutes. It is very effective for relieving tension.'

'Like this?' Bianca copied what Eva had just done and Eva nodded.

'Another acupressure you might want to try is Yin Tang. Press with your finger midway between your eyebrows.' She demonstrated and Bianca copied her.

'Let me show you one specifically for headaches too. This is called Wind Pool, or Gates of Consciousness.' Eva showed Bianca how to place each thumb in the hollow between the two vertical muscles on each side of her neck, under the base of her skull, and to press firmly for a minute. 'Tilt your head back and close your eyes as you do it,' she said. 'You should feel the tension ebb away and the pain lessen. You might need to practise it a few times before you feel the effect. There are other acupressure exercises you can do but concentrate on those two for now. They should help,' she advised.

'I will. Thanks again. I feel so much better now,' Bianca said. And she certainly did look more relaxed, Eva thought in relief as Bianca left.

Eva sat down on the stool, thinking over the session. Bianca had been friendly and relaxed with her this morning. She couldn't know who Eva was, what she had done, or she would never be able to act like that with her. She would be bitter, wouldn't be able to stop herself from saying something, surely. Eva desperately wanted to help Bianca to deal with the stress, wondering again if her actions were responsible. The guilt she felt was crushing her. She sat down, her head in her hands and took some deep, calming breaths.

I am resilient. I can make it through this difficult time. She repeated the affirmation in her head.

'Hey, is everything okay?' José was standing in the doorway looking at her in concern. 'You look shattered. Nothing else has gone wrong, has it?'

She took her hands from her face and forced a bright smile on her face. 'No, I'm just a little tired that's all.' *Because I think the daughter of the man I killed is staying here.*

It might not be his daughter, she thought, replacing the negative thought with a positive one. Tragically lots of people got killed in car accidents every day. It was probably just a horrible coincidence.

An inexperienced driver though. At night-time. And in Sutton where you lived.

It must be a coincidence.

The horror of it haunted her. The man lying on the ground, the screams of the man's wife as she arrived at the scene of the accident, the ambulance, the police car, Eva's devastation when she discovered that he had died.

The unbearable guilt that had blighted her life for years.

She had been cleared of any wrongdoing, she reminded herself. It had been dark and the man had stepped out into the road, right in front of her. She had no chance of stopping. A witness had said that in court. She had been completely exonerated.

But she had never stopped blaming herself.

'Didn't you sleep well?' José knelt beside her, his voice gentle. 'Is something troubling you?'

He was so kind, so understanding. She longed to rid herself of this terrible burden and tell him about it. Confess it all. The worry of how he would take it stopped her. She couldn't risk losing him.

She shook her head. 'I'm fine. It's just such a big responsibility, isn't it, having guests to look after? And I'm a bit uneasy about Saskia, she's such a flirt and seems to be getting very close to Carlos.' And she might tell him Eva's secret. Saskia had betrayed her before.

'They're adults, *cariño*. It's up to them what they do.'

He was right, she couldn't do anything about it. She felt powerless, so much was out of her control.

José's dark eyes were full of concern. 'Are you sure that nothing is troubling you, Eva? You seem so anxious.'

She had to give him some explanation. 'I just want the retreat to be a success and nothing else to go wrong. How do you feel about Carlos being here? At first I thought that he had come because he wanted to get to know you better and was curious about where his grandparents had lived but he's made a couple of barbed comments. Do you think that he will cause trouble?'

José gently stroked her cheek. 'Always such a worrier. Carlos has come to be nosey. We will give him a good time, and hopefully me and him can mend a few bridges. Two days and he will be gone. We will either never see each other again or we will become better acquainted.' He shrugged his shoulders. 'I can deal with either outcome.' He leant over and kissed her on the cheek. 'I must go and run the "grow your own food" session now, you rest and stop fretting. Our first retreat will be a success, you'll see.'

She returned his smile. 'I will,' she promised. How could she tell him that she was fretting because Saskia knew her

darkest secret, and she was worried that if she got too friendly
with Carlos she would tell him and it might get back to José?
What would José think when he discovered that she was
responsible for a man's death? And that there was the possibly
that the daughter of the man she had killed was here too. Did
Bianca know who Eva was? Was it all just a coincidence that
she was here or had she come to make trouble? Eva recalled the
look in her eyes yesterday, her angry words about the inexperienced driver who had killed her father. She had almost felt as if
the words were aimed at her, that Bianca had known it was
Eva's fault, but this morning Bianca had been friendlier.

A terrifying thought suddenly occurred to her. What if
Bianca did know and was only pretending to be friendly? What
if she had come to the retreat to get revenge?

Was she behind all the things that had gone wrong – the
goats trampling over the vegetable patch, Sombra being locked
in the studio and breaking the bottles of oils? And the Buddha
statue! Had Bianca only pretended to fall into it or had she
deliberately pushed it off the post on the terrace with the intention of hurting – killing – Eva? She shuddered. She felt
surrounded by people she couldn't trust and the doom-monger
wasps of foreboding were stirring in her stomach.

37

'I've decided to give the gardening session a miss, could you fit me in for a massage?' Saskia appeared at the door just after José left.

Eva looked up. 'No problem. I did think you might skip it and go back to bed. You looked shattered this morning.'

'Late night, sorry.' Saskia kicked off her flip flops and sat down on the massage bench. Then she looked sheepishly at Eva. 'Full disclosure. I spent the night with Carlos. And, well, we didn't get much sleep.'

Eva stared at her, her mind in turmoil. She'd been right to be concerned about how close Saskia and Carlos were getting. What if she told him about Eva's breakdown? About the awful thing she did?

'I didn't expect you to look quite so shocked,' Saskia said. 'Is it against the retreat rules or is it because he's José's cousin?'

Had she looked that disapproving? She hadn't meant to. As José had reminded her, they were both adults and could see who they wanted. 'I'm sorry, I was a little surprised, that's all.'

'I know we've only been here a couple of days but we've

really hit it off.' Saskia looked worried. 'You don't mind, do you? Will José mind? We'll keep it low key,' she promised. 'There's only a couple more days of the retreat anyway.'

'Do you think you'll see each other afterwards?' Eva asked.

'I don't know. I'm taking it as it comes. It's ages since I felt this way about someone. Not since Leo.' She put her hand over her mouth. 'I didn't mean anything by that and I won't mention anything to Carlos if that's what you're worried about. I promise.'

She sounded so sincere. 'I know,' Eva said. 'I'm happy for you.'

She warmed up the oils and started to massage Saskia's shoulders.

'That's wonderful,' Saskia sighed. 'You have magic fingers.'

'That's what Bianca said.' Would she still think that if she knew what Eva had done? Or did she already know and was playing games with her?

'Are you okay?' Saskia asked. 'You've gone quiet.'

Eva had to unburden herself to someone. She blurted out what Bianca had told her.

'I think it was her father I killed, Saskia. What if she knows it too and has come here to get some kind of revenge on me?'

'You can't keep thinking like that. I bet there are loads of road accidents in Sutton every year. You don't even know when Bianca's dad was... run over,' Saskia said.

She was right. 'I should have asked her more about it but I couldn't. I felt so guilty. And I was scared that if she knew it was me she would tell everyone what I did.'

'Stop torturing yourself. I'll talk to Bianca and see if I can find out more,' Saskia said. 'I'll be careful, I promise. I won't let on that I know anything, just show a caring interest. If we can find out what date it happened then hopefully we can rule you out.'

That would be such a relief. 'Thank you. That would take a weight off my mind.'

'Leave it to me. You can trust me.' Saskia got off the massage bench. 'Thanks for the massage. I feel much better now.'

As she watched her go, Eva hoped that she could trust her. She really needed a friend right now.

Feeling hot and sticky, she decided to freshen up and change before José and the others returned with the vegetables they'd picked.

Maybe I'm wrong about Bianca, she seemed friendly enough this morning. And everything could be just a coincidence, Eva thought as she turned on the shower. Everyone seemed to be getting on together and they were all enthusiastic about the sessions this afternoon and the trip to a restaurant in Toria to watch the flamenco dancers this evening. Eva and José often visited the restaurant and had seen the performance a few times so knew that the food was good and the dancers well worth watching.

She lathered herself and stood under the lukewarm cascading water, feeling the stress wash away. *Stop worrying, it's almost over. Two more days.* Sliding open the cubicle, she grabbed hold of the towel, wrapped it around herself and stepped out into the bedroom, padding barefoot over to the wardrobe. She paused as she saw a piece of paper peeping out from under the lamp on her bedside table. It looked like a note. Had José been in to talk to her, saw that she was still in the shower so left her a note? She walked over and picked it up then froze at the word written in black capitals.

MURDERER

Tremors running through her whole body, Eva sat down on the bed staring at the note, the word written in big, black capital letters burning into her mind. Murderer. There was no mistaking who it was from. Now she knew for sure that Bianca was here to cause trouble, to pay Eva back for causing her father's death. She had come to the retreat to get revenge.

38

José

He must speak to Eva later about the situation with Adrienne and Sean, José thought. He had wanted to explain earlier but she was so upset about things going wrong at the retreat he didn't want to worry her more. She had gone outside now to lay the table, they were having lunch on the terrace as it was such a lovely morning.

'Well, I didn't expect you to have such a good setup when I booked in here.'

Knife poised in mid-air, José stopped chopping the peppers for the quiche and looked around in surprise at Carlos's tone. 'And what did you expect?' he asked, keeping his voice steady and replying in their native language, as Carlos had.

Carlos shrugged. 'Papá said that the villa was run down, almost derelict.'

'So it was. You have seen the photos,' José said evenly.

Carlos shrugged. 'Photos can be manipulated.'

'What are you insinuating?' José put the knife down onto the chopping board, then leant against the work surface, arms folded as he studied his cousin. It was becoming obvious to him that Carlos had come here with a grudge, and was surprised how successfully José and Eva had transformed their grandmother's villa. A grandmother he had never made any attempt to get to know and a villa he had never visited.

'I think that you and your father pretended the villa was in a worse state than it was at our grandmother's funeral.'

'And why would we do that?'

'So that me and Papá wouldn't contest the will. And when Grandfather died you made sure that you were indispensable to Grandmother so that she would leave you the estate.'

'I was all she had. If you'd cared about her you could have come and visited her. Then you could have seen the villa yourself,' José retorted. 'But you never once visited her, checked on her. Even after Abuelo died and Abuelita was left to cope alone.' He tried to keep his voice low, not wanting the other guests to hear them arguing, but he couldn't let Carlos get away with saying such things.

'She never wanted anything to do with us. None of them did. My father was banished many years ago. My grandparents made no attempt to meet me.' That was true. José felt a flood of sympathy for his cousin not to have had the chance to get to know his grandparents, they had been wonderful people. What on earth had the row been about? It must have been something very serious to divide the family like this, to keep his *abuelos* apart from their eldest son and his family.

'They knew nothing about you until Abuelo's funeral. Your father never told them.' He softened his voice. 'It takes two to fall out. I am sure that my – our – *abuelos* would have loved to be part of your life.' He remembered the tears in his grandmother's eyes when she'd seen Tío Diego again and met her grandson for the first time. She was proud, both his grandparents were, but Abuelita had been pleased to see them. He knew she had. Carlos and his father had kept themselves distant though, had only given her a brief hug and then had gone. They could have made the first move, written to her, come to visit especially after their grandfather died, Abuelita would have welcomed it, he was sure. After all, it was his grandfather who had told Tío Diego to never darken his doorstep again, not her.

'That was their decision.' Carlos's voice was cold and angry. 'And you the golden boy, you kept close to her and now you have everything.'

José took a deep breath. 'You were left some money. And I was left a house to do up. A house that had been my second home for years. A house I have spent a great deal of money on.'

Carlos's lip curled. 'We were so surprised when Abuela died. She looked strong and fit at Abuelo's funeral, we thought she would live for many years more. And then, suddenly she was gone just two years later. It is strange that she went so quickly. That she would be so unsteady on her feet as to fall down the stairs.' His eyes narrowed. 'And that the fall would be so fatal.'

José felt rage surge through him. 'What are you suggesting?' he demanded. 'Spit it out and stop making vague accusations.'

Carlos glared at him, his eyes dark. 'I am not suggesting anything, *primo*, just remarking that the accident was a surprise to us. And that you've done very well out of Abuela's death.'

He turned and strode out of the kitchen leaving José clenching his fists with fury.

39

Carlos's accusation kept going over and over in José's mind. He had been so angry that it was all he could do not to strike his cousin. How dare he accuse him of harming his beloved *abuelita*?

His grandparents had been there for him all his life, showering him with love and kindness. This house had been his second home, and both their deaths had hit him hard. When his grandfather had died his grandmother had tried to manage by herself, a fiercely independent woman, she had always been too stubborn to ask for help. José had made sure that he visited her as often as he could, bringing food supplies with him, checking the house and grounds to see what needed doing and had asked Mario to keep an eye on her and report back to him if she was struggling or ill, giving him a spare key to the house just in case.

It was Mario who had found Abuelita collapsed on the floor, using his spare key when she didn't answer the door one morning, who had phoned for the ambulance and also phoned José. Mario's quick actions had saved her life, but she walked with a stick from then on. José visited as often as he could, and had moved her bed into the downstairs room telling her not to go up the stairs. She had been a proud woman and hated asking for help.

She found it difficult to sleep and was often awake early. When he'd been staying over one weekend she had woken at six and decided she wanted to look at the family album, so she had whispered to him later when he found her, but instead of waiting for José to get up and help her she had gone up the stairs to fetch it and slipped on the way down. José had heard her scream, jumped out of bed, raced down and found her in a crumpled heap at the bottom of the stairs. She was still breathing so he had called an ambulance, held her hand until it came, telling her that he loved her, willing her with all his might to live and she had told him to take care of El Sueño, to return it to its former glory in memory of her. He had shushed her, told her that an ambulance was on the way and she would be fine, that she was going to live for many more years. But he was wrong, she didn't survive the day. He had been heartbroken.

He had been grateful that she left him El Sueño because it had so many wonderful memories for him, and he vowed to keep his promise and restore it to its former glory but he would have preferred to lose his home, his job, everything he owned than his grandmother. She had been more of a mother to him than his own mother. It made him angry that Carlos suggested he had caused their grandmother's death so he could take her house. How dare he!

'What's the matter? You're pounding away at that pastry as if you were wishing it was someone's head you were thumping!' Eva said from behind him.

'Carlos!' José practically spat the words out.

Eva put her hand on his shoulder. 'What he's done?'

His anger melted a little under her gentle touch. They were good for each other, him and Eva, neither of them liked drama and confrontation. José had a quick temper but Eva always managed to soothe him, to help him feel calmer. While she was anxious, a worrier, and he offered her reassurance and comfort.

He left the pastry and turned to face her. 'He is jealous, and angry because of my inheritance.' He couldn't bring himself to tell Eva what his cousin had insinuated, it was an insult and would only cause her to fret, her anxiety levels were high enough. 'I wish he had never come here. I would like to tell him to go. I don't want him to be at this retreat a day longer, but I am trying to keep it pleasant for the other guests so I will bear it until Friday but then, I hope that I never see him again.'

'I guess that it's only natural that he would resent your close relationship with your grandparents but maybe he will come round,' Eva said. 'It would be so good if you two became friends. You two are the only cousins, the only ones to carry on your family name.'

'It is what I would like too but I think that is highly unlikely,' José said. 'Still, we have only one more full day to go so I will try to put up with it.' He frowned as he suddenly realised that Eva looked pale and drawn. 'Is everything okay, *cariño*? You look strained.'

She rubbed her forehead. 'It's all this tension, you and Carlos, Adrienne and Sean.' She smiled wanly. 'I will be so glad when this retreat is over.'

'Me too,' José told her. He couldn't wait for his cousin to leave. He shrugged. 'Soon it will be over. Now I must continue preparing our lunch.' He turned back to the pastry.

'Let me do the salad while you prepare the quiche,' Eva offered, 'the guests are all busy with another creativity session. I'll go out and check on them in a while.'

'That would be helpful, *gracias*. We picked it all this morning during our gardening session, it's in the salad basket. If you could wash and prepare it that would be a big help.'

Eva went over to the salad basket and took out the lettuce, washing it and spinning it in the salad spinner then chopping it and placing it in the big salad bowl. Next she did the tomatoes and then when they were washed and sliced she reached for the onions. 'How many onions do you want?' she asked.

'Just a few,' José said. 'I'll do them, they always make your eyes water. I'll just put the quiche in the oven and then I'll take over.'

'I can do them.' Eva picked up a handful of onions and peeled off the skin. 'They don't smell very strong,' she said as she chopped them, her eyes weren't watering at all. 'Have you been growing a new variety?'

José came over to her. 'No, they're the same ones.' He stared at the onions as Eva chopped them, she was right, there was no oniony smell. He paused, picked one up and sniffed it. Then he went over to the basket containing the salad items they had picked fresh from the garden this morning. He took out an onion and studied it. Could they be?

'What's the matter?' Eva asked.

José looked up at her. 'These are daffodil bulbs not onions.'

Eva's hand flew to her mouth. 'But daffodil bulbs are poisonous!' she gasped.

José nodded. 'In large quantities, yes. A small amount like this would give you an upset stomach. All our guests would have thought they had food poisoning and that would be devastating for our reputation.' His eyes sparked. 'Someone has done this on purpose to cause trouble for us,' he said grimly. 'And I'm going to find out who it is.'

40

Eva

Eva stared at him. Surely Bianca wouldn't go that far to get her revenge.

'Could someone have picked them accidentally?' she asked. 'Who was with you in the gardening session this morning? You all picked the ingredients for lunch, didn't you? Could someone have got mixed up? There are some daffodils growing near the edge of the vegetable patch.'

'Yes but they are well away from the vegetables. And I watched everyone. No one went near them,' he said. 'Someone must have gone back afterwards and picked some.'

Eva's mind was racing, she couldn't take this in. It was like she was in a nightmare and didn't know who to believe or trust. If someone had deliberately swapped the onions for daffodil bulbs hoping that José wouldn't notice and would serve them up in the salad, that meant they knew that everyone would be ill, poisoned. That was taking things to a whole new level. Whoever was trying to ruin things for the retreat had now raised the stakes. She shook her head. Surely not. It had to be a mistake. She felt her legs give way beneath her and pulled out a chair to sit down, her whole body shaking. 'I can't believe it. I can't.'

'There is no other explanation,' José said firmly. 'This is serious, Eva. Although I can't think who would do this, or why.'

Should she tell him about the note? Surely Bianca wouldn't poison a bunch of innocent strangers.

Could it be a mistake?' She was clutching at straws and she knew it. Too much had happened for it to be a coincidence.

'Hi, sorry to interrupt.' They both turned around at the sound of Saskia's voice. 'Ah, good you found the onions. I thought you might need them for lunch, that's why I brought them in.'

'You picked them?' Eva stared at her.

Saskia shook her head. 'No, I found them lying on the path near the vegetable garden, I guessed someone had dropped them in the gardening session earlier so picked them up and brought them in. I didn't want them to go to waste, you've had enough vegetables ruined.' She paused and looked from José to Eva. 'What's up?'

'They're not onions, they're daffodil bulbs,' Eva told her. 'Luckily we discovered them before we put them in the salad otherwise we could have all been poisoned.'

Saskia's eyes widened and her hand flew to her mouth. 'Oh my God! I'm so sorry. I had no idea.' She sank down on one of the chairs. 'I thought I was helping. Oh my God!' She looked like she was going to be sick. Eva felt faint with relief that it had been a simple accident.

José let out a long breath. 'At least we discovered the mistake in time, if you do find any other plants dug up like that again please don't touch them but come and tell me.'

Saskia nodded, her face still pale. 'I will.'

'Please don't mention this to anyone else. We don't want

anyone to worry that they might get poisoned while they're here,' José asked her.

'I won't. I promise. I really am sorry, I had no idea. I feel awful. I can't bear to think what could have happened.'

Eva touched her arm comfortingly. 'It's okay, Saskia, we understand that you didn't know. You were only trying to help.'

'I didn't even know that daffodil bulbs were poisonous,' Saskia said shakily. 'And there hardly seems any difference in them to the onions. How can you tell?'

'The smell gave it away for me.' *And thank goodness it did*, Eva thought.

'Why don't you go and sit on the terrace for a few minutes and relax,' José said gently. 'You've had a bit of a shock.'

Saskia nodded. 'Yes I will. Thanks.' She took the cold drink that José offered her and went outside.

'Poor Saskia. She's blaming herself,' Eva said. She knew what that felt like, how the guilt consumed you.

'Go and sit with her, you've had a shock too. I can finish off in here,' José told her.

'If you're sure.' Eva did feel a bit shaken up. She couldn't help suspecting that the daffodil bulbs had been deliberately dug up and left for someone to find. From now on she was going to have to be really vigilant. It was clear that someone was out for revenge and would stop at nothing – was even willing to cause harm to others – to ruin the retreat.

41

José

José had been relieved to hear Saskia's explanation about the daffodil bulbs until he remembered that he'd picked some onions that morning, with the rest of the salad. So where were the onions he had picked? They weren't in the vegetable trolley. Had someone removed them and deliberately left the daffodil bulbs on the path hoping one of the other guests would do just what Saskia did? Perhaps his jealous cousin? Was Carlos trying to ruin the retreat because he resented not being left a share of their grandparents' home? He hadn't even bothered to hide the fact that he thought José was making a fortune from it. If only he knew! Even Eva didn't know just how much restoring the villa had cost. It had not only used up all his savings, he was in debt for tens of thousands. If he didn't make this work, he would have to sell El Sueño and he couldn't bear to do that. He would feel like he'd let his beloved grandparents down.

Carlos's spiteful accusation this morning was still fresh in his mind. His cousin had said he'd come to see the villa and to connect with José, and maybe this had been true at first but José doubted it. He thought that Carlos had come to cause trouble, and that it was likely he was behind some of the things that had gone wrong. Perhaps he had shut Sombra in the studio hoping the cat would cause havoc, and could he have been behind the goats getting in? He hadn't even bothered to hide his pleasure that the vegetable patch had been ruined. José shook his head, Carlos was up in front with Saskia, he couldn't have sneaked back without José noticing him.

He was beginning to sound like Eva. There had to be a reasonable explanation. He thought back to the gardening session this morning. All the guests had taken part, everyone was picking different items for lunch today. Could someone have picked the daffodils then realised their mistake and left them there?

If so, what had happened to the onions José had picked and put in the vegetable trolley? It didn't make sense. Someone had deliberately moved them. And Carlos was the only person who had a motive to want the retreat to fail. He would be watching his cousin very carefully from now on. He didn't trust him.

42

Eva

The fresh salad was all prepared, in a big bowl on the table, when Eva came back in. José glanced up at her. 'Is Saskia calmer now?'

'Yes, she's stopped beating herself up, I think.' She washed her hands then opened the fridge to take the cheese out. 'The salad looks delicious. Shall we eat outside?' She always felt less anxious outside, she was starting to feel panicky being in the house with six guests knowing that at least one of them was a viper in the nest and could strike out at her any moment.

'Good idea,' José agreed. He prepared the salad dressing while Eva grated some cheese into a bowl, then took the rustic rolls she'd baked that morning out of the breadbin.

'Want any help?' Saskia, looking calmer now, popped her head around the half-open kitchen door.

'Thanks, it's all done now. Can you let everyone know that we're having lunch on the terrace in a few minutes?'

'Will do.' Saskia disappeared again.

Eva placed a jug of homemade lemonade on a tray with

some glasses and took it outside. Bianca, Nathan, Carlos and Saskia were sitting around the smaller table. 'Help yourselves, lunch is coming out now,' she said.

'I think Adrienne and Sean have gone for a walk,' Saskia said as Eva put the tray down in front of them.

'We can start without them, they know the meal times so will be along in a few minutes if they want to eat,' Eva replied pleasantly. She went back inside to fetch the tablecloth, crockery and cutlery, took them out and put them on the bigger table. José followed her out with the salad and rolls.

'Oh, that looks delish,' Bianca said enthusiastically as they all sat down at the table.

'Thank you.' Was Bianca wondering if she had found the note yet? Eva forced herself to meet Bianca's gaze, looking for some sign... of what? Resentment? Anger? Triumph? But Bianca had turned to talk to Nathan, who was seated next to her. No sign of guilt there, Eva thought. She was a bloody good actress.

Unless it wasn't Bianca, and it was Nathan – the idea hit her out of the blue. As if sensing her thoughts, Nathan raised his eyes to meet hers, staring coolly at her until she looked away. She felt a chill shoot down her spine. Was he getting revenge for Bianca?

Adrienne and Sean strolled around from the side of the house. She was no longer limping, Eva noticed. Did she actually hurt her ankle or had it just been a ploy to get José's attention?

'Just in time for lunch then,' Sean exclaimed. 'Great, that walk has given me an appetite.'

'We'll just pop in and wash our hands,' Adrienne said.

'I'm pleased to see that your ankle is better. Have you been up the mountain again?' José asked when they came back out and sat down to eat.

'It's a little weak but we walked slowly. We've been having a stroll around the area outside your villa. We saw Mario and he invited us in for a coffee,' Adrienne said.

'That was kind of him,' Eva replied. That was typical of Mario. He was so friendly and helpful.

'Nice property he's got. Smaller than this though and without as much land.' Sean picked up one of the rolls and started to butter it.

Mario's property was small, and he was continually working on it. His father, like José's grandparents, had been too old to take care of it properly and it was in a bit of a state when Mario moved in, so José had told Eva. Mario didn't have the income José and Eva had from their jobs and was struggling to find the funds to do the repairs to the old *finca*, which was why he was happy to be a paid handyman, chauffeur and whatever else for Eva and José.

'We had another look around your grounds too, and a quick peep through the casita windows. They're so pretty. If they'd have been ready Sean and I would have loved to stay in one.'

'In fact, we might return for another stay when they're available,' Sean said. 'This is the perfect place to get away from everything and unwind. You're completely off grid here.'

I hope they don't, Eva thought. She couldn't wait for Adrienne to leave, she didn't want her coming back!

'I agree. It's beautiful,' Nathan said. 'Will you be having larger groups in the future or keep to smaller ones?'

'We will have accommodation for twelve once the casitas and upper terrace room are refurbished,' José told her.

'What's the grid like up a mountain like this? Will you be able to provide enough electricity for more guests?' Carlos butted in.

Eva saw the look on José's face at the question, he was evidently still annoyed about Carlos's comments this morning. She could see that he was making an effort to control himself.

'Hopefully, we're on the highest band but it's hard to tell as so far there have only been the two of us living here. We've got a generator too, which will kick in if the electricity goes off. And we're looking into putting in solar panels next year,' José replied in measured tones.

'Sounds like you've got it all planned out,' Carlos said, pouring himself another glass of the homemade lemonade.

José shot him a look but said nothing. Why was Carlos questioning him? Eva wondered. He knew what the villa was like when José inherited it. They had shown him the album, there were plenty of pictures in there to prove what they had had to do.

'We did a lot of planning before we opened the retreat,' she said. 'We thought about every little detail. We want it to be perfect for our guests.' She glanced around the table, skimming past Bianca, who was looking down at her salad, and Nathan, who was staring at her inscrutably, on to Saskia's friendly face. *Focus, Eva!* 'That's why you are all here, why we gave you such a generous discount. So that we can make sure it is all as it should be before we officially open it to the general public.'

'I think that was a brilliant idea.' Saskia nodded. 'And I've got nothing to complain about. I'm sure no one else has either.'

'Thank you,' Eva told her. She glanced up and realised that Bianca was staring intently at her. Was she watching for some reaction to the note? Eva felt a shiver shudder through her and she quickly looked away. She tried to relax and join in with the conversation around the table but that single word was embedded in her mind. *Murderer*.

43

After lunch, Eva held a creative expression and mindfulness session but she found it very difficult to concentrate, all she could think of was that sinister note. What was Bianca planning next? Should she confess everything to José before Bianca revealed what she'd done? Or did something even worse. Her mind was in a whirl.

'I'd better check that your cat isn't around,' Nathan jested as he put a piece of paper down on the table ready to do some more painting.

Sombra. She hadn't seen the cat since yesterday, Eva suddenly realised. She guessed that he was keeping his distance because of the guests. She was a bit worried about him, he had shot out of the studio as if he'd been tortured and there had been no sign of him since. Sombra often disappeared for a day or two, and she knew that he was perfectly capable of feeding himself, she was always finding half-eaten geckos and mice around the garden. She hoped that being locked in the studio overnight hadn't freaked him out so much that he wouldn't come back though. She'd grown attached to the little cat.

'We can do better than that, I'll get you an easel from the shed,' Eva said. 'I'll be back in a minute.'

She hurried down the path, looking around to see if Sombra was sleeping anywhere. She paused at the fountain, Sombra often drank out of that, or curled up behind the bush next to it. She walked over to have a better look and gasped, quickly covering her mouth to stifle a scream – the water in the fountain was blood red! What on earth had happened? Her heart was pounding so much she thought it was going to burst out of her chest. Tentatively, she took a step nearer. Surely it wasn't blood? How could it be? Unless... She paused and clutched her throat. Sombra. Had he been hurt?

Keep calm, Eva told herself. *Stop letting your imagination run away with you. You're not in a horror movie. You're halfway up a mountain in sleepy Spain. Things like that don't happen here.*

But look at all the things that had happened. And the note.

Bianca or Nathan wouldn't kill Sombra.

'Hey, do you need some help?' She turned to see Nathan behind her, obviously wondering what was taking so long. 'What's up? You look as if you've seen a ghost.'

She couldn't speak, couldn't find the words, she merely pointed to the fountain. His eyes widened. 'Bloody hell!'

She held her breath, her eyes fixed on him, as he strode over to the fountain, bent down and sniffed the bright red water. 'It's okay, it's paint,' he announced.

Eva's breath whooshed out.

Nathan came back over to her, his face etched in concern. 'Are you okay? You look petrified. You thought it was blood, didn't you?'

She nodded, still unable to form any words.

'It's paint,' he stated again. 'Although I don't know why anyone would want to put paint in the fountain. It's a stupid thing to do.' His eyes searched hers. 'It's almost as if someone was threatening you.' A curious look came over his face. 'Have you been having trouble from anyone?'

She pulled herself together then. He seemed genuinely concerned. Maybe she had been wrong to suspect him. Perhaps he didn't even know about the note Bianca had sent her. For a moment she longed to confide in someone, to tell them how scared she was. He was Bianca's husband, he would be on her side even if he wasn't involved in the quest for revenge, she reminded herself. 'No, of course not. I've no idea how paint got in there either. I'll talk to José, he might have accidentally spilt some.'

Nathan raised an eyebrow. 'Strange place to accidentally spill paint.'

She nodded. 'I guess that's why I was so shocked at first.' She forced a weak smile on her face. 'I watch too many horror movies.'

'Yeah, me too. Then I see shadows in the dark and think the monsters are coming to get me.'

'Shall we go and get the easel then?' she said, wanting to change the conversation.

'Sure.'

They both walked over to the shed in easy silence but as Eva went to open the door a terrible thought stopped her in her tracks. What if the red water in the fountain was a warning?

What if Sombra was inside the shed? Hurt – or dead.

She trembled a little as she turned the handle, bracing herself for whatever sight might greet her eyes. As she flung the door open wide, she saw a pool of red on the floor. Screaming, she backed away in horror.

44

'Hey, it's okay. It's only paint. Again.' Nathan squeezed her arm reassuringly, then quickly scanned the shed, assessing the situation. 'There's the reason,' he said. 'Look at those pawprints. It looks like your cat has got locked in here, knocked over a tin of red paint then jumped in the fountain when he got free. He's a right little rascal, isn't he?'

He was right, there were pawprints all over the floor, and an upturned tin of paint in the corner. But how had Sombra got free if he had been locked in here?

'I'm guessing he got out of that window,' Nathan said as if he'd read her thoughts. He pointed to a trail of red pawprints that led up the wall to the open window on the side of the shed. 'Your cat certainly gets into some scrapes, doesn't he?'

Relief flooded through her. Of course, that's what had happened. She finally found her voice. 'You know what cats are like! Honestly I don't know about nine lives, I think he's got at least a dozen.' She looked over at the easels stacked against the wall. 'There's the easels. Maybe we should take a couple out in case anyone else wants one.'

Nathan nodded. 'Good idea, especially if your cat is

running around with red paws! We don't want his pawprints all over our paintings.' He laughed and Eva laughed with him. What an imagination she'd got! Thinking that was blood in the fountain, and that it was a warning for her. She really had been watching too many crime films.

What about the note? She hadn't imagined that, had she?

It wasn't a threat though, was it? It was Bianca telling her that she knew who she was, what she'd done. And Eva's guilt was making her suspicious about everyone and everything that happened. She had to talk to Bianca, impress on her how sorry she was.

'Ready?' Nathan had two easels tucked under his arm and was looking at her curiously and she realised that she'd been miles away, staring into mid-air. He must think she is nuts.

'Yep.' She picked up another easel, just in case. Then they went out and she bolted the door. 'I don't want Sombra getting in again. He makes too much mess.'

'Our cat's the same, she managed to get shut in our bath-room once and we came back to find her covered in shaving foam,' Nathan told her and they walked back over to the back terrace laughing about their cats' escapades.

'What's so funny?' Saskia asked as they approached.

Nathan told her about Sombra and she chuckled. 'I can just imagine your face when you thought that fountain was full of blood,' she said to Eva.

'I've got a vivid imagination.' Eva grinned, her eyes seeking Bianca so she could see her reaction but Bianca had her head down over her notebook and was busy writing. Or pretending to be.

Had she shut Sombra in the shed earlier, or was it all an accident? Eva didn't know what to think or who to believe. One thing she did know though was that she didn't feel safe.

45

'It's so lovely and warm here I don't feel like moving, but I could do with my neck and shoulders massaged, they're really achy,' Saskia said, stretching out on the sunbed by the side of the pool after lunch.

'Why don't you have a massage by the pool,' Carlos suggested. 'That would be okay, wouldn't it, Eva?'

Eva considered it, the sunbed which Saskia was lying on was very firm and if she only wanted a head and shoulder massage it wasn't too personal. Sean and Adrienne were relaxing in their room so she wouldn't have Adrienne scowling with disapproval. 'Sure, if that's what you want,' she agreed. 'I'll just go and get the oils.'

She returned with a hand towel and some lavender oil and got started. As she gently massaged the oil into Saskia's shoulders and neck, she could feel her friend relaxing underneath her touch. 'That's wonderful, so soothing,' Saskia said with a sigh.

Eva was pleased. She enjoyed giving a massage, feeling the stress and strain ease away from her clients as she worked the oils in with her fingers, and today, outside in the sunshine with the parakeets chirping in the trees, Nathan and Carlos chatting, and the air filled with the fragrance of orange blossom and jasmine, she felt her own tension easing away.

'Oh, I feel so much better now, thank you,' Saskia said with a contented sigh.

'You're welcome.' Eva wiped her hands on the towel, picked up the oil and placed it on the table planning to take it back to the studio in a while.

Adrienne and Sean came down to join them for refreshments. Adrienne sat on the side of the pool, dipping her feet in the water, while Sean disappeared upstairs, coming back down dressed in swimming shorts, a towel draped around his shoulders. 'I'm going for a swim,' he declared, throwing his towel onto an empty sunbed. 'I'm surprised not to find you two in the pool.'

'I prefer to sunbathe,' Saskia said, stretching out on a sunbed.

'I was about to go in. Fancy a five laps challenge?' Carlos asked, getting to his feet.

'I'm up for it,' Sean said.

'Count me out,' Adrienne said, taking her feet out of the pool. She walked over to the terrace then through the back door into the villa.

'Adrienne won't go in the pool, she can't swim. She's terrified of water. She almost drowned when she was a young child and the fear has never left her,' Sean said quietly.

So that's why she never went in the pool, Eva thought. She had wondered if she was scared of water. That was a shame, it robbed Adrienne of so much enjoyment.

'Coming in, José?' Carlos said, looking over at José.

'Not for me,' José replied.

'Not up to it?' Carlos challenged.

Eva saw José's jaw tighten but he smiled good-humouredly. 'I'm happy to leave you two to it.'

Carlos shrugged. 'Okay, Sean. Go!' Carlos shouted. He and Sean took off, racing to the pool, Sean in the lead. Suddenly

Sean lost his footing, skidded and fell flat on his side onto the tiles with a thud and a yell.

'Sean! Are you okay?' Carlos hurried over, then skidded too but managed to get his balance back. 'The floor is really slippery! There's oil or something on it.' He cautiously made the couple of steps to Sean and knelt down by him.

Sean groaned, sat up and held his head.

'Keep still, *amigo*. I think we need to get you checked over before you move. You could have broken something, that was quite a fall,' Carlos told him.

'What's going on? What's happened?' Adrienne gasped, she'd just come back out, a book in her hand, and seen Sean sprawled on the floor.

'Sean's slipped,' Eva explained as José joined Carlos at Sean's side.

'Does your head hurt? Does anything feel broken?' he asked.

'My head aches and my shoulder hurts where I fell but otherwise I'm okay,' Sean replied shakily.

'Let me check you over. Both Eva and myself have done a first aid course.'

José had insisted on it as they were out in the sticks and it could take a while for emergency help to reach them, so he said it would be best if they at least knew the basics. He checked Sean over and nodded. 'You seem okay but take it easy. Do you want us to call a doctor?'

'No, really, I'm fine,' Sean said, getting to his feet.

'Well, I'd avoid the pool for a bit,' José told him.

'Don't worry, I will. I'll do a bit of sunbathing,' Sean said, heading over to the sunbed. Adrienne stepped forward to help him, holding his arm for support as he sat down on the sunbed.

'This could have been really serious. Sean could have been concussed or broken something,' she pointed out, glaring angrily at José.

'It gets wet around the pool area, we did warn you all to be careful and not to run,' José told her.

Adrienne strode over to the spot where Sean had slipped, knelt down and ran her hands over the tiles. 'This isn't water. This is oil. Oil has been spilt here,' she declared.

'I don't see how that can be possible,' Eva started to say then she saw José frown as he stared at the bench. She followed his gaze and saw a small bottle of her massage oil under the bench. Adrienne had spotted it too. She picked it up and marched back with it, triumphantly placing it down on the table. 'See! The top is off and it's spilt out. No wonder Sean slipped!'

Eva looked at it in dismay. It was the lavender oil that she had used on Saskia. 'I don't understand how that got there.'

'You must had dropped it when you gave Saskia a massage by the pool,' Carlos replied.

'I didn't. I put it on the table out of the way,' Eva insisted.

Adrienne gave her an accusing look. 'Obviously you didn't! You really should be more careful. Sean could have been seriously injured. In fact, there have been a number of accidents where we have been put in danger. Your safety precautions here really aren't adequate.'

Eva bit her lip, knowing that Adrienne had a right to be annoyed but she had definitely put the bottle of oil on the table. Someone must have taken it and deliberately spilt it by the side of the pool so that one of the guests would slip on it. She looked at José for support but could only see disappointment in his eyes. If Sean had been injured they might be facing an expensive compensation claim that could put an end to their retreat before they even got it off the ground. 'Sorry. I'll go and clear it up,' she said. She fetched a bottle of soapy water and scrubbed the oil away, her mind going over and over. She was sure that she hadn't dropped that bottle of oil. But how else had it got there?

Saskia laughed and Eva glanced over at the pool where she

and Carlos were larking around. Carlos had suggested Saskia have the massage by the pool instead of the studio, and he was also the one who had suggested the race to the pool. And he'd held back and let Sean take the lead, she recalled. Could he have taken the oil and spilt it there? Was he trying to sabotage the retreat because he was jealous that José had turned their grandparents' old house into a lucrative holiday retreat? Had Sean been his intended target or had it been José? She wondered, remembering how Carlos had tried to encourage his cousin to take part.

It all made sense. Except why would Carlos put a note under her lamp calling her a murderer?

46

Later that evening Mario arrived to take them all down to Toria. José had reserved a table near the front of the restaurant so that they had a good view of the dancers, who arrived just as they had finished their meal.

A place had been cleared in the middle of the floor for the performance and a man sitting on a high stool played the guitar while two dancers stepped onto the dance floor. They were both dark-haired, the man in a white shirt and tight black trousers with a red cummerbund and the woman in a red dress with a flouncy hem from which peeped a black lace petticoat, black stockings and black patent shoes. They tapped and swirled to the music, the woman seductively sashaying her hips as the man spun her round.

'How amazing! I'd love to dance like that,' Saskia said.

'Me too,' Eva agreed. There was a flamenco dancing class in Toria, which she'd been thinking of joining once she had a bit more free time. Maybe she should make the time, what was it she was always telling the clients at the wellness centre, you had to make time to do things you liked as well as work. You had to make time for you. Maybe, once the guests had gone back home she should talk to José about doing a shared interest, like flamenco dancing. She could imagine him in those tight black trousers, with a cummerbund and a white shirt.

'I think you might be looking at that dancer a bit too much,' José teased, his eyes twinkling as he placed his hand on hers.

She smiled at him. 'I was thinking that maybe we should learn to dance like that.'

He nodded, his eyes still teasing. 'Maybe we should.'

Sean's shoulder was still sore so Adrienne pulled José up to dance, and they were soon both laughing as they whirled around on the dance floor. Sean didn't look very pleased but he said nothing, Eva felt guilty about the injury so kept him company, leaving the others to dance. Adrienne monopolised José for three dances, her head resting on his shoulder, her hips moving seductively against his, then Saskia rescued him, pulling him away to dance with her. After a while Bianca and Nathan sat down and started chatting to Sean, and Carlos came over to get Eva up to dance, then finally, she and José danced together.

'Sorry, couldn't get away from Adrienne. Got to be polite to the guests,' José whispered in her ear.

'Oh I don't mind, I just feel sorry for Sean,' she replied.

Everyone seemed to enjoy the evening and they were all in good spirits when they went back to the villa.

'I think this retreat is a great idea,' Saskia said, putting her arm chummily around Eva's waist.

'Thank you. I know a couple of things have gone wrong but hopefully it will all be smooth sailing now.' She held up crossed fingers.

Saskia shrugged. 'There's bound to be teething problems, that's what this trial run is about, isn't it?' she reminded Eva. 'At least this way you can find out what they are and put them right. I bet you'll be one of the most popular retreats in Spain in a couple of years' time.'

'We wish!' Eva smiled at her. Saskia had been so supportive, it was good to have her best friend back in her life. She couldn't believe that she had worried so much about Saskia coming to the retreat. Perhaps she should confide in her about the note? It would be good to talk to someone about it. She was sure that she could trust her now. Couldn't she?

47

Later, when the guests had left to go to their rooms, Eva realised that Adrienne had left her bag on the chair on the terrace where they'd all sat chatting for a while before going to bed. She picked it up to take up to her. As she reached the top step, she heard raised voices.

'How dare you! You're the one who had an affair and now you're accusing me!' Adrienne sounded furious.

'I'm not accusing you of having an affair but you have to admit that you can't keep your eyes off José. You're obviously attracted to him and not bothering to hide it. I guess you're doing it to get your own back, but it's a bit immature and not pleasant for Eva, who I can assure you has noticed.' His voice softened. 'We promised to put it all behind us, Adrienne.'

'A couple of days away in a villa in the Spanish countryside isn't going to put everything right, Sean.'

'You can't keep punishing me for this, Adrienne. Everyone makes mistakes. And if you hadn't been so obsessed with having a baby, making me feel a failure all the time, I might not have been driven into the arms of another woman.'

'That's right, blame me! You never will take responsibility

for your actions, will you?' Eva heard the sob in Adrienne's voice.

This was far too personal a conversation for them to know that she'd overheard. She turned around and quietly walked back down the stairs. She'd leave the bag in the kitchen.

José glanced up from the coffee decanter. 'Problem?'

'They're having a big argument. I didn't want to disturb them. I'll leave the bag here, I'm sure that Adrienne will come down for it in a bit.' She didn't want to repeat the conversation she had overheard, José must be aware of how Adrienne was being with him, and she didn't want to give the impression that she was jealous.

Sean came into the kitchen a few minutes later. 'Ah, there it is! Adrienne thought she'd left it outside,' he said, spotting the handbag on the table.

'She did, I brought it in and was going to take it up to her when we'd finished our decaff,' Eva said, not wanting him to guess that she'd overheard their argument.

'Thank you, that's very kind of you. See you both in the morning,' he said cheerily, grabbing the bag and going back out again.

'I guess they've made it up now,' Eva said to José. But her mind kept going over Sean's accusation that Adrienne was making eyes at José to get her own back at him. The phone conversation she'd overheard suggested that Sean might be still having an affair. Was Adrienne aware of it? Was she hoping to get back with José? She had obviously been more serious about their relationship than he had. Was she trying to recreate happy memories because she was miserable with Sean? Well, she could try but José loved Eva and would never cheat.

In bed that night she cuddled up to José, trying not to think about everything that had happened. They could get through this. The guests would be going home soon and it would all be over. As if sensing her unease, José sleepily wound his arm around her, she snuggled up and fell asleep.

A dog barking in the distance woke her a few hours later and she realised that José's side of the bed was empty. She guessed he'd gone to the bathroom, and turned over ready to go back to sleep when she thought she heard voices in the kitchen. Had one of the guests come down for a drink? The bedroom door was slightly open – José must have heard something too and got up to investigate. She pulled on her kimono, slipped her feet into her sandals and crept out. Then stopped in her tracks as she saw José and Adrienne in the kitchen, deep in hushed conversation. It looked secretive. Intimate. For a moment she wasn't sure what to do.

They're only whispering so that they don't wake anyone else up, she told herself. *Stop over-thinking. Adrienne is a guest, of course José would go to see what was wrong if he heard her up and about.*

'He was my first lover. I can't believe that he's forgotten me.' Adrienne's words flashed across her mind. She bit her lip. It was years ago. She'd had past lovers too.

But Adrienne didn't seem to be over José. Was Sean right and she was flirting with him to get her own back for the affair he had?

She stepped back a little as José put his arm around Adrienne's shoulder and she rested her head on his chest. What was going on? She stepped further back into the shadows as Adrienne kissed José on the cheek then walked out, along the hall and up the stairs.

'Eva. I thought you were fast asleep? Did you want a drink?' José asked as he came out of the kitchen.

Eva turned to him. 'Yes. I was about to get one when I saw you hugging Adrienne,' she snapped. She hadn't meant to say anything but the words came out before she could stop them.

José's face softened. 'She was upset because she's discovered that Sean is having an affair,' he explained. 'I was comforting her, that's all. As anyone would do.'

Was he telling the truth? She had overheard them arguing herself so knew that Sean was having an affair. It irritated her that José had hugged Adrienne, but maybe it was just a natural reaction if Adrienne had been upset. She probably would have hugged her too if she'd broken down in front of her.

'I've told you, *cariño*, it is all in the past. Adrienne means nothing to me.' José wrapped his arms around her. 'Soon she will go home and we will never see her again.'

She couldn't wait to go back to their normal life. No more looking over her shoulder, living on tenterhooks, doubting everyone. She felt like her nerves were constantly on edge.

*

*I've given you so **many** chances, so many warnings but still you won't acknowledge **what** you did to me. You think you can ignore me, ignore my note. You act as if nothing is wrong, pretend that everything is a coincidence, an accident, a mishap. But you don't really believe that. You're scared. I can tell. I saw your face when you thought that **was** blood in the fountain. You were scared that I'd harmed your **cat**. I would never hurt an animal. I don't want to hurt you but **you've** left me no choice. I can't let you get away with it. Because of **you** I lost someone I loved dearly. I didn't want to do this. I've given you chance after chance to show remorse but you **have none**. Now I will show no mercy either.*

48

THURSDAY – DAY FOUR

Eva

'Look at that!' Saskia held her arms out wide as she gazed down at the shimmery cobalt-blue sea in the distance. 'It's so beautiful here! I don't want to go home.'

She seemed so genuine that Eva felt guilty for not trusting her enough to confide in her.

'I've got a blister,' Adrienne complained. She was sitting on the spiky grass rubbing her heel. Eva sighed, trust Adrienne to wear fashionable sandals and a summer dress for the hike up to the chapel which was positioned halfway up the mountain. They were going in a different direction to the one they went the other day, up the side that faced the sea this time, and it was a steeper climb so they'd suggested that everyone wore sturdy boots or trainers, and carried a bottle of water with them. It seemed that Adrienne had ignored the warning and instead put on a pair of sandals. No wonder she had a blister. Eva unzipped her backpack and took out a small box. 'Would you like a plaster?' she asked, taking one out of the box and handing it to her.

'Thanks.' Adrienne took it from her and put it on her heel. 'I don't think I can walk much further,' she said. 'I'd better go back.'

'I'll come with you,' Sean said.

'Oh no, you stay here. I'll be fine to go back by myself,' Adrienne told him but Sean shook his head. 'I insist.' He turned to José. 'I know you've locked up so we'll go in the back gate and sit by the pool until you all come back.'

'No, let yourselves in.' José handed Sean his key. 'Help yourselves to a drink and snack. We'll be back in a couple of hours.'

Eva didn't like the idea of Adrienne and Sean being in the villa on their own but she knew that José was right, they couldn't expect them to sit outside and not be able to go up to their room. This was something they had to think about for future retreats. What if someone didn't want to go on one of the activities that took place off the grounds of the retreat. Did they leave them home alone?

'Everyone ready?' José called.

Eva turned back towards him and nodded. 'All set.'

She and José had walked to the chapel a few times over the years. It was a bit of a hike, but manageable if you stopped for breaks and a drink, and definitely worth it. The little chapel, cut into the mountain, was dedicated to the Virgin Mary hundreds of years ago when the Spaniards reclaimed the area from the Moors. Outside it looked like nothing, just a solid oak door in the rock, but inside it was beautiful. Every June the locals celebrated a Romería, when the icon of the Virgin was taken from the church in Toria up to the chapel, escorted by Romany-style caravans pulled by horses, donkeys and bulls, and pilgrims in traditional Spanish dress. The pilgrims spent the night up the mountain, partying after the traditional mass held in the chapel, then returned again with the sacred icon on the Sunday, taking it back to the church. The chapel itself was crudely constructed belying the beauty of the paintings on the wall and the statues inside.

'Oh my goodness, this is amazing,' Bianca said as they stepped inside, her eyes wide with wonder as they rested on the intricate gold altar. 'It's a wonder these things haven't been taken. Is it always kept unlocked?'

'It's open one day a week,' José told her. 'I messaged the keeper to say that we were on the way up so he opened it for us.'

After a look around the chapel they made their way back down to the villa. Everyone was leaving at midday tomorrow so this was the last full day, thank goodness, Eva thought. She couldn't wait for everyone to go back home and hoped that nothing would happen before they did. She was nervous about Bianca. She had left her that note for a reason so surely at some point she would make it clear to Eva that she knew who she was. Otherwise what was the point? Did she intend to denounce Eva tonight in front of everyone? Or tomorrow before they left? Should Eva tell José before that happened?

Maybe she should have a word with Bianca herself, try to explain how the accident had happened and how sorry she was. She'd thought of doing that a few times but her anxiety had kicked in. Every time she thought she'd plucked up the courage to talk to Bianca, an image of that man – Bianca's father – lying still in the road sprang into her mind and she couldn't bring herself to do it. She couldn't handle Bianca's reaction, scared that it would bring the horror of it all back. She couldn't risk sinking into that well of despair again.

When they got back to El Sueño, Adrienne and Sean were relaxing on the terrace with a cold drink. 'Did you enjoy the climb?' Adrienne asked.

'It was tiring but worth it, the chapel was beautiful,' Saskia told her. 'It's a shame you had to come back.'

'Oh I don't mind, it's been very relaxing here,' Adrienne replied, taking a sip from her glass of juice.

'Do tell us about it though, do you have any photos?' Sean asked.

Eva took out her phone and showed them a few.

'It looks beautiful,' Sean said but Adrienne barely glanced at the photos and didn't say anything. Eva wondered if she had been to the chapel with José all those years ago.

The guests all went to their rooms to freshen up while Eva and José made lunch. They'd prepared a goat's cheese salad before they went out that morning, but there were still the rolls and butter to put out, and the jugs of juice and flavoured water. It was a good couple of hours later, when lunch was finished and they had cleared away, before Eva returned to their bedroom to freshen up. As soon as she opened the door she sensed that someone had been in. Her heart thudding, she hurried over to the bedside table and sank when she saw a piece of paper sticking out from underneath the lamp. There was another note. Her hand shaking, she pulled it out. There were the familiar bold, black letters but this time there were three words.

Revenge is coming.

49

José

José tightened his lips as he scanned the online bank statement. They were drastically overdrawn. The improvements to the villa had cost much more than he had expected or budgeted for, and the bank were threatening to call in the loan he had taken against the house to cover the costs if he didn't clear a big chunk of the debt within three months. They really need this retreat to be a success, and good reviews from this week's stay to post on their website and Facebook page to encourage others to stay. Even if they went back to their jobs full-time there wouldn't be much left of their salaries by the time they'd made the repayments, and bang went their dream of not only running their own business but of starting a family too.

This morning he had been horrified to see a one-star rating on the retreat's Facebook page. There was no review so no way of identifying who had left the rating, but he was pretty sure that the culprit was Carlos. It was clear that Carlos resented him but to accuse him of causing his grandmother's death... The memory of his words made José's blood boil. So Carlos's dad had fallen out with his parents, that wasn't José's fault. And while Carlos couldn't have done much about it when he was a child, he could have made an attempt to get to know his grandparents when he was older. Especially after seeing how frail his grandmother was at his grandfather's funeral. But no, they had stayed long enough to pay their respects – and check whether they had any inheritance no doubt – then had disappeared out of all their lives again. Whereas José had loved and cared for Abuelita, done everything he could to make her life easier.

It had to be Carlos. Who else would it be? None of the other guests had any grudge against them, and everyone seemed quite happy with their stay, even though it hadn't gone perfectly. He wondered if Carlos was behind the things that had gone wrong, he wouldn't put it past him to try and ruin things. Maybe not the gate being left open but shutting Sombra first in the studio then the shed, digging up the daffodil bulbs – knowing that for the guests to all be ill would ruin the retreat's reputation forever.

Which was exactly what he wanted.

Now, as he hadn't succeeded in that he was resorting to bad reviews.

José rubbed the back of his neck with his hand to try and ease the tension. He felt as taut as a tightly wound spring, waiting to see what would happen next. Maybe bad reviews on websites like TripAdvisor? In today's online society it didn't take much to ruin your reputation. He bet that Carlos wouldn't hesitate to go down that route. He wished that his cousin had never come to the retreat.

He wished he would disappear and never come back.

50

Eva

Eva was shaking. This note was definitely a threat.

Her heart was racing and beads of sweat formed on her forehead as she remembered how narrowly the Buddha head had missed her.

Could Bianca – or Nathan, the thought occurred to her again – be planning to actually kill her? One life for another?

She closed her eyes as nausea swept over her.

'Eva, can... Hey, are you okay? You look like you're going to be sick.'

Eva could hear Saskia but her voice sounded muffled, as if it was in a tunnel. She remembered that she'd left the bedroom door ajar and guessed that Saskia was standing in the doorway. That distant voice again and the sounds of footsteps as Saskia walked across the tiles but Eva couldn't open her eyes. Couldn't breathe. Then she let out a big gasp, her eyes flying open as she tried to gulp in air. Her chest was hurting. She was going to faint.

'It's okay. You're having a panic attack. It will pass in a few minutes,' Saskia said, softly sitting down on the bed beside her. She took Eva's hand in hers. 'Take some deep breaths in through your nose and out through your mouth. In... Out... In... Out.'

After a couple of minutes focusing on her breathing, Eva felt her anxiety start to subside.

'Now let's try some grounding techniques.' Saskia passed her a clean tissue. 'Screw this up in your fist and concentrate on the feeling of it.'

Eva squeezed the tissue tight, taking in the whiteness of it, the softness of it, until her breath slowed down and the dizziness started to fade.

'I'm okay now. Thank you,' she whispered. Thank goodness it was Saskia who had come into the bedroom, not José, or any of the other guests.

'You still have the panic attacks then?' Saskia sounded concerned.

'I haven't had one for ages but...' She had to confide in someone and Saskia knew her history anyway. She had to trust her. 'Someone left a note under my lamp.' She took the crumpled note out of her pocket and showed it to Saskia.

'"Revenge is coming." That's a strange thing to say.' Saskia gave her a quizzical look. 'Have you any idea what it could mean?'

'It's the second note that I've received,' she admitted. 'The first one said "Murderer".'

Saskia gasped. 'What?' Then realisation dawned on her face. 'Do you think it's Bianca?' A guilty look swept over her face. 'I'm sorry, I meant to talk to her about the accident and forgot.'

Too busy getting it on with Carlos. Eva swiped away the resentful thought, this wasn't Saskia's responsibility. 'Who else can it be?' Eva got up and started pacing around agitatedly.

'What am I going to do? All this weird stuff that's happened, it's all down to Bianca. Maybe Nathan too.'

'What stuff?' Saskia asked.

'The broken oils, the goats getting into the garden, the slippery patch of oil by the pool causing Sean to tumble and hurt himself, Sombra being locked in the shed and getting covered in paint, the red paint in the fountain, the onions being swapped for daffodil bulbs... And the Buddha head,' she added.

'I brought in the daffodil bulbs,' Saskia reminded her.

'I know but how strange for them to be lying on the path like that. I bet Bianca dug them up and put them there for you to find. She's been trying to sabotage the retreat but now I think... she wants to hurt me.' Eva started to shake. She put her hand to her chest, gasping for breath.

'Slowly, breathe slowly,' Saskia said soothingly.

'I'm okay,' Eva said when she'd calmed down again.

'I can see that you've got in a right state over this, do you really think that Bianca – or Nathan – would hurt you? They don't seem the sort of people who would harm anyone. Nathan's a policeman, for goodness' sake.'

'If Bianca blames me for killing her father who knows what lengths she'll go to for revenge? That red water in the fountain, it looked so much like blood. That was a warning of what's to come. I'm sure it is.'

'Look, don't you think you might be getting this out of proportion? The notes are sinister and I can understand why you're creeped out but they don't actually threaten to harm you, do they? And the things that have happened, it could all be coincidental.'

That was exactly what Eva had tried to tell herself.

'Don't you think you should tell José about these notes? You're getting in a state and it might help if he knows.'

'Then I'll have to tell him what I did.'

'It was an accident, Eva. You didn't murder anyone, no matter what that note says.'

Saskia was right. She had to keep calm about this. Bianca could be playing with her mind, trying to scare her. That could be her revenge – to make Eva a nervous wreck and to ruin the retreat.

'Maybe they aren't planning on harming me personally. Maybe they want to make sure the retreat isn't a success,' she conceded.

'It's hard to believe that anyone as quiet and sweet as Bianca could be so conniving and malicious,' Saskia said with a frown.

'I know but her father was killed and if she blames me for it...' Eva reminded her, recalling the bitterness in Bianca's voice as she talked about her father's death. 'I guess sabotaging the retreat is a mild form of revenge really. I'll just have to make sure she doesn't succeed.' The retreat meant so much to her and to José. Especially José. He had worked hard to renovate the house, this was his dream. She wasn't going to let anything wreck it. She'd never forgive herself and she carried enough guilt as it was. She had to do something to prevent things getting any worse.

'I'm going to speak to Bianca, let her know how sorry I am. How much the guilt has haunted me all these years,' she decided. 'Then she might back off.'

'I guess you could try but personally I wouldn't. If she doesn't suspect you then you'll have made things worse.' Saskia gave Eva a comforting hug. 'I'd sit tight if I were you. There's only one more day of the retreat left then it will all be over. I don't think you're in any real danger. Bianca might be upset about losing her dad and want to get back at you, but she doesn't seem unhinged. She's got a good job, and is in a happy relationship. Why would she risk all that to harm you and end up in a Spanish jail?'

51

Eva thought over Saskia's words and decided that she was right. Talking to Bianca wouldn't do any good. Bianca had said that the driver who had knocked her father down had been exonerated from any blame, but she didn't accept that. It wasn't the truth she was after but revenge so it would do no good trying to talk to her, to explain how sorry she was. Grief did strange things to people. Besides, she had no proof that Bianca had done anything, so the other woman could always deny it. Then Eva would look paranoid and everyone, including José, would know what she had done. She decided to sit it out but keep vigilant. She was sure that Bianca wasn't about to give up yet. She hadn't written those notes for nothing.

After an hour's relaxation by the pool after lunch, José had arranged for Mario to take everyone down to Toria so they could 'see the sights'. Eva was pleased to have an empty house for a couple of hours so that she could stop looking over her shoulder, and she welcomed the opportunity to tidy around. With people coming in and out and up and downstairs all week the villa was looking a bit messy. She'd put a wash on too, she decided, she hadn't had the chance for a couple of days.

Tonight they were holding a final dinner for the guests. José told her he was planning a traditional Spanish meal with music and drinks on the terrace. She and José would make themselves available if anyone had questions about wellness or healthy eating, plus she had prepared a wellness plan for everyone and José had made a small booklet of easy-to-prepare healthy eating recipes.

One more evening to go, she told herself, then it would all be over. She was pleased that their guests would be going home the next day but she was sad to see Saskia leave. They'd become close again over the past few days and Saskia had been a big support. 'Let's keep in touch,' Saskia had suggested and Eva had agreed, even suggesting that Saskia fly over and visit them again out of season when the retreat wasn't running. Saskia had looked delighted. Maybe she'd been too hard on her old friend, shutting her out of her life like that for all these years. Yes, she'd let her down but she'd been very young and she had tried her very best to make up for it, Eva acknowledged.

The sound of a car horn burst through her thoughts. 'Mario's here!' Saskia announced.

Eva pressed the button to open the gates and Mario drove in. 'I have errands to fetch so will drop you off and leave you to wander around the town by yourselves,' he told them as they piled into the minibus. 'A lot of the shops are closed for the afternoon siesta but they will be open again about four-thirty. I will meet you all at the café by the fountain at five-thirty and bring you back home.'

'That sounds perfect, thank you,' Saskia said.

'See you later. Have a good time!' Eva called as she and José waved them off.

'Mario's a star. This is so good of him and so lovely to have a few hours to ourselves,' Eva said as the minibus drove through the open gates.

'He really is. We are lucky to have a neighbour like him,'

José agreed. 'Now I'm off to do some jobs in the garden, I'll be back to prepare the dinner for tonight. Our last supper,' he added with a grin before he went off.

Eva shuddered at his remark. With everything that had been happening, and her being on tenterhooks, it was a bad choice of words. Hopefully not a prophetic choice. *Don't be daft, Bianca's not going to go that far,* she told herself. *You're letting your imagination run away with you.*

She went indoors and quickly put the vacuum around downstairs and wiped down all the surfaces in the kitchen. She and José took it in turns to clean up the kitchen and he'd done it yesterday. Then she went to get the washing basket from the utility room and saw that there were only two guest towels in it. All six guests had brought their towels down every day to be replaced with clean ones but she guessed that they were intending to use the same ones tomorrow seeing as it was their last day.

She put the wash on then took the leaving packs she and José had made up, with activities and recipes they'd used on the course, and went upstairs to place one in each room. She was pleased to see that the guests had made their beds and the rooms were clean and tidy. Saskia's was the last room she went into and, remembering how untidy her friend used to be, Eva expected to see clothes everywhere but to her surprise it was very tidy too. She put the leaving pack on the table in the bedroom and felt something under her foot. Looking down, she saw a black felt pen on the floor, it must have rolled off the desk. She bent down and picked it up, then pulled open the drawer of the table to put the pen inside, catching her breath when she saw a pad of white notepaper. The same sort of notepaper the notes had been written on.

Don't jump to conclusions, Eva, it's a common enough notepad and pen. Saskia wouldn't write those notes, she's your friend.

She took the top off the pen and studied the nib. It was a fat nib, the same sort of nib that the notes had been written in. Slowly she sat down at the desk, ripped a sheet of paper off the pad and wrote the word *Murderer* on it.

She studied the word carefully, her mind waging a war with her thoughts. The letters were thick, and a bit smeary, like the letters in the notes. The paper seemed the same too.

Surely Saskia couldn't have been the one to write the note?

Saskia was the only other person, apart from Bianca, who knew that Eva was responsible for Bianca's father's death. Was she playing tricks with her mind? Hoping to drive her to a breakdown again? Or pushing her to tell José, hoping that when he knew the truth he would dump her like Leo had. Eva squeezed her eyes shut again as she remembered the rows, the goading, Leo's voice telling her that she was unstable, that the accident was her fault. Would José change too if he found out the truth? She couldn't go through that again, she couldn't let him find out.

She started to hyperventilate and squeezed her eyes shut.

I am not in danger. I'm just uncomfortable. This feeling will pass. She repeated the affirmation in her head until she could feel the panic fading.

It was years ago and Saskia had been so sorry, really distraught, had begged Eva to forgive her. Why would she come all the way out here just to betray her again?

52

José

José hunkered down and pulled up the last lettuce, adding it to the couple of tomatoes in his basket. There were barely any vegetables left, perhaps enough for a couple more days. Saturday, when everyone had gone home, he would fetch more seedlings and plant them. Until they grew, he would have to use vegetables and salad from the market, but at least they only needed enough to feed him and Eva.

If only Eva hadn't left the gate open. She knew to be careful, that the bolt was stiff and she had to pull it hard across. She had definitely been the last one through. Otherwise he might have thought that it had been deliberate – maybe by Carlos. His cousin hadn't even tried to disguise his pleasure that something else had gone wrong.

He sat down on a cut-off tree stump and thought about all the things that had gone wrong over the past few days, the heavy statue that had just missed Eva – that could have been aimed at him – the daffodil bulbs, the oil by the side of the pool, the blood-red water in the fountain. Sombra did have a habit of sneaking into places but were his paws covered in enough red paint to colour that water in the fountain so deeply? The more he thought about it the more he came to the conclusion that someone was trying to sabotage the retreat. And he could only think of one person who would want that. Carlos.

He looked around the land. It was beautiful here, with the abundance of fruit trees, the shimmering blue pool, the violet bougainvillea swaying in the breeze, the sugar-white sprawling *finca* that had been freshly painted earlier this year, the parakeets singing in the trees, the cicadas chirping in the long grass, the fresh mountain air. He had always loved it here with his grandparents, they had been an important part of his childhood, but Carlos had been denied that. He had never met them. Never eaten Abuelita's homemade marmalade or lemonade, recipes José used today, never helped Abuelo tend the vegetables or put a net under the olive trees and shake them to make the olives drop. Never been close enough to refer to their grandmother as 'Abuelita' – Granny. All because of a feud that had started before Carlos and José were born and which no one would talk about. He took his phone out of his pocket. It was time he found out what the big argument had been about.

His father answered on the fourth ring, he sounded a bit abrupt, as he did when interrupted at work. 'José? Is this important?'

'Would I phone you if it wasn't?'

He heard his father's sigh. 'What's happened?'

'That is what I want to know, Papá. What happened between you, Tío Diego and my *abuelos* all those years ago? What was the feud about?'

Another sigh. 'Why now? I am busy and some things are best left forgotten.'

'I need you to tell me now, Papá, because Carlos is here, he has come to El Sueño.'

There was a sharp intake of breath and then his father said, 'I will talk to you about it later, I'm about to go into a meeting.'

'Papá, the sooner you tell me the sooner you will go to that meeting because I will keep calling until you tell me. And don't even think about ignoring my calls because I will drive over and interrupt the meeting.'

There was silence for a moment and then another long sigh. 'Very well. If I must.'

Eva

Eva hurried back to her room, her heart pounding, the familiar sweaty feeling engulfing her. She knew it was the signs of a panic attack coming on and she had to control it before it engulfed her. Everyone would be back in an hour or so, she had to clear her mind, think this through before they returned. She shut herself in their bedroom, thankful that José was busy in the garden. Then after a few calming exercises she plucked up the courage to take the notes out from under the mattress where she had hidden them and put them by the piece of paper she'd written on in Saskia's room. It was the same paper and the same pen, she was sure of it, of course the writing was different, the writer had used capital letters to conceal their writing. If only she'd thought to look for a sample of Saskia's writing so she could compare them.

Her chest felt tight, her breath coming out in short gasps. *Focus, Eva. Focus. Calm yourself down.* She looked at the clock on her bedside table, focused on the shiny silver surrounding, the pulsating red numbers on the digital face and breathed slowly, then she concentrated on listening to the cicadas chirping outside. Her breathing slowed down. She put her three fingers on the inside of her wrist. Breathe. In. Out. In. Out. Finally, when she had calmed the panic that threatened to engulf her, she allowed her mind to go back to all those years ago, when Saskia had betrayed her. An act that had pushed her to the point of almost taking her own life. For the second time.

After the awful accident she'd been unable to sleep, whenever she closed her eyes all she could see was that man lying lifeless on the ground. Dead. And she had killed him. She'd been crying as the rain fell down on her, she felt for his pulse, talked to him, willing him to live. Someone had phoned an ambulance and she'd stayed with the man until it came, wanted to go with him but his wife had arrived by then and she went instead.

'I'm sorry. I'm so sorry,' Eva had told her but the woman hadn't replied, just got straight into the ambulance. Someone had told Eva's parents and her dad had come to get her, put his arms around and hugged her then taken her home. The police had come by later, told her the man had died but that she wouldn't be charged as a witness had seen the man step out into the road without looking. He'd had his hood up which had limited his view and he was too near the corner for Eva to see until she had turned it. If only he had crossed a little further along, if only his hood hadn't been up. If only Eva had stopped a little longer in the shop. So many 'if onlys'. She had heard that the man had a family and that had increased her guilt and distress.

She couldn't function. The doctor put her on antidepressants and she managed to pick herself up enough to go back to college. She squeezed her eyes as the memories flooded back. Standing on top of the college roof and Saskia fetching the principal, who talked her down. Her months in the psychiatric unit. Coming out and getting a job where no one knew her, no one knew what she'd done. Until thanks to Saskia talking to Rachel, the manager found out about her past. Saskia had been so apologetic, insisting that she'd only been talking about it because she was looking out for Eva, making sure she didn't have a relapse. Eva had believed her and accepted her apology but now it was happening all over again.

Why would Saskia do that though? It didn't seem as if she was too happy in her own job, was she jealous of how Eva had turned her life around and wanted to destroy it for her, like she had done before? She must have been delighted when Eva had that panic attack earlier, thinking that her plan was going to work.

Memories of how distraught Saskia had been all those years ago, begging her for forgiveness, flashed across her mind. And she had been so friendly and helpful this week. It couldn't be Saskia. It had to be Bianca. Or Nathan.

Whoever it was, their plan wasn't going to work. Eva was determined of that. It had taken her years to build herself up, to find ways of dealing with the guilt and moving on with her life and she wasn't about to let anyone destroy it. She sat up straight, pulled her shoulders back. She wouldn't confront Saskia or Bianca. No, she'd sit it out, say nothing, handle whatever came next. She wasn't going down without a struggle though. José and this retreat, their dream, meant too much to her. She would fight with all her strength to stop anyone taking it from her. She felt a surge of adrenaline gush through her. She was going to take control of her life and she wasn't going to let anyone destroy it.

54

Carlos

Carlos sat in the café, at a table in the corner that looked out on the town square. It was a pretty town with its quaint shops, the ornate fountain standing proudly in the middle with the steps leading up to it, lined by benches where several people were sitting chatting. He imagined his grandparents sitting there catching up on the news with their friends, or maybe his grandfather used to sit in the café drinking coffee, as Carlos was doing, while his grandmother shopped. Sadness overwhelmed him that he had never met them. And bitterness that José had known them so well.

Being at El Sueño where his grandparents had lived, and now sitting here in the town they would have shopped at, had brought out a mix of emotions in him. He had joined the retreat out of curiosity, wanting to see the home his father had been brought up in, to find out more about his grandparents, and see what his cousin had done with it. He'd been surprised at what José had achieved. The villa had been restored beautifully. When he sat on the back terrace at the villa, Carlos had imagined José playing in the gardens, swimming in the pool, helping their grandfather in the vegetable plot. He had been the favourite, the golden boy. The one they had adored and left their beloved home to. Whereas he, Carlos, had been the one they hadn't wanted to know. And all because of some stupid row before he was even born.

Had José walked around this town with their grandparents, he wondered, sat at this café having lunch? He took another sip of his coffee as he battled his emotions. When Mario had dropped them off they'd all had a look around together until the shops opened after their afternoon siesta. Then Saskia had gone off with the others, eager to look around the local shops but he had wanted to sit here and think.

'Hiya, sorry I've been so long.' Saskia put her bags on one of the empty chairs around the table and sat down on the one next to Carlos. 'I love this place,' she said enthusiastically. 'Eva is so lucky to live here. Not that it's my cup of tea as a permanent home but I'd love to visit again. I hope Eva lets me.' She turned to Carlos. 'Are you and José getting on okay? It would be good if you did. Maybe we could visit again together?'

Carlos rested his eyes on her face. She was so lively and upbeat, it was hard not to be drawn to her enthusiasm. He enjoyed her company and would like to see her again. 'I doubt if I will visit again,' he said.

'Oh that's a shame. You two have spent enough time apart. Can't you put the past behind you? It's not José's fault, is it, that your father fell out with everyone?'

'That everyone fell out with my father, you mean. And no one even bothered to acknowledge my existence.' He hadn't meant to sound so resentful but the words had spurted out before he could stop them.

Saskia sat back and studied him thoughtfully. 'Your grand-mother left you some money in her will, so she did think of you.

And José let you come here. He could have given the place at the retreat to someone else.'

'Yes, my grandmother eased her conscience with a few thousand pounds and my cousin allowed me to come and see how well he was doing so that he could gloat, rub it in how much he meant to our grandparents.' Carlos swigged back the rest of the coffee.

Saskia was silent for a moment, then she leant forward. 'Actually he's been very friendly to you, you've been the grumpy one. This argument isn't yours and José's. Let it go.'

She stood up. 'I'm going to catch up with the others. See you in a bit.' She picked up her bags and set off across the square.

It was easy for her to say that, Carlos thought, anger still simmering in him, José wasn't the one who had been abandoned. Ignored. His mind went back to his grandfather's funeral when his weeping grandmother, whom he had never met before, had been flanked by Tío Pablo and José. They had all acknowledged each other politely. His father had introduced him as his son and his grandmother had looked at him, her eyes full of tears. Something had stirred in Carlos then and he had wanted to go and comfort her but neither of them had made any move towards each other. He wished now that he had. Maybe things would have been different.

55

Eva

Mario brought the guests back just as José and Eva were laying the table for dinner. They were all chatting away, their arms full of bags.

'What a pretty little town,' Saskia said. 'I couldn't resist buying a couple of things from the shops, the clothes are so bright and cheerful.' She took a packet out of her bag and handed it to Eva. 'This is for you. As soon as I saw it, I knew the colour would suit you.'

Eva was taken by surprise and simply stared at her for a moment. 'Go on, take a look,' Saskia told her so Eva took the paper bag from her and opened it, drawing out a silky pale blue crocheted shawl. 'Oh thank you, it's gorgeous!' she exclaimed, automatically leaning forward to kiss Saskia on each cheek. This was so kind of her. She knew she had been wrong to suspect her, of course it was Bianca. It had to be.

Eva glanced over at Bianca, who was talking to Adrienne. 'It looks like you've all been busy shopping,' she said lightly. 'The shops have a wonderful collection of things, don't they?'

Bianca turned her head towards her and nodded eagerly. 'Yes they do, I could have bought so much but my suitcase is already full so I settled for a couple of scarves.' She took them out of the bag, they were both thin chiffon, one pale blue and the other a soft lilac. 'Aren't they pretty?'

'They're beautiful.' Eva couldn't imagine that designer-clad Adrienne would buy any of the local-made clothes and so was curious what was in the carrier bag she was holding. 'What did you get, Adrienne?' she asked.

Adrienne opened the bag and took out an exquisite white handbag, decorated with mother of pearl, holding it up for Eva to see. 'I couldn't resist this, it's so pretty and unusual,' she said. 'And I bought a scarf too.' She pulled a bright red silk scarf out of the bag. 'Isn't it gorgeous? I simply had to have it.'

Eva nodded. 'They're both lovely.'

Nathan had bought a cotton shirt and Sean a brown leather belt. She wondered if Carlos had bought anything, his backpack looked rather full, but thought it was best not to ask him. It could be a surprise gift for Saskia.

'I'm glad you all had a good time,' Eva said with a smile. 'You're back just in time for dinner so I hope you've worked up an appetite. We're eating in the dining room tonight. José has cooked a traditional Spanish meal as it's your final night.'

'I definitely have,' Sean agreed. 'Shall we put our shopping away and quickly freshen up then join you?'

Eva nodded. 'Come straight through to the dining room when you're ready.'

Everyone went upstairs to get ready, except for Carlos, who looked like he had something to say but didn't know how to say it.

'Is anything wrong?' she asked him.

'I saw something for here, the villa, and bought it but now I'm not sure how it will be received.'

He'd bought them a present? That was kind of him. 'Thank

you so much, I'll let José open it,' she said. After all, Carlos was his cousin.

'Let José open what?' José asked, coming out of the dining room in time to hear her words.

'Carlos has bought us a gift,' she told him.

She saw the surprise in José's eyes as Carlos put his hand in his backpack and brought out something wrapped in a plastic bag. 'It seemed a good idea at the time,' he mumbled.

'*Gracias.*' José seemed cautious, Eva thought as he unwrapped it. They both gasped as they saw the beautiful mosaic wall clock. It was something they'd been meaning to get for the terrace.

'You like it? I noticed that you didn't have one outside and thought it might be useful.'

'We love it. Don't we, José?' Eva exclaimed.

José nodded slowly. '*Gracias, primo.*' He took the clock into the kitchen without saying another word.

'Now I will go and freshen up before dinner,' Carlos said, going off down the hall.

Eva went into the kitchen. José had placed the clock on the table and was busy stirring the sauce.

'That was nice of him, wasn't it?' she asked. 'Do you think he wants to build bridges? It would be good if both families could bury the hatchet, wouldn't it?'

José stared down into the saucepan as he replied. 'It would. But I wonder if the hatchet is buried in too deep.'

56

It was almost over. Tomorrow everyone would be going home, Eva thought in relief as they all sat around the table tucking into the gazpacho – the popular cold Spanish soup – and homemade garlic herb bread. She was literally counting the hours until this nightmare was over.

'I hope you've enjoyed your stay with us,' José said. 'I know there's been a few hiccups but I can assure you that we will make sure these are corrected for future retreats.'

'I think it's been fantastic. And nothing major has happened really, has it?' Saskia asked. 'You've got to expect things like goats wandering around the garden when you live halfway up a mountain, surely?'

Sean nodded his agreement. 'We've enjoyed the break, haven't we, dear?' He squeezed Adrienne's hand. 'And we're going back home with lots of tips for healthy living and eating. Plus, I've fallen in love with this part of Spain and would definitely like to visit again.'

Everyone started talking then, sharing their experience of the last few days and what they would be taking from it. Everyone except Carlos.

'What about you, Carlos? What positive experience have you taken from the retreat?' Nathan asked.

Carlos levelled his gaze at José. 'Getting to know my cousin,' he replied.

Was he serious? Eva wondered. Then he had bought them that gorgeous wall clock and had made no snide remarks for a while.

José nodded. 'It's been good to get to know you too.'

Carlos raised his glass in a silent salute and José reciprocated. Up until today they had been at loggerheads with each other, but, even though nothing much had been said, she sensed the atmosphere had thawed between them. She wondered what had changed, was it because Carlos was going home tomorrow?

'It's been wonderful,' Saskia said enthusiastically. 'I'll write you a glowing five-star review as soon as I get back and recommend you to all my friends.'

Eva met her eye and Saskia smiled a warm friendly smile back. 'We must keep in touch. It's been great to catch up with you again.'

'We will definitely leave a good review too.' Sean nodded. 'It's worth coming for the food and the beautiful countryside. I feel very refreshed and relaxed. Don't you, dear?' He turned to Adrienne.

'I certainly do. I think I shall keep up my morning yoga and definitely be having more massages. I hadn't realised how beneficial they are.' She smiled at Eva.

'We've enjoyed it too, haven't we?' Nathan asked Bianca. 'You seem to be less anxious.'

'Yes, the acupressure and mindfulness techniques Eva has shown me have been very useful.' Bianca's eyes met Eva's. 'Thank you.'

Would she be saying that if she thought I was responsible for her father's death? Eva thought.

They all seemed so genuine. If it wasn't for those two

horrible notes Eva would have thought that she was over-reacting and everything that had happened had been a coincidence. But someone sitting around this table had sent those notes. One of these guests had it in for her and she had no idea how far they would go.

José brought out the second course, Spanish tortilla with a crisp green salad, followed by traditional Spanish caramel flan, which everyone enjoyed immensely. Dinner finished, they all moved onto the back terrace to chat and drink sangria, a selection of fruit juices or flavoured water.

José seemed very relaxed as they chatted away but Eva was on tenterhooks waiting for the next thing to happen. Whoever had sent her that note had done so for a reason. She wondered if they had just been toying with her but there was a danger that now everyone was going home tomorrow, things might get serious. Perhaps the note-writer intended to out her to everyone?

Or maybe they had got something more sinister planned.

57

José

It had been a pleasant evening, they had all sat chatting outside, the citronella candles helping to keep the mosquitos at bay – fortunately there weren't many this time of year – and the pool lights illuminating the terrace. Finally, one by one the guests went inside to have a shower and get to bed but José and Eva stayed out for a little longer, chatting and enjoying the mild evening. José felt relaxed, it was almost over. There had been a few hiccups but it had gone pretty well all things considered. He'd picked up some tips for future retreats and was feeling confident that they would make a success of it. He'd been hoping to have a word with Carlos but he'd disappeared with Saskia. They'd got pretty close, those two, and he wouldn't be surprised if they continued to see each other. *I'll talk to him tomorrow before he goes home,* he thought, his conversation with his father earlier that day playing on his mind. There were things that needed to be said.

He glanced over at Eva, who was staring out at the pool as if deep in thought. He knew that she was anxious despite her best efforts not to show it and to smile and engage with the guests, he had seen her do a couple of the acupressure points on herself when she thought no one was looking, pressing her three fingers on the inside of her wrist under cover of the table for one. She was probably worried that the guests might leave some bad reviews with what had happened but he was hopeful that they wouldn't. From the conversations tonight everyone had enjoyed the retreat and would be happy to recommend it to their friends. Perhaps that one-star review had been left by someone else, he had heard that there were people who randomly left bad ratings on business pages just for the hell of it. He was worried that it had all taken its toll on Eva though, she had been on tenterhooks all week and still couldn't seem to relax even though it was almost all over. He hoped the retreat hadn't been too much of a strain for her, so much of a strain that she didn't want to do it anymore.

'I think it's gone okay, don't you? Only tomorrow morning to go now. Not much time for anything else to go wrong.'

Eva dragged her eyes from the pool and turned them to him. She looked really troubled, he realised. He was about to ask her what the matter was when the pool lights went out. As did the terrace light. They were suddenly plunged into darkness. *Dios!* It was one thing after another, now the bloody electricity had gone off! Why couldn't it have lasted a few more hours? Just until tomorrow lunchtime.

'The electric...' Eva stood up. 'Why hasn't the generator kicked in?'

'I'll go and see if the fuse box has tripped first, if everyone's having showers it's a lot of electricity. Then I'll check the generator.'

Using his phone torch, José went to check the fuse box in the hall. The electricity used to go off a lot when they first moved in but since they'd had the house rewired and upped their electricity band it had been okay. There had been a lot of people using it this week though. The main breaker switch was down, he noticed. He pushed it up and it immediately tripped again. The problem was something to do with the house electrics then but why hadn't the generator kicked in? *Mierda!* Their water came from a well deep underground, they were too far from the town to receive the public water. It was pumped up with an electric pump so when the electricity went off the water did too. No one could have a shower, flush the loo, brush their teeth. This was the worst thing that could have happened.

'Has it tripped?' Eva was standing beside him.

He nodded. 'We'll have to get the electrician out tomorrow. I'll get the torch and go and check the generator.'

'What's happened? Adrienne was having a shower and the water's cut out. There's no electricity either.' Sean was coming down the stairs, using his phone torch as a light.

'Hey, what's happened to the electricity? I was charging my phone!' Nathan shouted down.

'There's no water either! I was in the middle of brushing my teeth!' This was from Carlos.

'I'm sorry, there seems to be a fault with the electricity but the generator should kick in any minute. I'll go and check on it,' José said. 'Meanwhile, we'll give you all a couple of candles to use, and there's plenty of bottles of water if anyone needs it.'

José went to take the big torch off its hook by the back door and groaned when he saw that it had gone. 'What did you do with the big torch?' he asked Eva.

'I haven't moved it,' she replied. She was using her phone torch to guide her way to the dresser, where she opened the drawer and took out a candle lighter. José waited while she put the candles on a tray and lit them then he went out to check the generator.

It was pitch black outside, without the pool or terrace lights, he really could have done with that big torch. He could only see a bit in front of him with his phone torch. He cautiously made his way down to the shed which housed the generator. He couldn't hear any sound from it, he hoped it wasn't broken, they'd only bought it last year and it hadn't been cheap but he'd wanted a good one to avoid situations like this. It was under guarantee but that wouldn't help get them electricity tonight. He opened the shed door and walked inside, aiming the torch beam on the ground in front of him so that he didn't trip over anything. Then he knelt by the generator hoping it might be something he could fix.

Eva

'To be honest, it's the water we're more bothered about. Adrienne is standing in the shower with soap suds all over her and shampoo on her hair. She's not very pleased, I can tell you,' Sean said as he went on ahead, still using his phone torch to light the way up the stairs, despite Eva carrying a tray full of candles.

No, Eva didn't think she would be. She prepared herself for the complaints as she reached the landing. Nathan and Bianca's door was open and Nathan was standing in the doorway. 'Any idea when the electricity will be back on? My phone is almost dead and I forgot to charge my power bank last night.'

'Hopefully soon, José has gone to check the generator.' She looked down at the candles on the tray. 'Have a couple of these to light up your room until he comes back.'

Nathan reluctantly took two candles. 'I don't really like using candles, they can be a fire hazard.'

'As I said, it shouldn't be long and the candles are safe, they are in metal containers. Make sure you extinguish them before you go to sleep though,' she warned.

'What about water?' Bianca demanded. 'I had to finish brushing my teeth with my bottled water but we can't even flush the loo.'

'I know and we're so sorry but I'm sure that José will be able to sort out the generator.'

'And if not?' Bianca looked cross.

'If not, then we have some big urns of water stored in the outside shed which you can use to flush the toilet,' she replied. They always kept a couple of urns of water in reserve in case there was a problem with the well, and thankfully they'd filled up a few more as a precaution before the retreat.

'This is like living in the back of beyond.' Bianca stormed back inside.

'I'm sorry,' Eva started to say again but Nathan had already slammed shut the door.

'It's probably best if I take these, Adrienne is not in a happy mood,' Sean said, picking up two candles from the tray and walking over to his room. Eva's heart sank. This couldn't have happened at a worse time, the guests had said earlier how much they'd enjoyed their stay, but now they were all going to be annoyed.

'I wondered if your electricity would cope,' Carlos muttered as he took a candle from her. 'This is all very inconvenient.'

Even Saskia wasn't sympathetic. 'I wanted to have a shower before I joined Carlos for the night,' she complained. 'I hope you can get the electricity on soon.'

'I'm sorry,' Eva said again. What could she do but apologise? She would be annoyed if she was on holiday and there was no electricity or water, especially this time of night when you wanted to shower and go to the loo before bed. If only it had happened a little later when everyone was asleep. Or earlier when everyone was shopping then they could have got an electrician out and got it all sorted.

Eva used her torch to light the way back downstairs and poured herself a glass of juice. José seemed to have been gone for ages, she glanced at her watch, over half an hour. What was keeping him?

And why hadn't the generator kicked in? They hadn't had it very long, it couldn't be faulty.

She shivered as she recalled the note she'd received this morning. *Revenge is coming*, it said. That meant the writer was planning something, just as she had dreaded. Was all this part of their plan? Plunge everywhere into darkness and then they could sneak about and do whatever it was they had plotted?

She thought back to when they were sitting on the patio, trying to recall if Bianca had disappeared at some point, but they had all been talking and at various stages someone had gone inside for something, or she or José had gone to get more drinks. If anyone had messed with the electrics then it would have gone off straight away rather than half an hour later when everyone had gone inside. Or at least she'd thought everyone had gone inside. Obviously whoever was responsible for the electricity going off had probably sneaked out of the side door, and down the path towards the shed to sabotage the generator too. She wasn't sure how they could stop the generator working though. It all sounded a bit far-fetched and if it wasn't for the notes, she would think she was crazy.

And now, here she was, isolated in the dark. The guests were upstairs, José was outside. She was alone in the house with a possible murderer. She hugged her shoulders as her eyes darted around the room, the candles glowing in the darkness, her ears pricked for the slightest sound. Was it Bianca out for revenge? If so, what had she got planned?

Her hands felt clammy and she broke out in a cold sweat as

she realised how vulnerable she was. She wasn't going to sit here and wait to be attacked, she would go and see how José was getting on with the generator. He might have stumbled and hurt himself. She had to keep her wits about her though, the attacker could pounce any minute.

*

Healthy food, healthy living, healthy thinking, that's all you've preached this week. You're so full of virtue. Have you forgotten what you did? Can you push it so easily out of your mind?

You have no guilt. You destroyed my life and now it's my turn to destroy yours. You think you've got away with it, but you haven't. The things that have happened so far have just been a warning but you haven't heeded them. You haven't acknowledged what you've done. Now it's payback. Now it gets serious.

59

José

José closed the shed door and walked back to the house, the narrow beam of the phone torch guiding his way, his mouth set in a grim line. The generator had been sabotaged. There was no doubt about it, this was a deliberate act. Someone had tampered with it, the same person had probably done something to cut off the electricity supply to the house. The question was why? Was it another attempt to jeopardise the success of the retreat or was there a more sinister reason? Were they actually planning to harm anyone? If so, who was it? Carlos?

Who else could it be? His cousin had practically accused José of causing their grandmother's death, although he now seemed to have thawed out a bit. Was his bitterness about José being left their grandparents' villa so all-consuming that he wanted José dead? If he did then, like everything else that had happened, he would want to make it look like an accident.

If only Carlos knew the story of the feud, he would surely understand why Abuelo had told Tío Diego to never darken his doorstep again. José had been planning on talking to Carlos in the morning, explaining it all to him and suggesting that they bury the hatchet and try to bring the family together. Was he too late? Should he have tried to tell him this evening?

An owl hooted as he made his way down the path, and something scuffled in the bushes. His heart skipped a beat. He stood still and shone the beam of light on the bushes but couldn't see anything. It was probably a rat, or a hedgehog. He moved the tiny light around, he couldn't hear anything now apart from the chirp of the crickets. Talk about a vivid imagination! A couple of things went wrong, perfectly normal things when you thought about it rationally, and he was convinced that his cousin wanted to harm him! It was ridiculous.

Swinging the small beam to the house, he saw lights glowing in the bedroom windows, candles. Eva would have given all the guests candles, and probably a bottle of water to use to wash and brush their teeth. He bet they were all disgruntled about the electricity going off and they were going to be even more annoyed when he told them about the generator. There was no way he would be able to get it fixed before they all left tomorrow. Which meant no showers, no charging phones, no flushing loos. *Dios mío*, what a mess.

The leaves rustled and he glanced around again before continuing along the path. Maybe Mario would allow the guests to shower at his, he was always willing to help. He would ask him in the morning. While it was a nuisance for the guests to have to traipse over there, he was sure they would rather be able to freshen up before they went home.

One of the paving stones wobbled under his feet. He shone the torch on it and saw that it was loose. He must fix that, he didn't want anyone tripping up and hurting themselves. Not that anyone would be walking around tomorrow, they were leaving before lunch, but he would have to call someone out to fix the generator so he must remember to point out the wobbly paving stone to them so they didn't trip over it. He continued up the path towards the house, the torch beam illuminating the way, his mind trying to sort out how he could lessen the impact of no electricity on their guests. He had a gas hob, so could still provide breakfast, but the oven was electric and... damn, the fridge and freezers. All the food would go to waste.

Suddenly there was a loud screech and something shot past his legs, almost tripping him over. He steadied himself and swung the torch in the direction the creature had run, breathing a sigh of relief when he saw the shape of a black cat diving into the bushes. Sombra! What on earth had scared him? He shone the torch in the direction Sombra had come from, catching his breath when he saw a streak of red in the pool. Was it blood? *Madre mía!* Had someone stumbled in the darkness, fallen in and hurt themselves? His mouth dry, his breath coming out in rasps, José covered the ground to the pool in a few leaps and focused the torchlight on the streak of red. Could it really be blood? It seemed to fill a large area.

He was at the side of the pool now, and the mass of red was almost within his reach. He let out his breath when he realised that it wasn't blood but something red floating on top of the water. He really was letting his imagination run wild! He knelt down to reach for it, his fingers almost grasping it when suddenly he felt a blow to his head and everything went black.

60

NOW

Eva

It was José!

Eva dived into the pool and swam over to the floating body, the familiar dark hair fanned out on the water around his head. *Please God, let him be alive.*

He was on his back, she noticed, did that mean he was alive? She'd read somewhere that drowning bodies were always face down. *Please don't let him be dead!* Her mind was in turmoil. What the hell had happened? What was he doing in the pool? José was a strong swimmer, if he had stumbled and fallen into it in the dark he wouldn't have any problem swimming to the side – even with his clothes and trainers on. Had someone pushed him in? Would they come back for her? They were both alone out here. Had anyone heard her screams? Would they come to help?

She'd reached José now and put her hands under his armpits to swim back with him when his eyes fluttered open. 'Eva?'

'Eva! Eva! Where are you? Are you okay?'

Saskia! She almost fainted with relief. 'We're in the pool! Help us!'

'What's happened?' She could just make out Saskia, using the beam from her phone, running down the steps towards them. 'I heard you scream.'

'I found José floating in the pool. Help me get him out, he's alive but he's hurt!' Eva shouted, her breath coming out in gasps. She was holding on to the bar of the narrow steps and supporting José at the same time. Then Saskia was in the water beside her, helping to lift José out and lay him down on the tiles by the side of the pool. Eva knelt beside him, relieved to see that he was breathing normally. Had he swallowed any water? Should she be doing something? The Heimlich manoeuvre?

'I'm okay. I'm okay,' José murmured. 'Just give me a minute.'

'What was he doing in the pool? Didn't he see it in the dark?' Saskia asked.

'I don't know...' Eva stopped as she saw that José was trying to sit up and reached out to help him. Her heart was thudding. He looked so disorientated.

'*Mierda*, my head hurts. That was some blow!' José muttered groggily.

'Blow?' Eva repeated as she and Saskia looked at each other, stunned. 'Did someone hit you on the head?'

José nodded, catching his breath. 'I saw something red floating in the pool. I thought it was blood so I went over to check it out. I bent down for a better look, shining my torch on the water, then I was hit on the back of my head. I can't remember anything else.'

'Someone hit you?' Eva repeated. She couldn't take it in. Someone had knocked José out, thrown him into the pool and left him to die. She had thought she was the one in danger but all the time it was José.

'You mean someone tried to kill you?' Saskia stammered,

her hand flying to her mouth. 'Someone here? One of the guests?'

Eva was shocked to the core. The notes that had been left, the things that had happened. Was this the revenge that the note-writer had threatened? Was Bianca responsible? Had she tried to kill José in revenge for Eva killing her father? Or was it Nathan, in revenge for the hurt she had caused Bianca? An eye for an eye, a life for a life. Hurting Eva in the cruellest way possible by taking someone she loved from her, as Eva had done to Bianca.

61

'What's happened?' Nathan was racing down the steps to them. 'I could hear a bit of a commotion out here so thought I'd better come and check.'

'José nearly drowned,' Saskia told him.

'What?' Nathan knelt down by José. 'You okay, mate?'

José nodded. 'My head's pounding but otherwise I'm good.' He rubbed the back of his head. 'Thank you for jumping in to help me, *cariño*. I was trying to float to the shallower end but I kept drifting in and out of consciousness.'

Eva nodded, fighting back the tears as she replied. 'I'm so glad I came out to look for you. I was worried because you'd been gone ages. I couldn't sit there waiting any longer, imagining that you were in trouble so I came out to check and saw you floating in the pool. I yelled for help and Saskia came.' She glanced at her friend. 'I thought you were with Carlos? Didn't he come out too?'

'He must be around the front of the house. He went out to try and get a signal on his phone a few minutes ago, said he had an important call to make, I came down to get a drink and heard you shout for help so ran out to see what had happened.'

As if he'd heard them, Carlos came sauntering around the corner, using his phone as a torch as they all did. 'Hey, what are you all doing out here? Are you going for a midnight swim?' he shouted.

'José's been for one, but it wasn't intentional. He was knocked out and fell in,' Saskia told him.

'What?' Carlos quickened his pace and stood at the top of the steps. 'Are you all right, *primo*?'

'I am. Thanks to Eva. And Saskia.'

'I heard Eva shout for help,' Saskia explained. 'It's a wonder you didn't hear.'

'I was on the phone, out the front.'

'There was something red in the pool, I thought it was blood,' José repeated.

'Something red?' Nathan repeated, frowning. He shone the phone torch over the pool. 'There it is, floating over in the corner.' He went over, bent down and pulled it out of the water. As he spread it out on the ground they could all see that it was a thin red scarf.

Eva recognised it immediately. It was the red scarf Adrienne had bought in Toria today, which she had been wearing that evening.

'It's Adrienne's,' she stammered.

'She must have left it on the chair and the wind's blown it into the water,' Nathan said quickly.

Too quickly? Had Bianca or Nathan thrown the scarf in the water knowing that it would spread out and look like a pool of blood? Was she, or both of them, responsible for the electricity going off? Had they hit José over the head and pushed him into the pool?

'Where is Bianca?' she asked. It was strange that Bianca, Adrienne and Sean hadn't heard the commotion yet Nathan had. Had he been hanging around to see if his plan had worked and José would drown?

'She's in bed. I told her I'd come down and see what was going on. I didn't want her coming out in the dark.' Nathan shot José a look of alarm as he stumbled to his feet. 'Take it steady, mate. I'm wondering if you should go to hospital for a check-up. It must have been a hard blow to your head to knock you into the pool like that.'

'I agree. And there's secondary drowning to consider. You seem fine but if some water has got into your lungs it could be fatal,' Carlos added. He seemed genuinely concerned.

'What?' Eva felt like she was going to faint. She thought she'd saved José but it seemed he could still die. 'I'll phone an ambulance.'

'No. There's no need for that. I'm fine. Honestly. I didn't swallow any water. When I fell in I was conscious enough to keep my mouth closed, bring myself back up to the surface and float on my back.'

'It's concussion that I think is the bigger worry,' Nathan said. 'Do you know the signs?'

'Yes, headache, dizziness, nausea, confusion, problems with vision...' Eva rattled off.

'I've got a headache but nothing else, don't worry,' José said.

Eva was worried though. 'I really think we should get you checked over. You got hit on the head and almost drowned. Also...' She glanced over at Nathan. 'Shouldn't we call the police? This sounds like attempted murder.'

She heard Nathan draw in a breath. 'Why? What exactly happened?' he asked sharply. 'Did someone attack you, José?'

'I felt a blow to the back of my head.' José related the events to him. 'I don't know if it was someone or something that hit me but it was a hard enough blow to knock me out.'

Nathan frowned. 'Could it have been something else? A tile from the terrace perhaps?'

'We're far away from the terrace here,' Eva told him.

'Yes but it's not inconceivable.' Nathan stood up straight,

and even in the torch light Eva could see that his expression was serious. 'You need to be certain, José, because not only is that a serious crime to accuse one of your guests of, it has other repercussions.' He looked from one to the other of them before continuing. 'If we call the police that means none of us can leave Spain until they've investigated what happened and come to a conclusion whether it was attempted murder or not. Personally I need to get back. And I'm sure the others do too. However, if you're sure that someone deliberately whacked you on the back of the head, then that makes this attempted murder and of course it should be investigated,' Nathan said firmly.

'Look, let's check out the pool area and make sure nothing has fallen down and narrowly missed you,' Saskia suggested. 'I mean, I know a few things have been going wrong, but attempted murder? It's a big accusation.'

José nodded slowly. 'I think that might be best. No point calling in the police and delaying everyone when it was probably an accident.'

Eva swallowed as José's eyes met hers. What if someone had tried to kill him? Would whoever was trying to sabotage the retreat go that far?

One of her father's sayings came to mind. 'Listen to your gut. It won't lead you wrong.'

Right now her gut was telling her that someone had knocked out José, pushed him in the pool and left him to die. And the only person she could think of who had a grudge against them was Bianca. Was Nathan in on it? Is that why he'd suggested that they didn't call the police?

62

Eva looked worriedly at José. 'Do you think that someone deliberately hit you?' she whispered.

He shook his head, bewildered. 'I don't know, Eva. All I remember is bending down to look into the pool then a bang on the back of my head and falling into the water.' He reached out and squeezed her hand. 'Thank you for your quick action. I owe you my life.'

Tears filled her eyes and she swallowed the lump in her throat. She didn't know what she would do if anything had happened to José. Bianca – or Nathan – was responsible, she was sure of it. She should have told José about Bianca, about the notes. She shouldn't have let things go this far.

'I hope it was an accident. Otherwise somebody hates me very much and wants to kill me – and that's a horrible thought,' José added, his voice grim.

'Maybe it's not you they hate but me,' Eva whispered. 'Maybe they want to kill you to make me suffer.' She had to tell him. She couldn't let Bianca get away with this. The woman was dangerous.

José's startled eyes shot to her face. 'What do you mean?'

Eva swallowed, trying to find the words to explain to him what had happened all those years ago. Before she could say anything though, Nathan returned. 'I've searched everywhere but I can't find anything. Are you sure that you didn't just hit your head on a branch then fell into the pool? It's dark out here. It's perfectly feasible that you wandered into one of the low branches, the bump on the head and fall into the pool might have left you a bit confused.'

'You could be right...' José looked unsure. 'I guess it is a bit far-fetched to think that someone lay in hiding and whacked me on the head.'

Eva wasn't convinced. José said he'd been kneeling by the pool when he was hit on the head, how could he get confused about that?

'Look, quite a few things have gone wrong since we've been here. And you almost drowned. I can understand why you're feeling fraught. Why don't we all go back to bed and talk about this in the morning,' Nathan suggested.

It seemed the sensible thing to do. They had no evidence that someone had hit José did they? Besides, Nathan was a policeman, he didn't think anything suspicious had happened.

Or was he protecting Bianca? Or even himself.

After checking that José was feeling okay, and warning Eva again to look out for signs of concussion, Nathan, Carlos and Saskia said goodnight and went upstairs, using the torches on their phones to see the way as their candles were already in their rooms. Eva took a box of paracetamol from the cupboard and slipped them in her pocket, then put a bottle of water from the kitchen and two glasses on a tray, doused all the candles apart from one in a metal holder which she put on the tray too and took into the bedroom, standing it on the chest of drawers to provide some light for them to get undressed.

'You could probably do with these,' she said, pouring a glass of water and handing it to José with a couple of paracetamol.

'Thank you. My head is pounding.' He took the glass, popped the two tablets in his mouth and swallowed them down with the water.

'I can't believe that Bianca, Adrienne and Sean have slept through all this,' Eva said as she and José both undressed and climbed into bed.

'Bianca knew that Nathan would deal with it, and Adrienne and Sean's room is on the front so I guess they didn't hear anything,' he said wearily.

He was right. Carlos hadn't even heard anything until he came around to the back.

She turned to José to question him further but his eyes had already closed. She'd let him sleep and talk to him in the morning, she decided. She went over to the chest of drawers, blew out the candle and used her phone torch to guide her way back to the bed. Tomorrow everyone would go home. It was almost over. There was still time for something else to happen, she thought, as she got into bed. She couldn't afford to let her guard down yet.

63

FRIDAY – DAY FIVE

José was soon snoring softly besides her but Eva's mind was too busy to sleep. She had almost lost José tonight. If she hadn't come out when she did... it didn't bear thinking about. Was it really just another accident? So many accidents. So many coincidences. Well, in a few hours it would all be over, everyone was going home. Would the person responsible give up now they had almost killed José or did they have another trick up their sleeve?

If only she knew for certain who it was and could confront them. Bianca was still her main suspect. The woman had a reason to hate Eva so a strong motive to threaten revenge, and cause her – or someone she loved – harm. Perhaps Bianca noticed that Adrienne had left her scarf behind and had thrown it in the pool to draw José's attention so he would investigate further. In the dark, with only a torch beam for light, she could understand how it would have looked like a pool of blood. Was Bianca waiting in the bushes to sneak out and hit him over the head with something as soon as José got close enough to the pool? Or did Nathan do that?

It couldn't be Saskia. There was no way Saskia was capable

of sneaking behind José and hitting him over the head. Why would she want to kill him? And she'd helped Eva get José out of the pool.

That doesn't mean she was innocent. Eva couldn't afford to eliminate anyone. José could have died tonight. Perhaps Saskia had sneaked Adrienne's scarf off the back of the chair, put it in her bag then dropped it in the pool later, hidden in the bushes for José to spot it then whacked him over the head. Seeing Eva rush out and jump in to rescue him, she could have helped too, so that she wouldn't be considered a suspect. She'd had the same paper and pen the note-writer had used after all. And she was getting very close to Carlos. Maybe they were working together. He clearly had a grudge against José.

She dismissed the thought. She couldn't believe that Saskia would hurt her or José. It had to be Bianca – maybe with the help of Nathan? He was a policeman, he should want to investigate this surely? Why didn't he question the events more? Everything pointed towards someone wanting to jeopardise the retreat but Nathan didn't seem to see anything suspicious. Was that because he was the perpetrator or knew who was?

Should she have shown the notes? If she did then everyone would know what she'd done and she couldn't bear that. They were all going home tomorrow, maybe it was best to say nothing. José was okay, thank goodness. Soon everyone would be gone and the nightmare would be over. Surely whoever was responsible for sending her those notes wouldn't risk doing anything else after this.

Finally, Eva drifted off but her sleep was punctuated by wild and confusing dreams, someone was chasing her and she was running, running, trying to get away but the person – she couldn't see if it was a man or woman – was catching up with her, was almost upon her. She dashed into a nearby building, slammed the door shut, locked it, her hands shaking as she pulled the rusty bolt across, her breath coming out in gasps. She reached in her pocket for her phone so she could call for help then realised that she'd lost it. She must have dropped it when she was running. She had to stay there until the pursuer had gone.

She could smell smoke. Something was burning. Turning towards the small window high on the back wall, she saw that it was open, and lying on the floor underneath it was a bundle of flames. It was a burning rag, she realised. The pursuer had thrown it in. They were trying to smoke her out. If she opened the door they would get her but if she remained where she was she would burn to death. Smoke was filling the room. She coughed. The smoke would kill her before the fire did. She had no choice. She had to open the door.

'Eva! Eva! Wake up. The room is on fire!'

José was shaking her. She coughed and opened her eyes, realising that she wasn't dreaming. The room was full of smoke and there were flames leaping up by the closed door, blocking their way out.

'The candle! You left the bloody candle burning!' José shouted as he ran into the bathroom, coming back out a few seconds later with a wet towel around his mouth and another one in his hand which he threw at her. 'Put this over your mouth!'

'I didn't! I remember blowing it out!' she protested. She ran over to the patio windows to unlock them so they could escape into the garden but the key had gone. *Oh shit!* Someone had set fire to their bedroom and taken the key so they couldn't escape.

'I can't open the windows, the key's gone!' she yelled as José came back out of the bathroom, dragging the big urn of water they'd put in there to use for washing and flushing the loo. They'd give one to each of the guests too.

'Stand by me and when I say "Go" run out and grab the extinguisher in the hall!' he shouted.

The wet towel now tied around her head, covering her

nose and mouth, Eva sprinted over to José as he heaved up the huge bottle of water. The top was already off – he must have used it to wet the towels – and he was struggling not to spill it. She put her hands on the bottom to take some of the weight, then moved them to the side as he swung his arms back and emptied out the water over the flames nearest to the door.

'Go!' he yelled. The flames had spluttered and diminished enough for her to run and yank open the door handle. Thank goodness there was no lock on this door, just a bolt on the inside. Hoping that José was behind her she sprinted the couple of steps down the hall to get the fire extinguisher, tugged it off the wall and raced back with it.

To her dismay the flames had flared up again and were blocking José's exit. She could hear him coughing inside. She had to get him out of there quick! She pulled the pin out of the top of the extinguisher, aimed it at the flames, squeezing the handle and sweeping it from side to side. As the fire extinguished José came hurtling through the smoke and threw himself onto the floor in the hall, almost bent double with coughing.

'José! Are you okay?' Eva bent down by him. Her chest hurt, her eyes stung and her throat was scratchy but José had inhaled more smoke than she had. He'd been in the bedroom longer, it was only a couple of minutes but every minute counted with a fire. Smoke was the silent killer. His face was blackened by smoke, his eyes peering out as if he was wearing a mask. She was sure hers was the same.

'It's a good job I woke,' he wheezed. 'A few minutes longer and we'd have been dead.'

'I did extinguish that candle. I swear I did,' she insisted. She walked over to the door and gazed in horror at the burnt patch on the big rug resting against the bottom of the blackened chest of drawers.

'Maybe you thought you did but it was still alight a bit and flared up again,' José told her.

'I double-checked, I always do,' she insisted. José always teased her about how cautious she was but she knew how easily accidents could happen, and then you had to live with the consequences for the rest of your life. 'Besides, it was in a metal holder. Even if it was still alight – which it wasn't – it wouldn't burn through to the chest of drawers.' She always put candles in metal or glass holders. She always played it safe. 'And someone has taken the key out of the patio doors so we can't open them.' They always left the key in the lock so that they could open them up and go out into the garden when they awoke in the morning.

She stared down at the rug, suddenly realising that it had been moved. It had been running along the side of the bed, not at the bottom like that. Then she noticed that the candle holder had gone. Fear coursed through her. 'Someone came in when we were sleeping, José. They took the key out of the patio doors, moved the rug to the chest of drawers, took the candle out of the holder, relit it and closed the door. They wanted to burn us alive in our beds.' She was shaking and sobbing. This couldn't be happening. She was in some kind of living nightmare.

64

'Hey, are you guys okay? I heard you coughing and I smelt smoke.' Nathan came padding along the hall towards them. His gaze took in their blackened appearance then swept over to the open door, resting on the burnt rug, before darting back to them. 'Blimey! Did you knock over your candle or leave it burning all night?'

'No. Someone else did,' Eva told him. 'Someone sneaked in, lit our candle while we were sleeping, closed the door and left us to be burnt alive.'

'Shit.' Nathan had paled. 'You mean one of the guests? One of the people here?'

'Who else could it be?'

'What's the commotion?' Carlos was walking towards them, hair tousled, sleepy-eyed.

Nathan quickly explained. Carlos looked shocked. 'Are you sure you didn't leave the candle alight? It's a bit of an accusation to say someone did it deliberately. That means it had to be one of us.'

José coughed again, clutching his chest. 'Eva is certain she doused it.'

'Yes I am! Besides, the candle had been taken out of its holder. Someone relit it and left it to burn down into the wooden chest of drawers. If they had left it in the metal holder it would have just gone out. And they took the key out of the patio doors so we couldn't escape through them,' she added.

'First the pool, then this. It's a bit of a coincidence, I admit. But why would anyone here want to kill you?' Carlos asked.

'I have no idea.' José ran his hands through his hair, frightened eyes staring out of his blackened face.

'Don't you have a smoke alarm?' asked Nathan, he'd slipped into 'policeman on duty' mode.

'We do and it's got battery back-up,' Eva said, wheezing. 'There's one upstairs and one downstairs.' Only none of them had worked, had they? She bet they'd been tampered with.

'*Mierda.* I should have checked everyone else was okay.' José sprang to his feet then was seized by another bout of coughing.

'I'll go,' Nathan said. 'You wait here.'

José hunched back down on the floor, wracked by a coughing fit. Eva sat down beside him and he wound his arm around her shoulder. She leant her head on him and they sat there silently, trying to take it all in. Someone in this house had tried to kill them.

Nathan returned a few minutes later looking very grim. 'Everyone else is okay and I checked your smoke alarms...' He paused.

Eva swallowed. 'What is it?'

'Both alarms were turned off.'

65

Even though it was what she suspected, dreaded, to actually hear Nathan say the words sent a shudder through Eva. There was no doubt about it. Someone had tried to kill them. Someone had switched off the smoke alarms then sneaked in and set fire to their bedroom.

The other guests had come down now, still dressed in their nightwear, groggy and wide-eyed at what Nathan had told them. Eva studied them, trying to pick up any signs of guilt. Adrienne and Sean holding hands, Bianca literally shaking, Carlos looking worried, Saskia horrified. Which one of them wanted her and José dead? And it had to be both of them the attacker had a grudge against because they had both been sleeping in the bedroom, they could have both died. Plus the statue could have landed on either of them too, she reminded herself.

'Nathan told us about the fire. I can't believe it.' Saskia threw her arms around Eva. 'I'm so glad that you're okay.' She shot a worried look at José, who was having another coughing bout. 'I think he needs to get checked out, his chest sounds awful. The almost-drowning and the fire might have seriously damaged it.'

Eva was worried about that too, but José had refused to go to hospital, saying he was fine and wasn't leaving her here alone.

'Almost drowning?' Adrienne and Sean exchanged astonished looks. 'When was this?'

'Last night,' Eva told them. 'Look, I'm sorry if this causes your flights to be delayed but I'm going to call the police. Someone here is responsible for the fire in our bedroom tonight. Someone here tried to kill José, then both of us.' Her voice wobbled as she said the words and there were collective gasps of horror from their guests.

'I understand that you both must be feeling really shook up but don't you think this could all be a terrible accident? José could have tripped and fallen in the pool. And you could have forgotten to extinguish the candle. It's easily done,' Sean pointed out.

'We didn't even light our candles, we used the torch on our phones, I was so worried that the candle might cause a fire,' Bianca said.

Eva shook her head, her voice breaking as she reminded them that the candle had been taken out of the holder and the rug moved, and that the key had been removed from the patio doors and the smoke alarms had been switched off. 'Are you seriously suggesting that all this was coincidental?' she asked.

'Maybe the smoke alarms not working is something to do with the electricity going off,' Adrienne suggested.

'Well, that definitely wasn't an accident,' José said. 'When I went to check on the generator I discovered that it had been sabotaged.'

'All this was a set-up to kill either me or José. Or both.' Eva could hear the tremor in her voice.

'That's a very strong accusation. Why would any of us want to kill you?' Sean demanded, his voice clipped.

'He's right. I know you've been through a terrible shock both last night and this morning but there's nothing that points to attempted murder. No one here has a grudge against you or a motive to want to harm you,' Nathan said.

Eva swallowed. She had to say it. She couldn't let her get away with this. José could have died last night. They both could have died today.

She took a deep breath. 'Yes, they do.'

All eyes turned on her, including José's. Nathan raised his eyebrows. 'Really? Who?'

Eva pointed to Bianca. 'She does.'

Bianca went pale 'What?' Her eyes wide, she looked from Nathan to Eva. 'Why are you saying that? I didn't even know you until Monday. How could I possible have a grudge against you? Why would I want to kill you or José? You're crazy!' She was trembling.

Nathan put his arm around her shoulder. 'I think you'd better take that back,' he warned Eva. 'Why on earth would Bianca want to harm you?'

Eva steeled herself to meet Bianca's eyes, to say the words that would probably be the death toll for her and José's relationship. 'For revenge. Because I killed her father.'

66

José

José listened in astonishment as Eva continued. 'You discovered that I was the driver who knocked your father over and you came here for revenge.'

He looked at Bianca and saw that the colour had drained from her face. Was this true?

'I'm so very sorry,' Eva continued, 'but it was a terrible accident. I had a witness to prove it, you know that. It was late at night and your dad stepped out in front of me, he was wearing dark clothing, barely visible, I didn't even see him until it was too late.' Her voice broke into a sob.

'It's true. And the guilt almost destroyed her,' Saskia added. 'She was totally devastated.'

José looked at Eva incredulously. She had been carrying this all these years and had never said a word about it to him yet it was clear that Saskia knew all about it. 'You killed Bianca's father?'

'Yes but it was...'

'No, you didn't.' Bianca's voice was firm. 'The person who

killed my father was a male. A young teenage driver who had just passed his test and was showing off to his friend who was a passenger. He took the bend too fast, and yes, my father stepped out into the road without looking, and yes he was wearing dark clothing, but he never had a chance at the speed the driver was travelling.' Her voice was bitter. 'I've no idea who you ran down but it wasn't my dad.'

'I can't believe you haven't told me this, Eva,' José said incredulously.

'I couldn't. The guilt of what I'd done almost destroyed me. It was an accident. I wasn't even charged but the knowledge that someone had died because of me has eaten into me all these years.' She stared at Bianca, confused at what the other woman had said. 'Then when you told me about your father, and it was in the same area...' She paused. 'How many years ago was your father knocked down?'

'Fourteen,' Bianca replied.

'Your accident was twelve years ago,' Saskia said softly.

'Maybe you should have spoken to Bianca about this before and checked the details,' Adrienne remarked. 'It seems to have all been a misunderstanding.'

Eva looked stunned. 'But the notes...' she stammered.

Bianca stared at her. 'Notes?'

'Someone left me some threatening notes...'

José drew in his breath so sharply everyone turned to look at him. 'When was this?' he demanded. 'You have said nothing to me.' He couldn't believe that Eva had kept such huge secrets from him.

'I thought it was Bianca and I didn't want to worry you,' she said. 'I'm sorry.'

Nathan stepped in. 'I think I need to see these notes. This sounds serious. We may have to call in the police after all.'

José was stunned and angry as Eva went into their bedroom to get the notes. How could she keep this from him? He could have been killed. How many more secrets was she keeping? He felt like he didn't know her anymore.

You are keeping a secret too, he reminded himself, thinking of the enormous loan he had taken out.

Who was responsible for these threatening notes? Who did they want to kill? Eva or him? Or both of them? His thoughts went to Carlos. His cousin had looked furious when he had accused José of causing their grandmother's death. Did he hate José enough to kill him even if it meant Eva would die too?

Eva returned a few minutes later and held out a piece of paper. 'This was the first one.'

José stared at the word written in black capitals on the piece of paper. 'Murderer,' he read out loud.

Eva nodded. 'That's why I thought it was you,' she told Bianca.

José's gaze went straight to his cousin. Carlos had accused him of causing their grandmother's death. Was this his doing? Carlos's face was blank as he returned his gaze.

'And this is the second note.' Eva held it out.

'Revenge is coming!' José read it then looked again at Carlos. 'You!' he whispered. 'You're the one responsible for this. You sabotaged the generator, hit me on the back of the head and left me to drown in the pool, then when that didn't work you set fire to our bedroom.'

67

Eva

Eva was stunned at José's accusation. 'Carlos?' she repeated, shaking her head in disbelief. 'But why? And the note...' Why would Carlos leave Eva a note saying she was a murderer?

'That's ridiculous!' Saskia exclaimed, jumping to Carlos's defence.

'The note was left for me. Carlos accused me of causing our *abuelita* to fall down the stairs,' José said through clenched teeth. 'He who never came to see her, never tried to get in touch, has had the nerve to say that I wanted her dead so I could inherit El Sueño. He's jealous of how close I was to our grandmother and how much of a success I – we' – he turned to Eva – 'have made of this place. I've never got around to making a will, if I were dead then the villa might go to him.'

Saskia looked from José to Carlos, doubt flickering across her face. 'Is this true?'

'What? That I tried to kill him because I wanted this place?' Carlos looked shocked. 'Are you mad? Apart from the fact that I would never kill anyone, especially my own cousin, I live in a modern apartment in Rome. I do not want to live halfway up a mountain in an old house that is falling down and has constant problems.' He looked at José in bewilderment. 'We had had a few words, yes, and I was wrong to hint that you had something to do with our grandmother's fall. I apologise. I was angry and hurt. But to accuse me of this terrible thing...'

'Well, someone tried to kill us!' Eva shouted, trembling. 'Have you any idea what it's been like this week, everything that's gone wrong and then receiving those notes? I've been petrified but I've carried on, trying to make you all welcome, to help you, to make the retreat a success. This is our dream, we have worked so hard for this! We've toiled from dawn to dusk, ploughed any spare money we have into this house but ever since you all arrived it's been one disaster after another. Someone has gone out of their way to try and sabotage our retreat.' She could feel her chest tightening, her anxiety rising but she was going to let whoever it was know exactly what they had done. 'And then, not content with all the trouble they caused, they decided to take it further. To try and kill us.' Her voice was wobbling. She shifted her gaze onto every one of them in turn. 'Someone wanted us dead.'

There were gasps of horror and disbelief as the guests digested her words but Eva wasn't fooled. They all looked so innocent but one of them was guilty. She couldn't bear to be in the same house as them any longer. She opened the front door and ran outside, sitting down on the bench and sinking her head in her hands. She had tried to be strong but the anxiety was swallowing her up and building into another panic attack. She couldn't breathe, it felt like a vice was tightening around her chest.

68

José

Everyone stood in stunned silence when Eva ran out.

'I need to go to Eva,' José said, following her. He didn't want to be with any of them either. He wanted them to get out of his house and go home. He didn't want to see any of them again. Maybe him falling in the pool, and the candle burning the chest of drawers was an accident, but someone had sabotaged the generator, someone had sent Eva notes, someone had been causing trouble all week. As soon as he had comforted Eva he was going to phone Mario and ask him to take everyone to the airport. He didn't care that it was hours too early for their flights. He wanted them all out of his house. And that included his cousin.

Eva was sitting on the bench trembling and struggling to breathe. She was having a panic attack, he realised, and small wonder with everything that had gone on.

He sat down beside her and put his arms around her. 'Take deep breaths,' he said gently. 'In, out, in, out...'

She breathed with him and finally he felt the trembles ease.

'Take your time,' he said softly. 'But I would like to know why you haven't told me about these threatening notes.'

'I thought it was Bianca...' Her voice trailed off.

'Another thing you haven't told me. I can't believe you have carried this around with you all these years and didn't tell me, not even when you thought the daughter of this man you accidently ran down was at the retreat,' he said. 'I thought we were close yet you were unable to share this with me.'

She swallowed. 'I couldn't talk about it. Even though I was exonerated from any blame the guilt almost killed me.' She gazed into the distance, as if she was scared to look at him and see his reaction. 'When it happened, I couldn't stop thinking about that poor man and his family. I had a complete break-down. I had to go into a psychiatric unit. It took me a long time to recover.' Her voice breaking, she told him all about it and how it was discovering wellness and mindfulness techniques that had finally helped her deal with it. 'I learnt how to deal with the guilt but never how to stop thinking about it. It was always there, eating away at me.'

He wound his arm around her shoulder and pulled her closer, kissing her gently on the forehead. 'I'm so sorry you had to go through all that.'

'It was a nightmare. Then when Bianca came here and told us about her father it brought it all back. I thought it was her father I'd killed. Saskia did too.' She closed her eyes as the memories flooded back, swamping her.

'How did Saskia know about this... accident?' he asked, he guessed that this was why Eva had been so anxious about Saskia coming to the retreat, because she didn't want to be reminded of what had happened. He could understand that but he wished she had told him about it, he might have been able to help her, reassure her.

'It happened when we were at college together. I was in

such a mess. I had a full-on meltdown at college. I was desper-ate.' She swallowed. 'I couldn't cope...'

'Go on.' He kept his voice soft, reassuring.

'I climbed up to the roof of the college building' – she licked her lips – 'stood on the edge, willing myself to jump. I just wanted it all to end, for the pain to go away.'

She must have been so desperate to want to end her life, he thought, his heart going out to her. He couldn't bear to think that she might have gone through with it and then he would never have met her. 'What happened?'

'Saskia saw me and alerted the college principal. They called the police and a policewoman came up and talked me down. That's when I was sent to the psychiatric unit.'

He hugged her tight and they sat in silence for a few minutes before he asked, 'If you and Saskia were such good friends back then, and she knew all about this, why didn't you both keep in touch? Was it because she knew and you wanted to forget all about it?'

Eva shook her head and clenched her eyes tight. She took a few deep breaths before opening her eyes but stared ahead, as if she was scared what she would see on his face as she revealed her darkest secret to him. 'My boyfriend didn't take it too well. We split up. And while I was in the hospital recovering, Saskia went off with him. She said she didn't mean it to happen, she was simply comforting him at first, but then they realised they had feelings for each other.'

'Ouch!'

She nodded. 'I was devastated at the time but as Saskia said, we'd split up.' She turned to him. 'Then when I finally recov-ered and got myself a job, started to settle down, I discovered that Saskia's neighbour worked there and Saskia had told her everything about me, soon it was all around the company. I couldn't cope with them all knowing and had another relapse and took an overdose. Mum found me in time.' She licked her lips. 'Saskia was distraught, full of apologies, begged me to forgive her again but I couldn't, it was too much of a betrayal. Saskia wrote me notes, came to see me and I forgave her eventually but I moved away and we lost touch.'

José released her and turned to look at her, still holding her hand. 'Eva, you don't think Saskia is behind all this, do you?'

Her eyes shot to his face. It was exactly what she'd been wondering since she'd discovered that it wasn't Bianca or Nathan. 'Saskia? Why would she do all this?' That was the question that she'd been asking herself.

He shook his head. 'I don't know but she seems to have a history of causing trouble for you. Maybe she's jealous of how well you've got your life together and wants to ruin it. Like she's done before. And she knew about the accident, she knew that leaving you a note saying "murderer" could push you over the edge again.'

69

Eva

Thoughts raced through her mind, memories of the past, Saskia being her friend then destroying her, pleading to be forgiven then betraying her again. And the notes, written on the same paper and with the same pen that Saskia had in her room. Saskia was the first one who came out when she found José in the pool. Could she have been watching, waiting to see if anyone found him?

Was José right and Saskia was behind all this? Hadn't she suspected as much herself?

'There you both are!' They turned around at the sound of Carlos's voice. 'I think that you are right, both of you, and that someone is trying to harm you,' he announced.

Eva and José stared at him speechlessly.

'I've just been checking out your bedroom and I've found something. Some incriminating evidence.'

José found his voice first. 'What is it? Does it prove who did it? Does Nathan know about it?'

'I think it proves it beyond doubt but no, I haven't told Nathan. I wanted to tell you first.'

Finally they were going to find out the name of the person behind this terrible campaign against them. Eva felt José squeeze her hand as they waited for Carlos to show them what he had found that proved someone had been in their room. Was it Saskia? It couldn't be Carlos, as José had believed, or he wouldn't have been looking for evidence. She bit her lip. *Please don't let it be Saskia.* She had enjoyed having her friend back in her life, she had seemed so genuine. She couldn't bear it if she had betrayed her again. And this time it would be much, much worse because before Saskia hadn't really meant to harm her. Leo had blamed Eva for the accident, said she should have been watching the road more carefully, and he hadn't been at all sympathetic when she'd had her breakdown. He'd ditched her, leaving Eva heartbroken. Yes, Saskia had gone off with him but he and Eva had already been finished. As for the neighbour, Saskia had been friends with her for years, she didn't realise that she would gossip about it. She said she'd been genuinely concerned for Eva.

'What is this incriminating evidence?' José asked.

Carlos opened his hand and there in his palm lay a gold crucifix. 'I found this by the patio doors. The chain has broken. I'm guessing whoever dropped it started the fire.'

José's eyes rested on the gold chain dangling from his cousin's fingers. He recognised it. He had seen it many times.

Eva gasped. She recognised it too.

'You know who it belongs to?' Carlos asked.

'Mario.' The words snapped out of José's mouth. 'It belongs to our neighbour Mario.'

70

Eva looked at the gold crucifix, hardly able to believe it but José was right, it belonged to Mario. Their friend and neighbour.

'Surely not! Mario is our friend, he would never harm us. There must be some mistake.' Mario was kind, helpful, he had always been there for them. He was taking their guests back to the airport today. It couldn't possibly be him. There must be some mistake. She shook her head. 'I know Mario wears a crucifix like that but other people must have one too,' she said even though she knew that this crucifix, with its distinctive design, was definitely Mario's. He'd told them his father had left it to him, and it had been his grandfather's before that.

'None of our guests wear such a crucifix. What other explanation is there? This is Mario's crucifix and he has keys to the villa,' José said angrily. 'He has done all this.'

'We must call the Guardia,' Carlos said. 'This man is a danger to you both.'

'What I don't understand is why? Mario has been a family friend for years. He looked after our *abuelita*. Why would he want to harm us?' José looked devastated.

'I don't know, but we have to contact the police. They'll get to the bottom of this,' Carlos insisted.

'The police?' Sean had come outside and was standing behind them. 'You will need firm evidence before you call the police.'

Carlos looked over this shoulder at him. 'We have it. We know who it is that has been trying to harm my cousin and Eva.'

'You do? Great. Please come back into the house and tell us all. We've all been accused so you owe it to us to tell us who the real culprit is. Nathan can let you know if you have enough evidence for the police.' He looked at them ruefully. 'I'm sorry. I know this has been awful for you both, and I sympathise, I really do, but if we get the police involved then none of us will be able to go home until they've done an investigation so we'll all be stuck here. I don't know about anyone else but Adrienne and I have important business meetings to attend. And the others might not be able to afford to pay for another flight.'

'José and Eva have almost been burnt alive. I am calling the police,' Carlos said firmly, taking his phone out of his pocket.

'At least tell me what evidence you have so I can go and tell the others,' Sean replied.

José told him about Carlos finding the crucifix, and how Mario had a spare set of keys to El Sueño because he used to come and help José's grandmother.

Carlos had already called 112 and was talking in rapid Spanish. 'They will be here shortly,' he said when he'd finished the call. 'And they said that no one must leave the villa.'

Sean went inside to report the latest developments and when José and Eva finally came back in they were all looking very worried.

'Look, I sympathise, of course I do. And I'm pleased that you're both okay,' Adrienne said. 'However, Sean and I can't afford to miss our flight. You know who the culprit is so what does it matter if we go home?'

Sean nodded. 'She's right. We have to go. We've already packed and have ordered a taxi to the airport. You have our contact details, if the police want to speak to us, although I don't see why they would.'

Eva could see their point. They had to fly all the way to the USA and needed to leave earlier than the others. The holiday had been bad enough without them missing their flights.

'I guess we can't legally keep you here,' she said.

'Thank you. I hope that Mario is locked away for many years. I can't believe that he's done such a terrible thing. He seemed such a nice man,' Adrienne said. She and Sean went upstairs to get their luggage.

'I think the rest of us should get dressed, the Guardia will be here soon,' Carlos said. 'Hopefully after seeing the crucifix they will arrest Mario.'

Eva felt sick. Not only had the retreat gone drastically wrong, it was their neighbour, someone they thought was a friend, who had betrayed them. Worse than that, tried to kill them. Why? Was he jealous of the success they had made of El Sueño while he was struggling to repair his villa? This retreat had turned into a nightmare.

The Guardia arrived shortly after Sean and Adrienne left, and took statements from everyone, then, after saying that the other guests were free to go they went around to talk to Mario. They came back to say that he wasn't at home but they would put out a call for him to be detained.

'Do you think Mario realises he'd left his crucifix behind and has done a runner?' Eva asked.

'I don't know. He could simply be out on an errand. Either way they've put out a warrant out for him. They will get him,' José reassured her, his face grim. He and Mario had been such good friends for years, this must be such shock to him, Eva thought sadly.

Nathan and Bianca came down with their luggage. 'I hope

it all works out for you but we need to go now or we will miss our flight.' Nathan glanced over at Saskia. 'Would you like to share a taxi to the airport with us?'

She held on to Carlos's arm. 'I'm not going back yet. Carlos wants to stay until Mario is arrested and so do I. I can't stop thinking that Eva and José could have been burnt alive. It's horrible.'

She did look terribly upset and Eva felt guilty for suspecting that she was behind it all.

If there was one good thing that had come out of this, it was that Carlos and José had called a truce, Eva thought. She had to say something to Bianca before she went, she decided, she owed her an apology.

'I am so sorry that I accused you of everything, Bianca. I really am from the bottom of my heart. I hope that you can forgive me.'

Bianca looked at her steadily for a moment, her expression inscrutable, then she stepped forward and, to Eva's surprise, hugged her.

'I forgive you and, actually, I want to thank you,' she said, releasing Eva and stepping back. 'The young man who knocked my father down recently contacted us, expressing his regret. He said he was young and inexperienced and has never got over what happened to my father, that he lives with the guilt every day.' Her eyes clouded. 'I refused to accept his apology. I didn't believe him, I was so eaten up with bitterness at how he had destroyed my life. His letter has played on my mind for months.' She licked her lips and Eva could see that this was painful for her. 'But after learning how the accident you were in has affected you, still affects you after all these years...' She paused. 'I'm sorry but I overheard you talking to José about your break-down. And now I realise that although he was careless, the young man didn't hit my father deliberately and maybe he *was* eaten up with guilt too, like you are. So when I get back home I intend to write back to him and tell him that I forgive him.'

Tears sprang to Eva's eyes. She couldn't bear to think of someone else going through the trauma she had suffered all these years. 'Thank you,' she said simply.

71

Carlos

Carlos watched as the other guests said goodbye, his mind in turmoil. He didn't know what had made him search the bedroom, but it had shaken him to see his cousin and Eva's blackened faces, they could have died. When Eva had confessed about receiving those notes he realised that someone probably had knocked José over the head and tried to drown him. That maybe the things that had happened this week – he felt ashamed to remember that these things had amused him – had been deliberate and someone had tried to ruin the retreat. So he'd gone to investigate, to see if he could find any clues. He had been shocked when he spotted the crucifix lying by the patio doors, immediately recognising it as Mario's because of its distinctive design. The chain must have broken and the crucifix dropped off. He wondered if Mario had noticed it was missing yet. If he was panicking and searching everywhere for it. Looking at José now, coughing and weak, and Eva so pale and traumatised, he felt furious at Mario for what he had done.

The notes puzzled him. That couldn't have been Mario, he

didn't know about the dreadful accident in Eva's past. Even José didn't know. Saskia was the only other person who had known about it. Had she written them, maybe to push Eva over the edge? Had she been working with Mario? He had seen them both talking together a few times.

Surely not. He couldn't believe that Saskia would do such an awful thing, she was Eva's friend. She seemed so warm, so open. It was her words yesterday about letting the past go that had made him think about his bitterness towards José and realise that his cousin was just as much a victim of the family feud as Carlos was and that it was time the feud was ended, at least between them two. That was why he'd bought a present for José and Eva, as a sort of peace offering.

He had to find out if Saskia had anything to do with it before he fell any harder for her.

'I'm not going home until Mario is caught,' he'd told her. 'Will you stay too? We can book into a B&B if José and Eva prefer us not to stay here.'

She had agreed straight away. 'I don't want to leave Eva like this.'

She couldn't be guilty otherwise she would want to get home quickly before Mario was caught and incriminated her.

But if Saskia hadn't written the notes, who had?

72

José

'You must both stay here, we would like you to, wouldn't we, José?' Eva said when Carlos told him about his and Saskia's plan to book into a B&B.

'Of course. You are very welcome here,' José agreed. He hesitated, wondering how to word what he wanted to say. 'I need to talk to you, *primo*, about why the family fell out with your father. I've spoken to my father about this and he's finally told me what it was all about.' He met Carlos's gaze. 'It isn't a pleasant story.'

Carlos looked guarded. 'My father is a good man, he wouldn't do anything very bad. So what was his crime? Did he run off with a family heirloom?'

'No, he ran off with my father's bride-to-be, your mother.'

'*De verdad?*' Carlos looked stunned. 'Is this true? All this has been because my mother chose my father over yours?'

'It's a bit more than that.' José nodded towards the sofa. 'Let us sit down and I will tell you all what my father told me.'

'Maybe I should leave, this all sounds a bit personal,' Saskia said.

Carlos shook his head. 'No, I want you to be here.'

They all at down, José and Eva on one sofa, Carlos and Saskia on the other, and José repeated the story his father had reluctantly told him.

'Papá and your mother, Tía Isabella, were childhood sweethearts. Our two families had been friends for generations, so their wedding was planned with great joy. However, your father loved Isabella too. And I guess that she loved him more than my father because on the morning of their wedding Tío Diego turned up and begged her not to go through with the wedding, not to turn her back on their love.' José got up and paced around the room, imagining the scene, the devastation it must have brought to both families. 'They went off together, left Papá standing at the altar in the church, rejected in front of all his family and friends.'

Carlos looked astonished. 'That is bad, of course it is, but is it bad enough to be cast out of the family all this time? For my – our grandparents – to even turn their back on me?'

'There is more.' José took a breath. 'Papá stormed out of the church and back home – both our fathers were living at home – just in time to see your mother and father about to leave. He grabbed Tío Diego and punched him. They had a terrible fight. Then, Abuelo arrived and tried to pull them apart. In the scuffle Abuelo was punched in the face by your father, who said that he was aiming at my *papá*. Abuelo was furious, Abuelita distraught. Abuelo told your father to get out and never darken his doorstep again. Your mother begged him to understand, said that they had been in love for a long time but both families were so caught up in the wedding plans that they couldn't tell them, couldn't bring themselves to disappoint everyone.'

There was silence for a few minutes, as if they all needed time to digest his words. Then Carlos said, 'This is bad, yes. My father did wrong, my mother too – but love, it is a powerful emotion. My father and mother are still together and happy. They obviously loved each other, and Spanish weddings, they are a big affair. I can understand how my mother felt she couldn't back out.' He frowned. 'What I can't understand is why it has been such a big secret all these years though. I would have thought Tío Pablo would have told you all about it as it seems he was the injured party.'

José thrust his hands in his pockets. 'I asked Papá this and he said that a couple of years later he met Mamá and fell in love. He didn't tell her what had happened but after the ceremony she heard one of the guests remark that they were glad it went ahead this time. She demanded what he meant and she was upset, believed that she was his second choice, second best. Papá swore that wasn't true but Mamá was so distressed that they vowed to never talk about it. Years went by and no one attempted to end the feud, I think perhaps your father and mother were too ashamed, and my father didn't want to upset my mother, so it carried on.'

'That's quite a story,' Eva said softly. 'Don't you both think that now it's time to end it? None of this is any of your fault.'

She was right, it was time the family was brought back together. He wished it had happened when his *abuelos* were still alive. He wondered how Carlos felt. Was he still angry about his inheritance? Abuelita did leave him and Tío Diego some money though, she didn't cut them off completely. 'I am happy to do so if Carlos is.'

Carlos held his gaze for a moment then he stood up and walked over to him. 'I would like my cousin in my life,' he said. And they both hugged.

73

Eva

Two Guardia came back later to say that they had arrested Mario and taken him for questioning. Apparently Mario had said that while he was behind some of the things that went wrong at the villa, he hadn't tried to drown José or start the fire in their bedroom.

'He is lying, we found his crucifix,' José protested.

'Señor Gonzalez said that this woman' – the policeman looked at his notes again – 'Adrienne Wallis, planted it to frame him. He lost his crucifix a couple of days ago. He thinks she took it.'

'How could she?' Eva asked, puzzled. 'She hardly knows him.'

'They've been working together. Señora Wallis offered Señor Gonzalez money to sabotage the retreat. Apparently you gave him a key to your house so he was able to let himself in when you were out and do things such as' – he looked down at his notes – 'unlocking the back gate and leaving it open for the goats to get in.' He looked back up. 'However, he is adamant that he made no attempt to hurt or kill anyone. And he has an alibi for last night when the fire happened, he had been away at a friend's house. Witnesses have confirmed this.'

Eva was bewildered. So that's what Adrienne had been talking about in Spanish to Mario.

'Did Mario say why he did these things?' she asked.

'He didn't want your place to become a holiday home, lots of people and noise would ruin his quiet life,' the policeman replied.

Carlos had been explaining to Saskia, who didn't speak Spanish, what the policeman was saying. She looked stunned. 'Eva said that Adrienne was an old girlfriend of yours. What did you do to her to make her hate you so much?' she asked.

José shook his head wordlessly. 'I've no idea. I haven't seen her for years. I didn't even recognise her when she turned up.'

'Oh that must be it. You didn't remember your big love affair. That would have annoyed her,' Saskia said.

'It was no big love affair, it was a holiday romance. I don't understand why she hates me. Or why Mario would work with her. Why didn't he just come and tell us his fears about the retreat then we could have reassured him? I thought we were good friends.'

It certainly was a mystery. And one that they possibly wouldn't get answers to. No wonder Adrienne had been anxious to get to the airport. She knew that the police probably wouldn't be able to touch her once she got back to America. She'd almost killed them both and got away with it. What Eva wanted to know was why.

The police asked for the full names of Adrienne and Sean, and for photos of them so that they could forward them on to the airport police.

'I think they'll have already boarded,' José said, glancing at his watch. 'Their flight leaves in ten minutes.'

74

José

Adrienne. José couldn't take it in. Why would she want to kill him? What had he done?

He needed answers.

Then the police phoned and said they had Adrienne and Sean, the plane had been about to take off when the police had stopped it, boarded it and taken them both. Sean had been detained as a precaution until they'd questioned Adrienne. José wanted to question Adrienne too and find out why she had done this. And to question Mario.

Later that night there was a knock on the door. It was Mario. He looked tired. And ashamed. 'I owe you an apology and an explanation,' he said.

José was so angry and hurt he was tempted to refuse to listen, to tell Mario to go away and never speak to him again, but he was also curious about why their former good friend and neighbour had betrayed them so he agreed to hear him out.

They sat out on the terrace and listened while Mario explained that he had been worried about the amount of visitors the retreat would bring to the mountain. How he liked his peaceful home and didn't want it ruined. Then Adrienne had arrived, flirted with him, made him feel good, sympathised with him, offered to pay him a lot of money if he could make sure the retreat wasn't a success, so he'd gone along with it. He needed the money badly for repairs to his *finca*, and he wanted to keep his quiet life.

'I opened the gate to let the goats in, I shut your cat in the studio, and the shed, put red paint in the fountain.' He bowed his head. 'I sabotaged the electricity and the generator too and Adrienne hid the torch you kept by the back door. It was all her idea, she said that the guests would be so annoyed not to have electricity or water they wouldn't want to come here again, and would recommend people not to come to the retreat. I swear it was never to harm you. I didn't knock you out and throw you in the pool. I didn't set fire to your bedroom.' He looked at them now and José could see the distress in his eyes. 'I would never do that. That was Adrienne. She planted my crucifix there so it would look like it was me. She is an evil woman. She must hate you.'

75

José

The police phoned José on Saturday morning to tell him that they had released Adrienne without charge. He listened to their explanation in a mixture of disbelief and relief. He was glad that Adrienne wasn't guilty, he couldn't bear to think that she had actually tried to kill him... them. But if it wasn't her, who was it?

Eva stared at him, uncomprehending when he repeated the conversation to her. 'Why?'

'Apparently there is no evidence that she had anything to do with the pool or fire incident. A police officer is coming to talk to us about it,' he explained.

His phone rang again. He glanced at the number and frowned. He didn't recognise it. Perhaps it was someone wanting to ask questions about the retreat, they couldn't afford to turn away business. He swiped to answer. '*Hola*, El Sueño Relaxation Retreat. Can I help you?'

There was a pause. Then a familiar voice said. 'José, it's Adrienne. Can I speak to you? I'm in the café down in Toria.

I'm due at the airport in an hour so haven't got long but I want to explain. Please say you will come.'

José's mind was in a whirl. He never wanted to see this woman again, but part of him wanted answers. Just as he had with Mario.

'Who is it?' Eva asked.

José muted the call. 'Adrienne. She wants to meet me and explain. What should I do? She's leaving for the airport in an hour.'

'What do you want to do?'

'I'd like to know why she did what she did.'

'Then go and meet her,' Eva said.

'Will you come too?' he asked.

Eva shook her head. 'I doubt if she will talk freely if I'm there. And to be honest I never want to see her again. I would like an explanation for what she did too though.'

'I'm not looking forward to this.' José grimaced then wrapped her in a hug. 'I will be back soon,' he promised.

As he set off, his mind was a mixture of emotions, anger that Adrienne had tried to destroy the retreat, that she had such a grudge against him, and curiosity about who had hit him over the head and started the fire. If it wasn't Adrienne, who was it? Everyone had gone home so the culprit had escaped justice. That made him really angry.

Adrienne was sitting at the table outside the corner café, a half-drunk cup of coffee in front of her. She looked pale and tired, he noticed. She looked up as he approached and gave him a wan smile.

He kept his expression stony as he pulled out a chair and sat down beside her.

'I'm sorry,' she said softly. 'Things got a bit out of hand.'

'Out of hand!' He could barely keep the fury out of his voice. 'Why the hell did you come here just to try to destroy our business? And I'm still not convinced that it wasn't you who attempted to kill us even if the police have released you.'

'I didn't come to destroy your business. I came because I wanted to see you again. I've never forgotten you. But you had forgotten me. You didn't even recognise me. Do you know how that felt?'

'*Madre mía,* Adrienne. Not this again! We had a brief romance ten years ago.'

'I loved you. I thought that you loved me. It hurt that you'd forgotten me so easily.' She looked at him, tears glistening in her eyes. 'Why did you lead me on, seduce me then abandon me when I needed you most?'

He was stunned. 'I did no such thing. We both knew that it was a holiday romance, that you would be going back to America in a few months.' His voice hardened. 'And you were as eager as I was, Adrienne. I certainly didn't seduce you.'

'You were my first lover, you knew that.' Her voice choked and her eyes filled with tears. 'You were so gentle with me, so tender. We were inseparable.'

Dios, was the woman crazy? 'A long time ago we had a good time together for a few months, you went back home, we both carried on with our lives, moved on. We have had no contact with each other since.'

'Except I couldn't carry on with my life, could I? Because I was pregnant with your baby!'

Her words shocked him. 'What! You never told me.' Anger was rising in him now. 'Where is this child? My child? Why haven't you told me this before?'

'I came to tell you when I realised that I was pregnant. I flew back over and came to your apartment to surprise you. I thought you would be happy to see me, and to find out that you were going to be a father. I thought you were missing me like I was missing you and we would be together.' She leant forward and jabbed a finger at him. 'But you had already replaced me

with someone else. I saw you, both of you, through the open
window.'

'You came back and spied on me yet you still didn't tell me
about the baby?'

'How could I when you were all over *her*? I was so upset I
went back to my hotel room and cried. I was distraught, I
couldn't think straight. I couldn't eat or sleep. The next day I
had a miscarriage. Alone. In my hotel room.' She glared at him.
'Can you even imagine what that was like for me?'

José felt for her, that was a terrible thing to happen. 'I am
very sorry that you went through that but I didn't know. You
didn't tell me.'

'What would you have done if I had?' She practically spat
the words out. 'You had already replaced me! She swallowed,
tears glistening in her eyes. 'I lost my baby because of you. I was
too distraught to get medical help and ended up with a bad
infection which ruined my chances of ever having children
again. Sean and I have been trying for years, and that's what the
doctor told me. Our struggle to have a child has ruined our
marriage, driven Sean to have affairs. I hate you for that.'

'I knew nothing about this. You didn't tell me that you were
pregnant,' he pointed out again.

'I didn't get the chance! You were with someone else. I had
to cope alone. The grief nearly destroyed me, that's what caused
my miscarriage. You murdered our baby. And ruined any
chance I had of having future children. Then, when I came to
the retreat you didn't even recognise me! You put me through
all of that then erased me from your mind.'

Murdered our baby? José remembered the notes that had
been left under Eva's lamp. 'You left the notes, didn't you? They
weren't for Eva, they were for me. You left them under the
lamp.'

'I thought it was your lamp. You slept on the right side when we were together,' Adrienne said. 'I wanted you to know what you'd done.'

'I didn't do anything, Adrienne. We were finished. You went back home. I didn't know about the baby. I didn't know you'd come back to Spain. Yes, I took up with someone else, but I was young and single, we were over. It wasn't a crime,' he protested. He stood up. 'I can't believe that you have carried all this bitterness around with you for years, you came to our home to get revenge, befriended our neighbour to get him onside, then tried to kill us both.'

Adrienne shook her head adamantly. 'You're wrong. I didn't try to kill any of you. Yes, I left the notes. And yes, Mario and I made a few things go wrong. But that's all. I swear. I knew the daffodil bulbs would cause everyone to have an upset stomach, that's why I swapped them for the onions. I knew that such a small amount wouldn't kill you.'

'And the Buddha head?' he suddenly remembered. 'Did you deliberately push Bianca so that she would topple into it, hoping it would fall on Eva and kill her?'

Adrienne's eyes flashed. 'It was a warning, I knew Eva would get up before it landed on her.'

José shook his head. 'You're mad. Totally insane.' He leant forward. 'I don't know how you've managed to convince the police that you didn't try to kill me, but if it wasn't you then who the hell was it?'

Adrienne pushed her chair back as a taxi pulled up. 'It was Sean. I told you he was jealous. That's why I didn't want him to find out about us. You destroyed our chance of having a family, something Sean wanted more than anything. He saw how close we were and kept questioning me. Finally I had to tell him everything, including how you were responsible for us not being able to have children. I guess it pushed him over the edge.' Her eyes flashed with anger. 'You've only yourself to blame for this,

José. You can't mess around with people's feelings and expect no consequences.'

José stared at her, dumbstruck, as she walked over to the taxi and got inside. A couple of minutes lates the taxi drove away, taking Adrienne to the airport where she would catch a plane back to America.

Sean.

Had she been telling the truth?

If she was it was too late, Sean was probably already on the plane on his way back to America.

He glanced down at the table as his phone rang. It was Eva.

'The police are here,' she said.

'I'll be ten minutes,' he told her.

76

Sean

Sean packed his bags and took a final look around the hotel room he'd booked into while Adrienne was taken in for questioning. The police had taken them both off the plane but soon revealed that it was Adrienne they wanted for questioning. He had been astonished to hear that they suspected her of attempted murder and that she'd been conspiring with Mario to ruin the retreat. She was facing a tough jail sentence, but it was her own fault, she was unstable. Unhinged. They'd been happy once, when they were first married, before the desire to have a baby had taken hold of Adrienne and changed her into someone he barely recognised. He'd wanted a child too, but Adrienne had been obsessed. When she'd discovered that she couldn't have a baby she'd been heartbroken. She never mentioned that she'd once had a miscarriage, but he'd seen it on the consultant's notes by chance during one of their appointments. He never questioned her about it, everyone had a past.

Adrienne had become more and more obsessed over the years, and increasingly bitter. The failure to have children ate away inside her and although he had begged her to confide in him, to talk to someone and get help, she had insisted that she didn't need it and had thrown herself into her work. They'd grown distant and he'd found himself drawn to someone else. He'd had a couple of short affairs but they didn't last long. He didn't want to jeopardise his marriage. Then he met Leila and fell hard. Adrienne found out and was so distressed he'd finished it, but he couldn't get Leila out of his mind and had gone back to her. Now she was pregnant, carrying a baby boy, the scan had shown, and wanted him to leave Adrienne and live with her. He wanted that too but Adrienne had threatened to ruin him financially so he had agreed to give their marriage another go. She'd seen this retreat and he'd agreed to go along and try to reconnect with each other.

He knew from the way Adrienne had looked at José that she was interested in him, but it wasn't until he overheard them talking that he'd realised that they'd had a relationship years ago and started to wonder if José was the father of the baby Adrienne had miscarried. When she kept flirting with José he was pleased, hoping they would rekindle their love affair and then maybe he would be free to be with Leila, until he realised that José wasn't interested in Adrienne. Sean was desperate to be with Leila so when he'd seen Adrienne's scarf on the back of the chair he thought of a way to be free of her. He threw the scarf in the pool knowing that Adrienne would come down for it, see it floating in the water and try and reach it then he would come behind her and push her in. He'd already told the others that Adrienne was scared of water and couldn't swim so no one would be surprised that she'd drowned.

Instead, it was José who had spotted the scarf. When he saw him bending over the pool Sean come up with the idea of framing Adrienne, believing that when their past relationship came to light it would look like she'd flipped and pushed him in out of anger because she'd been spurned. José was a good swimmer though so it would have to be more than a push in the pool. Spotting the shovel by the wall, he'd grabbed that, crept up behind José and hit him over the head, causing him to fall, unconscious, into the pool. Watching him come back up and float on the top of the water, Sean had felt sick, suddenly realising what he'd done. He wasn't a murderer. He'd been about to jump in the pool himself when Eva had come out and saved José.

Sean had hidden in the shadows until he could sneak back up to his room unnoticed. Luckily Adrienne was fast asleep. He was shaking about the terrible thing he had almost done, ashamed at how low he'd stooped. He vowed he was going to leave Adrienne as soon as they got back home. She was poison. He wanted a new life with Leila and their baby. He would hire a good lawyer and file for divorce, put their condo on the market and buy a place for him, Leila and their baby. Finally he was going to have the life he wanted. The police had given him his passport back this morning so he'd booked himself onto the next flight to the US. He was free now to join Leila and their baby boy.

He zipped up his case, turning around as there was a knock on the door. It was probably the porter to help him with his luggage. 'Coming,' he shouted.

He wheeled his case over to the door and opened it, the smile on his face faltering when he saw the two Guardia Civil standing outside.

'Señor Wallis, we are arresting you for two counts of attempted murder,' one of the officers said in perfect English.

Sean's mouth dropped open. 'That was my wife and Mario, not me. You know that. You've arrested her.'

'Other evidence has come forward that suggests it was you.'

Sean's head was swimming, he struggled to keep his voice steady. 'What evidence?' They were bluffing, they had to be.

'A spade with your fingerprints on it that was used to hit Señor Lopez over the head and push him into the pool.'

Damn, he should have wiped that spade clean. He thought quickly.

'Of course my fingerprints would be on the spade, we all did some gardening on the retreat. I used the spade a few times.'

'And your pen was under the bed in the Lopez's bedroom. We believe that you were responsible for starting the fire that almost killed them both.'

77

Eva

Eva could barely believe what the police were saying. They had arrested Sean. They had proof that he had hit José over the head with a spade and pushed him into the pool, and that he had caused the fire in their bedroom. Sean was the one who had tried to murder them.

'It doesn't make sense,' she stammered. 'What grudge did Sean have against you? Unless... he found out about you and Adrienne and was jealous. Which is crazy, it was so long ago.'

José hesitated. What he was about to say next he would have preferred to say to Eva alone, but Saskia was owed an explanation for the notes, for a brief time they had all thought it was her. He kept his gaze on Eva. 'Adrienne told me that she came back from America not long after we finished because she had discovered that she was pregnant. Only by then I was dating someone else and she saw us together. She was upset and went back to her hotel without speaking to me. The next day she had a miscarriage.' He tried to keep his voice steady although he was sure the emotion he felt was written on his face. 'Later when she and Sean tried to start a family, she discovered that an infection she'd had as a result of this miscarriage had ruined her chances of having children and blamed me for it. Hence the notes saying "Murderer". Adrienne left them for me.' He looked at Saskia. 'She said that she used the notepad and pen in your room so that no one would know it was her.'

Saskia's eyes widened. 'She tried to frame me? Surely you didn't suspect me?' she asked Eva, her voice wobbling a bit.

Eva bit her lip. 'I didn't know what to think,' she admitted. 'I told myself that it was a common notepad and pen so it didn't mean you wrote the note.'

'Covering her back, she called it,' José continued. 'All the things she did with Mario's help were payback. She didn't want to see me happy when she and Sean couldn't have the children they wanted.' He could see the horror in Eva's eyes and hoped he hadn't lost her. 'Apparently Sean was suspicious when he saw Adrienne watching me, and he caught us talking, so she had to confess we had a relationship all those years ago and the baby she miscarried was mine. So he blamed me too for them not being able to have children. This was his revenge.'

He met Eva's gaze. 'I am sorry, cariño, I only discovered all this myself today.'

Carlos stood up. 'I think that me and Saskia should leave you both to talk.'

Saskia nodded. 'We'll go for a drive.' She walked over to Eva and hugged her. 'See you both later.'

Eva's mind was a whirl. She could hardly believe all this. Adrienne had got pregnant, she and José had been having a baby. She could see the hurt and anger on José's face at this shocking news. What would have happened if Adrienne had told him, she wondered. Would he have married her? She was sure that he would have wanted to be a father to the baby.

It was a long time ago, she reminded herself. She had had her secrets too.

'I am sorry that you have to find out this way,' José said softly.

'It's not your fault. We all have a past.' She walked towards him and they both embraced. 'At least it's over now.'

It wasn't until much later, when they were both in bed, that she remembered overhearing Sean's phone conversation, his words 'I miss you too' making her think he had been having an affair. She must have misheard. If he'd been having an affair, why would he be jealous about José and angry enough to want to kill him?

José murmured and she moved closer, snuggling into him. What did it matter? How could you understand the way a deranged mind worked, and Sean had to be deranged to do such an awful thing. At least he was locked up now, and Adrienne was on her way back to America. She and José had to put it behind them and make the retreat a success otherwise they would have both won.

*

I'm tired of men thinking they can treat me how they want. Using me, taking from me, then betraying me. First José and then Sean, my own husband. I've known he was having an affair for a long time, that was nothing new, it wasn't his first affair. I decided to ignore it concentrating on the bigger picture. We had a good life, a beautiful home, this affair would peter out just like the others did. But the months went by and still Sean was seeing the Slut. I knew that this time I had to fight really hard to save my marriage. I couldn't let her take him from me. I tackled Sean and he promised he'd finished with her. He knew that it would be financial ruin to divorce me. We agreed to make a fresh start but I didn't trust him. I'd been keeping an eye on what José was doing for years and when I saw that he and Eva were offering a trial run at their retreat I talked Sean into booking us in, convincing him how good it would be to relax and reconnect with each other. The truth was I wanted to make sure that the retreat wasn't a success. How dare José make a new life with someone else after he had destroyed mine.

I was furious when José didn't even recognise me. It was an insult after everything he had put me through. I was even more

determined that the retreat wouldn't be a success. I wasn't plan-
ning anything serious, I just wanted to make sure that the guests
had an awful time, that would teach him. Let him have his dream
shattered too, like he'd shattered my dream of having a baby. I
didn't want to actually harm anyone.

Then I discovered that Sean was still in touch with the Slut
and that she was pregnant. I was devastated. Sean had wanted a
baby for so long, and I couldn't give him one so I knew that now
I had no chance of keeping him. He would leave me to build a
new life with her and their baby. And it was all because of José. I
couldn't believe it when I saw Sean hit José over the head and
push him into the pool. I knew that Sean was capable of being a
bit underhand but murder! I wonder if he would have left José to
drown if Eva hadn't come to the rescue. At first I was only going
to blackmail Sean, threaten to tell the police unless he dumped
that Slut and had nothing to do with the baby. Then a better idea
came into my head. A way to get revenge on them both. Shame
about Eva but she was collateral damage.

First I took the batteries out of the smoke alarms, then I
sneaked into their room and took the candle out of the holder and
relit it. I moved the rug so it would catch fire once the chest of
drawers started to burn. I checked that the patio doors were
locked and took out the key, holding it with a tissue so as not to
leave fingerprints. I threw it under the bed. Then I closed the
bedroom door and went back up to my room knowing that soon
the candle would be burnt down to the wooden chest of drawers.
But before I did that, I took Sean's pen out of my pocket where
I'd slipped it earlier, wiped it clean with the tissue and dropped
it under the bed. Then I put Mario's crucifix by the patio doors. I
knew that Mario was away that night so he had an alibi and
wouldn't be charged, but I wanted Sean to think he'd got away
with attacking José. I wanted him to have a taste of a new life
before it was taken away from him. Revenge is sweeter that way.

EPILOGUE

THREE YEARS LATER

Eva

It was a gorgeous sunny afternoon so they'd had lunch on the terrace. Eva picked up the jug of sangria and took it outside to where José, Carlos and both sets of parents were sitting talking. Saskia was sitting beside them, baby Elena in her arms while José was holding their son, Luis. This morning both babies had been baptised in the local church and the families had come back to El Sueño for lunch. She and José had got married two years ago, and Carlos and Saskia last year. Eva and Saskia had been delighted when they both realised they were pregnant, both babies being born a few weeks apart. Finally the Lopez family had buried the hatchet and come together to celebrate the two babies being baptised. The atmosphere was a little strained but Eva was sure that they would get there. The love of their grandchildren was strong enough to beat old grievances. She wished that had been the same for José's grandparents, but then they hadn't known of Carlos's existence for years, had they?

The atmosphere was a bit tense. José's mother had taken the

lead, greeting Carlos's mother and father warmly and the two men were being polite to each other. It was early days but the feud was over. Carlos and José were close, his marriage to Saskia bringing them even closer, and now their babies had cemented the bond. Both she and Saskia were determined that these cousins would grow up together, knowing both sets of grandparents. Family was important.

Thank goodness Carlos had come to their first retreat and he and José had patched things up. It had been awful at the time, she still couldn't believe everything that had gone on. Sean had been arrested and finally admitted hitting José over the head with the spade but denied having anything to do with the fire. The evidence was stacked against him though so he had been convicted of attempted murder and was imprisoned for a long time. He deserved it, but it turned out that he had a mistress and baby daughter, so they were victims too. She couldn't understand why he had done what he'd done but Adrienne had said he was a jealous man and who knew what jealousy drove you to do. Mario had been officially cautioned but Eva and José had decided not to press charges. He had sold his villa and moved away, too embarrassed to live by them any longer. It was his betrayal that had hurt the most, they had thought that he was their friend but instead he resented them, betrayed them, and all for money.

El Sueño was growing. They were now running retreats all through the summer months and both enjoyed it. It would be lovely to bring their son up here and maybe another child too. Carlos and Saskia lived in Rome but were frequent visitors, regarding El Sueño as their second home.

Eva put the tray of cool drinks down on the table and glanced over at the scene in front of her. Both grandmothers were sitting beside each other, holding a baby each and cooing over them. The two women both glanced up at each other and smiled.

'*Familia, donde la vida comienza y el amor nunca termina,*' José whispered in her ear. Family, where life begins and love never ends.

It had taken a long time for the Lopez family to come back together but now she had a feeling they wouldn't be torn apart again.

José

He really did have it all, José thought as he waved goodbye to their guests. Abuelita would be so happy so have seen the family together, in her home. All day he'd had the sense of her watching them all and smiling. The two brothers together again, with their families. She would have loved the babies, new life she'd have said. He wished she could have been here.

'I did it, Abuelita,' he whispered. 'I brought your home back to life, and your family back together – me and Eva.' He knew he wouldn't have done it without Eva. She had been a tower of strength. He'd confessed to her about the debt they had been in after that awful first retreat, not wanting there to be any more secrets between them, and she had worked with him to pay it off. They had both been determined that Sean's attempted murder and Mario and Adrienne's attempts to ruin the retreat would not succeed, instead it had spurred them on to make it a success. And it was. He was so lucky to have Eva, and their baby.

There was one secret he hadn't told Eva though. Hadn't told anyone. He had seen Adrienne all those years ago when he had left the apartment with his new girlfriend. She had been hiding in the shadows and he hadn't acknowledged her because he was with someone else and he wasn't comfortable with how Adrienne was sneakily watching them. He guessed she had come back for another stint at the hotel and wanted to pick up where they had left off but he didn't want to, he had moved on. He was young and selfish then but if he had known that she was having his baby he would never have ignored her. Then she might not have miscarried. He felt bad about that but if he had known he would probably have married Adrienne, because he wouldn't have wanted to let his grandparents down. Thank goodness that hadn't happened. Especially after what he had read today.

Nathan had sent him a link to an article, saying he might be interested in reading it. It was an article from an American newspaper about a woman who had just been convicted of attempted murder. And there, staring out of the screen at him, was Adrienne. Stunned, he'd started to read. Adrienne had met someone else, fallen in love with him, but they had split up and he'd taken up with another woman. She had tracked them down and set fire to their house in the middle of the night. A neighbour had raised the alarm and the fire brigade had arrived in time to save them. The neighbour's CCTV had clearly shown Adrienne putting a burning rag through the letterbox. Bile rose up in the back of José's throat. She had tried to burn them alive.

Was it Adrienne who had set fire to their bedroom? Sean had always denied it although he admitted hitting José over the head so he would fall into the pool. And Adrienne had confessed that she had deliberately pushed into Bianca to cause the Buddha head to fall off. He was shaking at what could have happened. Should he tell Eva?

Why worry her? he decided. It was all in the past, there was no point in dragging it all up again. He had a wonderful life with Eva and their baby son. As for Adrienne, she'd got what she deserved in the end.

He closed the computer down and went to join his wife and son.

A LETTER FROM KAREN

I want to say a huge thank you for choosing to read *The Retreat*. If you enjoyed it, and want to keep up to date with all my latest releases, just sign up at the following link. Your email address will never be shared and you can unsubscribe at any time.

www.bookouture.com/karen-king

I've set a few romance novels in Spain, where I now live, and thought it would be interesting to set a psychological thriller there too. I mentioned this to my former editor, Isobel Akenhead, and she thought it was a great idea, suggesting that I did a darker version of my romance novel *The Year of Starting Over*, which is partly set in an artist's retreat in the Andalucian countryside. We both thought a sprawling white villa, surrounded by orange, lemon and olive trees, with a sparkling blue pool halfway up the mountains would be the last place anyone would expect danger, the peaceful setting being a great contrast to the darkness of the events that take place there. I chose a wellness retreat, the whole ethos of wellness, mindfulness and relaxation luring the reader into thinking it was safe – but someone has come for revenge.

The extremes people will go to for revenge amazes me, the newspapers are full of stories of the dark and devious acts people have done as revenge for being spurned or for imagined or real grievances so I thought this would make a good premise for a novel.

I hope you loved *The Retreat*, and if you did, I would be very grateful if you could write a review. I'd love to hear what you think, and it makes such a difference helping new readers to discover one of my books for the first time.

I love hearing from my readers – you can get in touch on my Facebook page, through Twitter, Goodreads or my website.

Thanks,

Karen

karenkingauthor.com

facebook.com/KarenKingAuthor

x.com/karen_king

ACKNOWLEDGEMENTS

There's a lot of things that go on in the background when writing a book, and a lot of people who help with the process. I'd like to thank my fantastic former editor, Isobel Akenhead, who discussed this idea with me and helped me flesh it out, and my new editor, Jayne Osborne, for her expertise and advice, also all the Bookouture editing team of Dushi Horti and Becca Allen for their hard work and constructive advice. A special thanks to Aaron Munday for creating yet another stunning cover. And to the fabulous social media team of Kim Nash, Noelle Holten and Sarah Hardy, who go above and beyond in supporting and promoting our work and making the Bookouture Author Lounge such a lovely place to be. You guys are amazing! Also to the other Bookouture authors who are always willing to offer support, encouragement and advice. I'm so grateful to be part of such a lovely, supportive team.

Thanks also to all the bloggers and authors who support me, review my books and give me space on their blog tours. I am lucky to know so many incredible people in the book world and appreciate you all.

Massive thanks to my husband, Dave, for all the love and laughter you bring to my life, for being a sounding board for my ideas and for supplying the much-needed logic to some of them. Thanks also to my family and friends who all support me so much. I love you all.

Finally, a heartfelt thanks to you, my readers, for buying

and reviewing my books, and for your lovely messages telling me how much you've enjoyed reading them. Without your support there would be no more books.

Thank you. Xx

Made in United States
Troutdale, OR
12/27/2023